Sweet Talk

Judith Keim

BOOKS BY JUDITH KEIM

THE HARTWELL WOMEN SERIES:

The Talking Tree – 1
Sweet Talk – 2
Straight Talk – 3
Baby Talk – 4
The Hartwell Women – Boxed Set

THE BEACH HOUSE HOTEL SERIES:

Breakfast at The Beach House Hotel – 1
Lunch at The Beach House Hotel – 2
Dinner at The Beach House Hotel – 3
Christmas at The Beach House Hotel – 4
Margaritas at The Beach House Hotel – 5 (2021)
Dessert at The Beach House Hotel – 6 (2022)

THE FAT FRIDAYS GROUP:

Fat Fridays – 1
Sassy Saturdays – 2
Secret Sundays – 3

SALTY KEY INN BOOKS:

Finding Me – 1
Finding My Way – 2
Finding Love – 3
Finding Family – 4

CHANDLER HILL INN BOOKS:

Going Home – 1
Coming Home – 2
Home at Last – 3

SEASHELL COTTAGE BOOKS:

A Christmas Star

Change of Heart

A Summer of Surprises

A Road Trip to Remember

The Beach Babes – (2022)

DESERT SAGE INN BOOKS:

The Desert Flowers – Rose – 1

The Desert Flowers – Lily – 2 (Fall 2021)

The Desert Flowers – Willow – 3 (2022)

The Desert Flowers – Mistletoe & Holly – 4 (2022)

Winning BIG – a little love story for all ages

For more information: **http://amzn.to/2jamIaF**

PRAISE FOR JUDITH KEIM'S NOVELS

THE BEACH HOUSE HOTEL SERIES

"Love the characters in this series. This series was my first introduction to Judith Keim. She is now one of my favorites. Looking forward to reading more of her books."

BREAKFAST AT THE BEACH HOUSE HOTEL is an easy, delightful read that offers romance, family relationships, and strong women learning to be stronger. Real life situations filter through the pages. Enjoy!"

LUNCH AT THE BEACH HOUSE HOTEL – "This series is such a joy to read. You feel you are actually living with them. Can't wait to read the latest one."

DINNER AT THE BEACH HOUSE HOTEL – "A Terrific Read! As usual, Judith Keim did it again. Enjoyed immensely. Continue writing such pleasantly reading books for all of us readers."

CHRISTMAS AT THE BEACH HOUSE HOTEL – "Not Just Another Christmas Novel. This is book number four in the series and my introduction to Judith Keim's writing. I wasn't disappointed. The characters are dimensional and engaging. The plot is well crafted and advances at a pleasing pace. The Florida location is interesting and warming. It was a delight to read a romance novel with mature female protagonists. Ann and Rhoda have life experiences that enrich the story. It's a clever book about friends and extended family. Buy copies for your book group pals and enjoy this seasonal read."

THE HARTWELL WOMEN SERIES – Books 1 – 4

"This was an EXCELLENT series. When I discovered Judith Keim, I read all of her books back to back. I thoroughly enjoyed the women Keim has written about. They are believable and you want to just jump into their lives and be their friends! I can't wait for any upcoming books!"

"I fell into Judith Keim's Hartwell Women series and have read & enjoyed all of her books in every series. Each centers around a strong & interesting woman character and their family interaction. Good reads that leave you wanting more."

THE FAT FRIDAYS GROUP – Books 1 – 3

"Excellent story line for each character, and an insightful representation of situations which deal with some of the contemporary issues women are faced with today."

"I love this author's books. Her characters and their lives are realistic. The power of women's friendships is a common and beautiful theme that is threaded throughout this story."

THE SALTY KEY INN SERIES

FINDING ME – *"I thoroughly enjoyed the first book in this series and cannot wait for the others! The characters are endearing with the same struggles we all encounter. The setting makes me feel like I am a guest at The Salty Key Inn...relaxed, happy & light-hearted! The men are yummy and the women strong. You can't get better than that! Happy Reading!"*

FINDING MY WAY- *"Loved the family dynamics as well as uncertain emotions of dating and falling in love.*

Appreciated the morals and strength of parenting throughout. Just couldn't put this book down."

FINDING LOVE – *"I waited for this book because the first two was such good reads. This one didn't disappoint.... Judith Keim always puts substance into her books. This book was no different, I learned about PTSD, accepting oneself, there is always going to be problems but stick it out and make it work. Just the way life is. In some ways a lot like my life. Judith is right, it needs another book and I will definitely be reading it. Hope you choose to read this series, you will get so much out of it."*

FINDING FAMILY – *"Completing this series is like eating the last chip. Love Judith's writing, and her female characters are always smart, strong, vulnerable to life and love experiences."*

"This was a refreshing book. Bringing the heart and soul of the family to us."

CHANDLER HILL INN SERIES

GOING HOME – *"I absolutely could not put this book down. Started at night and read late into the middle of the night. As a child of the '60s, the Vietnam war was front and center so this resonated with me. All the characters in the book were so well developed that the reader felt like they were friends of the family."*

"I was completely immersed in this book, with the beautiful descriptive writing, and the authors' way of bringing her characters to life. I felt like I was right inside her story."

COMING HOME – *"Coming Home is a winner. The characters are well-developed, nuanced and likable. Enjoyed the vineyard setting, learning about wine growing and seeing the challenges Cami faces in running and growing a business. I look forward to the next book in this series!"*

"Coming Home was such a wonderful story. The author has a gift for getting the reader right to the heart of things."

HOME AT LAST – *"In this wonderful conclusion, to a heartfelt and emotional trilogy set in Oregon's stunning wine country, Judith Keim has tied up the Chandler Hill series with the perfect bow."*

"Overall, this is truly a wonderful addition to the Chandler Hill Inn series. Judith Keim definitely knows how to perfectly weave together a beautiful and heartfelt story."

"The storyline has some beautiful scenes along with family drama. Judith Keim has created characters with interactions that are believable and some of the subjects the story deals with are poignant."

SEASHELL COTTAGE BOOKS

A CHRISTMAS STAR – *"Love, laughter, sadness, great food, and hope for the future, all in one book. It doesn't get any better than this stunning read."*

"A Christmas Star is a heartwarming Christmas story featuring endearing characters. So many Christmas books are set in snowbound places...it was a nice change to read a Christmas story that takes place on a warm sandy beach!" Susan Peterson

CHANGE OF HEART – *"CHANGE OF HEART is the summer read we've all been waiting for. Judith Keim is a master at creating fascinating characters that are simply irresistible. Her stories leave you with a big smile on your face and a heart bursting with love."*

~Kellie Coates Gilbert, author of the popular Sun Valley Series

A SUMMER OF SURPRISES – *"The story is filled with a roller coaster of emotions and self-discovery. Finding love again and rebuilding family relationships."*

"Ms. Keim uses this book as an amazing platform to show that with hard emotional work, belief in yourself and love, the scars of abuse can be conquered. It in no way preaches, it's a lovely story with a happy ending."

"The character development was excellent. I felt I knew these people my whole life. The story development was very well thought out I was drawn [in] from the beginning."

DESERT SAGE INN BOOKS

THE DESERT FLOWERS – ROSE – *"The Desert Flowers - Rose, is the first book in the new series by Judith Keim. I always look forward to new books by Judith Keim, and this one is definitely a wonderful way to begin The Desert Sage Inn Series!"*

"In this first of a series, we see each woman come into her own and view new beginnings even as they must take this tearful journey as they slowly lose a dear friend. This is a very well written book with well-developed and likable main characters. It was interesting and enlightening as the first

portion of this saga unfolded. I very much enjoyed this book and I do recommend it"

"Judith Keim is one of those authors that you can always depend on to give you a great story with fantastic characters. I'm excited to know that she is writing a new series and after reading book 1 in the series, I can't wait to read the rest of the books."!

Sweet Talk

The Hartwell Women Series - Book 2

Judith Keim

Wild Quail Publishing

Sweet Talk is a work of fiction. Names, characters, places, public or private institutions, corporations, towns, and incidents are the product of the author's imagination or are used fictitiously. Any resemblance to actual events, locales, or persons, living or dead, is coincidental.

wildquail.pub@gmail.com

www.judithkeim.com,

Published in the United States of America by:

Wild Quail Publishing
PO Box 171332
Boise, ID 83717-1332

ISBN# 978-0-9909329-6-3

Dedication

For loving mothers everywhere

CHAPTER ONE

The sign for Sarita, California, appeared ahead of me. I let out a sigh of relief and loosened my tight grip on the steering wheel. It had been a grueling drive from Maine.

A car behind me beeped its horn, and I slowed to allow it to pass. I glimpsed a blond-haired man with handsome features. Our gazes met, and then he was tucking his silver Mercedes convertible into the line of cars ahead of me. A soft, giddy laugh escaped. California was the land of beautiful people. That man, whoever he was, had just proved it.

While searching for Treasures, the art gallery I now unexpectedly owned with my old college roommate, I drove past the cluster of small colorful shops along the water and continued up into the rolling hills overlooking the village. Her call for help had come at a time when I was vulnerable, following my failed marriage of little less than a year.

The carved wooden sign announcing the gallery beckoned. Second thoughts overcame me as I pulled into the parking lot. I rested my head against the steering wheel. Maybe now, with the New Year beginning, my life would take a wild swing for the better. God, I hoped so. This move had to drag me out of the mental and emotional pit I'd wallowed in for the last several months—months in which I'd despaired of any real happiness, while pretending to be fine.

The drive cross-country had seemed unending. I stacked the CDs I'd all but memorized on the journey and put them in the console between the front seats. I crinkled together the M&M wrappers that lay scattered across the passenger's seat and grabbed the empty water bottle. My travel-weary legs supported me as I climbed out of my SUV, stood, and stretched.

The door of the art gallery opened. I tossed the garbage in a trash can at the curb and hurried forward. A tall woman with curly chestnut hair strode toward me with a wide smile that lighted her face. A young girl skipped along behind her.

"Allie!" Kristin Lewis held her arms open to me. "You made it!" Her voice lilted with happiness. "Daisy and I have been watching for you all afternoon."

I returned her embrace, and turned to the young girl hanging back. My breath caught at her beauty—blond curls, wide blue eyes, and tiny, perfect features.

Kristin smiled at her daughter. "Daisy, you remember Allison Hartwell, don't you? She's your godmother!"

"My *fairy* godmother?"

I knelt before her and gazed into round blue eyes, fringed with enviable long lashes. My heart swelled. "Sometimes, it's good to believe in magic."

Clad in pink tights, red shirt and a green plaid skirt, she nodded. I hugged her gingerly, careful to avoid crushing the teddy bear she carried. I hadn't seen her for over a year and she'd grown taller. Her little arms reached around me for a brief moment before she turned away.

I stood and faced Kristin, silently assessing my old friend. Normally vivacious and healthy, she looked exhausted. Dark circles smudged the white skin under her eyes. A smile wavered on her face. "I know, I know. I swear I haven't slept in months. I was terrified I'd lose the business, have to start all over again, and be forced to move Daisy out of the school and her special class."

"Didn't the money I sent help?"

"Yes. It allowed me to pay off enough bills to order more

inventory, but our troubles go much deeper than that." Tears shimmered in her eyes. "I can't believe she took off on me."

I filled with sympathy. Last fall, amid heartbreaking sobs, Kristin had poured out the story of her lover's betrayal. Lisa Vaughn had taken off with all their savings, claiming it was her money. It'd left Kristin unable to pay her bills and without the means to build holiday inventory for the gallery. I'd known Christmas season was the best time for retail and had offered Kristin a loan. Instead, she'd suggested a business partnership. I'd jumped at the chance. My short marriage to Willard Jackson III had ended months earlier when he'd left me for his old girlfriend whom he'd kept on the side. Temporarily living at home with my parents after the break-up was not my idea of unwedded bliss.

"We sure know how to pick 'em, don't we?" I said, attempting humor.

Kristin laughed, and her face brightened, smoothing out the lines of worry. "This time it'll be better. I trust you, Allison. You've got a good head for business, and our friendship will make it so much easier." Her lips quivered. "I don't know what I would've done if you hadn't agreed to step in. Daisy is happy at her school, and we have a good life here."

Daisy spun around and around, her arms held out like the wings of a rare butterfly. *Such a precious child,* I thought, well aware that at birth Daisy had been deprived of oxygen and had suffered minor brain damage.

"How's she doing?"

Kristin's lips curved. "Remarkably well. She's a slow learner, but the teachers say once Daisy's learned something, it's locked in for good."

"Does she miss Lisa?"

Kristin's expression turned grim. "She hasn't said one word about her since Lisa left. It makes me wonder why." Her fists clenched at her side. "God! I was so stupid! Why didn't I see what was coming?"

Wondering how to respond, I teased my lip. I knew all about being made to look like a fool.

Daisy whined and tugged on Kristin's hand. "Mommy? I wanna go inside."

"In a second, honey." Kristin gave me a sheepish look. "I'm sorry, Allie. I got so wrapped up in the past, I forgot my manners. Let me help you bring your things inside."

"Do you mind if I take a moment to go into Treasures? I want to look around and savor the moment." Enthusiasm bubbled through me, chasing my fatigue away. "I can't believe I'm part-owner of the gallery. It's what I've always wanted—to have a store full of beautiful things. It's going to be so much fun helping people buy them."

Kristin's expression turned wry. "Oh, honey, believe me when I say that feeling will go away!"

"I hope not," I replied seriously. The promise of starting a whole new life away from Maine had kept me driving almost non-stop to reach California. I was out to show everyone I could succeed at running a business of my own. I also wanted to prove I could get along without a man. And while I was working at that, I intended to have a good time.

Kristin and Daisy followed me into the gallery. The sound of door chimes danced in the air behind us. My gaze swept from one end of the open, airy room to the other. An exotic aroma filled my nostrils, and I noticed a stick of incense smoldering nearby.

Brightly lit display cases lined the off-white walls, illuminating intriguing items inside. A few large pieces of artwork in various designs and materials sat on glass pedestals. They were highlighted by small, discreet spotlights from above. Hand-blown glass, paintings, pottery, jewelry, and metal sculptures in a variety of shapes and colors, twinkling in rainbow hues like shards of glass, caught my attention and kept my gaze darting about eagerly. Beautiful art hung on the wall and fine crafts, works of art in their own right, filled in spaces throughout the room. My fingers itched to handle some of the smaller pieces and erase the dust that lightly coated them.

"It's like a fairyland," I said softly, clasping my hands. "I can hardly wait to start."

Kristin clapped me on the back. "Let's get you settled in the apartment. Then you can wander down here to your heart's content. Tomorrow, we'll be open, but it won't be very busy. Not in January, after the holiday rush."

We went to my car to collect the luggage. Daisy, lost in her own world, gamboled around us like a long-legged filly exploring clover in a field.

"Are you sure you don't want to change your mind about renting a house?" said Kristin. "You can bunk in with Daisy and me permanently."

I shook my head. "Thanks, anyway, but I'm anxious to be on my own, especially after living back home with my parents for a few months." I tilted my head at the huge U-Haul trailer behind my SUV. "Besides, I've got to put all these hardly-used wedding presents to use. You can't believe all the stuff—everything from dishes to towels to chairs."

Kristin smiled. "Okay. Tomorrow Rob Henrickson will show you the house you've agreed to rent. It's right up the street. Like I told you, it's a great place. You'd never find anything else so nice, so close to the gallery."

I followed Kristin to a side entrance of the building and climbed the wooden stairs inside to the second story.

"Here we are." Kristin indicated the rooms with a sweep of her arm. "Home sweet home."

The living room was tiny but orderly. Book cases lined the wall on either side of the brick fireplace. They contained books and an assortment of art objects that obviously had come from the gallery downstairs. A red couch matched the color of designs in the Indian rug that lay before the hearth. Two dark-blue, overstuffed chairs flanked the fireplace.

"Cozy," I commented.

Jumping up and down with excitement, Daisy tugged on my arm. "Wanna see my room?"

"Sure, honey." I set my suitcase down and allowed Daisy to lead me to a snug room that contained a white, four- poster bed and a menagerie of stuffed animals. A pink and purple patchwork quilt lay atop the bed. The same patterned fabric was gathered and mounted high on the double windows that looked out to the water of Richardson Bay.

"This is it," announced Daisy proudly.

"It's very pretty. Just like you." Any girl would be thrilled to have a room like this. Everywhere I looked, a doll or a teddy bear winked a cheery hello. Daisy played with doll furniture in the large wooden dollhouse I'd sent her last Christmas.

"She's spoiled, but I can't resist all the girly things I never had," said Kristin softly.

I smiled at her. "Funny, how things work out."

The grin on Kristin's face evaporated. "Lisa emptied the company savings account, but she couldn't get hold of anything else. Daisy should be taken care of. That's one thing I did right. That, and naming you godmother. If anything happens to me, I want you to take care of Daisy."

My heart skipped a beat. My plans had no room for children. They made me uneasy with all their demands.

Fatigue set in as I sipped the red wine Kristin had handed

me. I followed her onto a deck overlooking the huge, fenced backyard. I'd had no idea she owned so much land behind the gallery.

"What's that?" I pointed to a compact cottage nestled near a corner of Kristin's property. From this angle, it looked like an oversized play house. A bright red door sat amid soft gray clapboard siding A number of small inviting windows glistened orange, reflecting the shimmering colors of the setting sun, and I had an overwhelming urge to run downstairs and peek inside.

"That's where Lisa did her work." Kristin's expression grew grim. "Right now, it's a mess."

"Are her paintings selling?" Lisa's bold, poorly-executed oil paintings had never appealed to me.

Kristin shook her head. "She blamed me for that, of course, even though I opened the gallery based on her paintings. They didn't sell even then. The business didn't take off until I filled the place with the works of people like Dawson Smith."

We sat in the kitchen to eat a simple meal of hamburgers and a garden salad. Kristin coaxed Daisy into eating a few bites of food while ignoring her high-pitched whining.

I did the dishes while Kristin got Daisy ready for bed. Overhearing the pleading hum of Kristin's voice and the now familiar whine from Daisy, I wondered how Kristin managed. I'd once thought of having children of my own, but seeing how difficult it could be, I was happy Will and I hadn't had any.

When Kristin reappeared, I fought and finally gave in to a yawn. "Sorry, I can't help it."

"I'm sorry. I've forgotten my manners again. You must be exhausted. The sleep couch is already made up for you. The bathroom in the hallway is yours."

We pulled out the folding couch, and Kristin handed me a pillow. "Sleep tight."

As I prepared for bed, I thought about the house down the street. I hoped it was as nice as the pictures I'd seen. Privacy was important to me, though at the moment I was so tired I thought I'd be able to fall asleep in the midst of a roaring crowd. I slid under the soft blankets and lay back against the pillow, breathing the cool night air from the open window, satisfied I'd exchanged Casco Bay for Richardson Bay.

In the night, a high-pitched scream shot shivers of alarm down my spine. Confused and dazed, I jumped out of bed.

Kristin poked her head into the living room. "It's okay. Daisy often has nightmares."

Trembling from the adrenaline that still raced through my body, I climbed back into bed and lay there, letting my heartbeat slow to its normal rhythm.

Sunlight slanted through the windows onto my face, begging me to open my eyes. Sleepily, I blinked my way into my first full day of my new life. The smell of coffee wafted over to me from the kitchen. The calls of birds in the trees outside cheered me. Eager to see what the day would hold, I rose and padded into the kitchen in bare feet.

Kristin sat at the kitchen table, sipping coffee, newspaper in hand. She looked up at me and smiled. "I'm sorry about disturbing you last night." She rose and handed me a cup of coffee. "Daisy has nightmares pretty often. I think it's the medicine she's on, though the doctor denies it."

"It must be difficult raising her alone."

"Sometimes I wonder if I made a mistake by not telling her father about her. At the time, I was still trying to figure out so many things. Later, I came to think it was better that he remain unaware."

She stared out the window and turned back to me.

"Everyone wants to know who he is, but at this stage of my life, I'm not telling anyone. It would hurt other people. I was in bad shape when I got pregnant—partying and screwing around because I hadn't come to terms with the fact that I was gay. You can imagine how I felt when I found out I was pregnant at the same time I finally admitted I much preferred women to men. It was such a horrible time in my life. The only good thing to come out of it was Daisy. God knows, my family dumped me in a hurry." The corners of Kristin's mouth turned down.

I knew her ultra conservative parents from our college days. It hadn't surprised me that they'd made it clear they'd never accept her, her life or her child.

"After this business with Lisa," she continued, "I don't know if I could ever be really close to someone again."

I sighed with sympathy. "I know how you feel. I've decided not to date. Then I know I won't get hurt."

"Hah! That's never going to work. With that honey-colored hair and those blue eyes of yours, you're a knock-out. I remember what it was like in college—the guys followed you around with their tongues hanging out."

I remembered too, and at twenty-nine, I wondered what they'd seen in me. Will had made me feel so ugly, so worthless.

"Mommy?" Daisy called from the bathroom.

Kristin let out a sigh and went to her.

Daisy looked like a sleep-rumpled angel when she entered the kitchen.

I smiled. "Morning."

Daisy glanced at me and, silent, climbed up onto a chair.

As Kristin poured Daisy's cereal into a bowl, I studied their features. They looked nothing alike. I couldn't help wondering who Daisy's father was.

After breakfast, Kristin took off with Daisy, down the hill

to the school bus stop with a promise to be right back.

I showered and dressed, then hurried downstairs to Treasures.

In bright daylight, the store looked dusty and tired, as if some things had been sitting on shelves too long. Fighting dismay, I realized it would take more than a dusting to make it fresh. I could see now that the gallery could use more inventory, a broader variety. Some items needed rearranging to cover bare spots. Worry threaded through me, knotting my stomach. I hadn't received a year-end report from Kristin, like she'd promised. She'd been too busy to prepare it.

I wandered through the gallery, picking up various items, reading their information cards, gathering details I'd need for selling. I turned on the background sound system, delighted by the soft, soothing music, and walked into the back office, eager to discover what I could about the financials. I was sitting at the desk, leafing through the papers on top of it, when the sound of sirens rent the air. I checked my watch and frowned. Kristin hadn't returned. A feeling so strong, so awful gripped me. I raced to the door.

At the bottom of the hill, I could see an ambulance.

I started running.

A small crowd had gathered at the bottom of the hill. Kristin was nowhere to be seen. With its red lights flashing, the ambulance pulled away from the curb.

"What happened? Where's Kristin?" I managed to get out.

A young woman came over to me. "Are you the new business partner she was telling us about?" She grasped my hands. Tears shone in her eyes.

"Yes," I answered numbly.

"I'm Cindy Cartwright. I live down the street. Kristin collapsed. They're taking her to the Greenbrae Hospital."

My knees turned to marshmallow. "Omigod! No! I have to

go to the hospital right away."

"Do you need help? "Cindy gave me a worried look. "I'm not sure you should drive."

"I'd better go on my own. I have no idea how long I'll need to be gone. Just tell me how to get there. And, Cindy, give me your phone number in case I need your help with Daisy."

Cindy took a paper and pen out of her purse and quickly wrote down the information I wanted. She repeated the directions and handed me the paper. I said a quick good-bye and ran up the hill.

My SUV, with the trailer still attached to it, sat in the parking lot beside Kristin's old blue Honda. I ran inside for the keys to her car. I'd seen them hanging on a hook in the kitchen. I grabbed them and my purse.

Outside, I unlocked her car, slid behind the wheel and turned the key. The car coughed and then roared to life.

Trying to remember everything Cindy had told me, I pulled out of the parking lot and headed for the hospital. Cindy had said it would take approximately fifteen minutes to get there. The ambulance was about ten minutes ahead of me.

The red light ahead of me flashed a warning. I glanced both ways to make sure no cars were approaching and raced through it. Pleading to heaven for Kristin's recovery, I hardly registered the passing landscape.

The sign for the hospital's emergency entrance appeared. I swerved into the nearby parking lot. The car's tires squealed in protest as I whirled into an empty space.

An ambulance was backed up to an entrance. I got out of the car, and seeing no one else, stealthily crept through the door, into a space marked Resuscitation Room.

Clinging to the wall, I drew in a shaky breath. Kristin lay on a table. A doctor and two others circled her. Shivering, I stared at Kristin, unable to believe this pale, still woman was the same person I'd chatted with that morning.

The doctor shook his head at a paramedic. "We'll declare the time of death as 9:27 AM."

"She's dead?" My wail echoed off the walls.

Surprised, the staff turned to me. The paramedic rushed over to me. I held onto him, grateful for his strength.

"I'm her friend and her business partner," I explained to the doctor who approached us.

"Here, have a seat." The doctor gestured toward a metal folding chair sitting against the wall. I collapsed on it, feeling as if I'd never have the energy to rise again.

The doctor took my hand. "What's your name?" Kindness softened his voice.

"Allison Hartwell," I finally managed to get out past the lump in my throat.

"I'm awfully sorry about the loss of your friend. We did everything we could to save her. She'd been without a pulse for some time and despite all the intervention, we were unable to start her heart again."

"Was it a heart attack?"

He shook his head. "I'm suspecting a cerebral hemorrhage, something congenital, but we'll leave a final diagnosis up to the medical examiner after he completes his autopsy."

The room whirled in front of me. "I..I think I'm going to faint."

"Put your head between your knees," the doctor said, gently pushing my head down.

I felt something being placed in front of my nose and jerked away from its stringent odor.

"Better now?" a female voice asked.

Tears slipped down my cheeks. I'd never been worse in my life.

"Would you like to talk to one of our counselors?" the

brown-skinned nurse asked gently.

I shook my head, numb to the bone.

"We need to get some information on the patient. And we need to know the next of kin."

A thought, like a blow to the gut, hit me and I doubled over again.

Omigod! Daisy was mine now.

CHAPTER TWO

After taking care of paperwork at the hospital, I returned to the gallery and called the school. I was transferred to the school psychologist.

Roberta Rosenberg listened to me and said, "I'm so sorry this has happened. Kristin spoke to me about your arrival, Allison. She filled out paperwork so you'd be authorized to pick up Daisy from school when she couldn't. She was so happy to have you come here."

I nodded foolishly, as if she could see me. "Can you help me? I'm not sure what to do. How am I going to tell Daisy?"

We agreed to let Daisy complete her normal daily activities. She'd have enough to cope with later and I needed time to calm myself to make final arrangements for Kristin.

"Remember, Allison," said Roberta kindly, "the truth is important, put in such a way as not to be overly frightening. And not only should you keep Daisy on a normal schedule, but you, yourself, need to go on with your life, melding hers with yours. You both will have a lot to handle in the next few months. Routine will help. And, of course, we all understand that you need to be able to make a living. You'll have to provide for her financially as well as emotionally and physically. I'm here to help you both. Call me anytime."

I hung up, as frightened as I'd ever been. Deadened, I called my older sister in Boston and sobbed out the news of Kristin's death. "I don't know what I'm going to do, Samantha. I don't know a damn thing about raising children. How can I be a good mother to an eight-year-old—a difficult one at that?

I'm so scared I won't do a good job with her." I held back another sob. "And how am I going to support both of us? I have an awful feeling the Christmas season didn't help as much as we thought it would."

"One thing at a time, Allie," Samantha said, in the voice she must use to others in her consulting practice. "Didn't Kristin have friends? They can help you with Daisy. As far as the business goes, you'll have to sort through things when you can. It's good that both of you had already signed the partnership agreement I drew up. That means you, Allison, now own the house and land, along with the business."

Instead of feeling relieved, I felt trapped. There was no escape now. I'd made a promise to Kristin and I meant to keep it. Her family had written her and Daisy off. I would not, could not do that. Now I solely owned a business that might not be doing as well as I'd been led to believe and I was mother to an eight-year-old I hardly knew. I wanted to crawl back into bed and forget the day had ever happened.

Poor Kristin, poor me and poor, poor Daisy.

Feeling as if I were acting in a play gone awry, I stood waiting for the afternoon school bus with the other neighborhood mothers. I didn't belong here. They knew what they were doing. I did not.

I looked for Cindy, but she was not among them. Ignoring the sympathetic glances cast at me, I stayed on the outer edge of the group, preparing myself for the emotional scenes that were sure to come.

Ice crept through my veins when the yellow bus rolled to a stop in front of us. The door opened and two boys, pushing each other, got off. They were followed by several girls, then another group of boys.

My throat grew dry. I leaned forward, searching for Daisy.

Through the window I spied blond curls and let out a sigh of relief. Daisy emerged and gazed at the dispersing group of mothers and students with surprise.

I stepped forward and waved. "Hi, Daisy!"

She studied me uncertainly, then her lips curved and she waved back.

"Where's Mommy?" She accepted the hand I held out to her.

I took a deep breath and forced a smile. "Hey! Did you have a good day at school? Mrs. Rosenberg told me they were showing a movie in your class today."

Daisy's eyes lit up. "The movie was called Bambi and it was all about a baby deer."

I listened to her chat about the different characters in the story, grateful I'd found a topic to distract her. My heart clutched when I realized the movie dealt with death too.

We reached the gallery's parking lot, and Daisy raced ahead of me to go inside.

"Upstairs," I called to her, and she ran around to the side of the building.

"I want to tell Mommy about the movie," she announced, climbing the stairs to the apartment ahead of me.

I followed her. My feet felt as if they were blocks of cement. How do you tell a little girl her mother is dead? The school psychologist had suggested being direct.

"Where's Mommy?" Daisy's brow wrinkled.

I took her hand and led her to one of the overstuffed chairs. She stood in front of me, her lips quivering.

"I want my Mommy."

"Come here, Sweetheart," I said softly, sitting and drawing her into my lap.

"Why are you crying, Allie?" Daisy traced the wetness on

my cheeks with a tiny finger. "What's wrong?"

I took a deep breath, praying I would find the right words.

"Where's Mommy?" Daisy's eyes welled when I still couldn't answer. "I want Mommy."

"I know you do," I began, holding back sobs. "But sometimes things don't work out the way you want them to. Mommy got very sick—so sick she couldn't get better. Oh, honey, your Mommy is in heaven." I couldn't think of another way to say it.

Daisy frowned. "In heaven? Like my pet bird?"

"You and Mommy talked about that, remember? Do you know what heaven is?"

Daisy's eyes widened as understanding dawned. "I don't want Mommy in heaven. I want her here!" She pounded at me with angry fists. It hurt my heart more than my body. Falling back against me, she let out a haunting high-pitched wail I'd remember for the rest of my life.

Sobbing earnestly now, I held onto her and rocked her in my arms. After some time, she wiggled out of my arms and stood scowling at me, her hands on her hips. "I don't want *you*. I want Mommy."

"I know you do. I wish she could be here, too. But if she couldn't be with you, Mommy wanted me to help."

Her face screwed up. "No! No! No!" She threw herself down on the floor and kicked in a tap, tap, tapping rhythm. It felt as if she were pounding a nail into my heart. I sat on the floor beside her. When she finally lay quiet, I reached for her.

She scrambled to her feet. "Go away! I hate you!" she screamed and ran into her mother's bedroom.

My heart pounded in nervous beats. I let her go. I was so bad at this.

Following the psychologists instructions to keep things as normal as possible, I went into the kitchen and fixed spaghetti, one of Daisy's favorite things. She reluctantly came to the table but neither of us ate; we simply pushed food around on a plate and stared at each other helplessly.

Afterward, Daisy lay on the couch like a rag doll, staring blindly at the television. I sat next to her and started to rub her back.

She whirled away from my touch. "Don't do that!" she shrieked. "You're not my mother!"

Crying, she got up off the couch and raced into her room.

Wringing my hands, I stood in the hallway outside her room. "Daisy?" I called softly, "Are you all right?"

She burst through the doorway and wrapped her arms around my legs, weeping. I scooped her up and held her against me, wishing I could take the hurt away.

When she stopped crying, Daisy allowed me to undress her and tuck her into bed. I stayed with her until she fell asleep. The hell with following a normal routine, I thought, picking up her dirty clothes and tossing them into the hamper in her room. Daisy could have a bath in the morning.

Mentally and emotionally exhausted, I pulled out the sleep couch, got ready for bed and collapsed onto the mattress. I rubbed my eyes, still swollen from all the tears I'd shed. They felt as if sandpaper were being scraped against them. I couldn't believe all that had happened. I'd come to California full of plans for a successful business and a happier life. Now it all lay in jeopardy.

My eyes closed, but it was some time before I slept.

A high-pitched scream awoke me. Groggy, I got to my feet and staggered into Daisy's room. "Daisy?"

The soft glow from the nightlight in her room made her eyes look owl-like in her small-featured face. When she saw me, she threw herself back on her pillow. "No! Not you! Mommy!"

I let out a sigh. Nobody wanted Kristin more than I. Lowering myself on the edge of the bed, I took Daisy's hand in mine. "Sweetheart, we'll get through this. You and I, together. Do you want me to stay with you for a while?"

She shook her head and stared at me. "Can I come sleep with you? "she asked in a little voice that touched me.

"Sure, honey. C'mon."

Taking her hand, I led her to the pull-out couch, giving up on the idea of further sleep for me. She settled beside me and after moving restlessly, fell asleep clutching her teddy bear. Watching her sweet little face relax in sleep, I marveled at her perfect features. Her eyes were still swollen from crying. I wiped a lingering tear away and silently vowed to do my best to take care of her, like Kristin wanted.

In the morning, Daisy surprised me by saying she wanted to go to school. She cooperated about taking a bath, had a melt-down over what clothes to wear, ate half her breakfast and refused to wear a coat, even though a morning fog proved to be chilly. By the time we were outside and headed to the bus stop, I felt as if I'd been forced to climb several of San Francisco's hills.

Cindy came forward to meet us. She gave me a worried look as Daisy left my side to climb onto the school bus. "How did it go?"

I blinked back tears. "Fine," I lied. "It'll take a while for both Daisy and me to get used to all the changes." When I waved good-bye to Daisy, she simply stared at me.

Cindy noticed and clucked sympathetically. "Like you said, she needs time. Come meet some of the other mothers."

Six other women were gathered there. After introductions were exchanged and sympathy expressed, I climbed the hill to the gallery, determined to find any information I could about Daisy's father.

In the gallery office, I found a drawer full of Kristin's personal papers. Leafing through them, I discovered Daisy's birth certificate. No mention was made of a father.

I was sitting at the desk, attempting to figure out the password to get into the financial files, when I heard a deep masculine voice call, "Hello! Anyone here?"

I went out to the front.

A man stood there, his arms wrapped around a tall, ceramic form.

"Can I help you?" I watched as he set a large vase down on the floor.

"Hi! I'm Dawson Smith." His hair was silver, not only at the edges, but remained a thick and bountiful presence throughout his soft curls. "You must be Allison Hartwell. Kristin told me all about you."

I smiled and held out my hand. Dawson shook it and returned my smile. The creases at the corner of his eyes deepened, adding to his friendly demeanor. I guessed him to be in his fifties.

"Where's Kristin?" he asked.

I blinked rapidly, willing the sting in my eyes to go away. Tears defiantly rolled down my cheeks. "Kristin died yesterday. They think it was a cerebral hemorrhage. The announcement should be in the paper today."

He staggered back. "Dead? But I talked to her a couple of days ago. She wanted me to bring in more work on consignment." He closed his eyes and drew a deep unsteady breath, his pain obvious.

"I'm sorry. It's hard for me to believe too."

"Give me a few minutes. This has really thrown me for a loop." He took a seat behind the counter and rested his head in his hands.

To give him time alone, I knelt beside the vase. About two

feet tall, its glazed surface shone in various shades of blue. "The colors are beautiful."

Dawson rose to his feet and came over to me. "Kristin always loved my work. My pieces are unusual for Raku because they're so large."

I'd heard about Raku pottery, and read what I could, but knew little about how it was actually made. Forcing myself to focus on business, I asked, "What is Raku, exactly?"

His eyes grew moist. "It's something Kristin was really into." He cleared his throat. "It's a process of firing done by rapid heating and cooling of the pottery. Sometimes, after the pots have been fired and are still very hot, we place them in piles of leaves or straw or other combustible materials for what is called a post-firing. It makes for interesting finishes."

"Now I remember." I smiled and recited, "The glazes are thick and very alkaline. The pots are dipped into them or the glazes are poured over the pottery or brushed onto it." Admiring it, I trailed my fingers over Dawson's vase.

"It takes a lot of care to handle the hot pieces, especially when they're this big."

I glanced at him. Beneath his T-shirt his arm muscles bulged. For a man his age, he was in very good shape. His eyes met mine and I read real sadness there.

"I still can't believe Kristin is gone." He shook his head. "Should I take this piece back or do you want to keep it?"

I rose. "I definitely want it. But you're going to have to help me. You mentioned this is on consignment. What price would Kristin place on this? And, if I remember correctly, the consigner gets sixty percent and the gallery gets forty. Right?"

"A vase like this would usually be marked fifteen hundred dollars."

I studied it with new respect.

Dawson and I found the consignment book and filled in the

date, description and price under his name.

"Thanks for your help." I had to learn so many things—things Kristin would have shown me.

"I'm so sorry about Kristin. She was someone special."

"How did you two get to know each other?"

He jabbed a thumb at the blue Honda sitting in the parking lot. "That old car of hers. Back a number of years ago, it broke down along the road. I stopped to help, fiddled with some wires under the hood and followed her here to make sure she got home safely. She invited me to stay for dinner. That was the beginning of our friendship." He smiled sadly. "She made really good meatloaf."

"You're kidding!" When she and I were college roommates, Kristin's idea of cooking was to heat a can of soup.

"I'll miss much more than that. Let me know when there will be a service." Dawson gave me a little salute and turned to go.

I watched through the front picture window as he walked slowly to his truck, climbed in, and took off.

As I continued to go through the consignment records, it soon became apparent that money was still owed to a few people. Pulse pounding, I searched through the checkbook to see if it was simply a matter of poor recordkeeping. But no checks had been written to those people in the last several months.

I'd started my search for the proper computer password when the phone rang. I picked it up. "Treasures Gallery" I chirped, remembering when I would have been excited about saying it. Right now, it seemed like a noose around my neck.

"Allison? Is that you?"

At the sound of my mother's voice, I burst into tears.

"Oh, honey, I'm sorry I missed your call yesterday. Samantha phoned and told me all about what happened. I'm so sorry. I've been thinking this whole trip to California was a bad idea. Now that you have a little girl to take care of, why don't you consider coming home where you have family to help you?"

For a moment, that's exactly what I wanted to do—run home to my family. "No, Mom. I can't do that. Daisy is happy here, with her school and all. It wouldn't be fair to her."

"Are you going to stay in Kristin's apartment? What about the house you rented?"

I felt my eyes widen. In all the confusion, I'd completely forgotten about the house I'd agreed to rent. I'd already put first and last month's rent down. "I...I don't know what I'm going to do about it. Right now, I have to make it through another day." My voice cracked. "It's going to take time for me to sort things out."

"Oh, my darling, I'm sure you'll do fine, but I worry so when one of my children is in trouble. "

I was in trouble, all right, though the sound of my mother's voice had made me feel stronger. Daisy, bless her heart, would never have that satisfaction again.

CHAPTER THREE

The rumbles in my stomach couldn't be ignored. I left the office and climbed the stairs to the apartment to grab something for lunch. Standing alone in the middle of the living room, the overwhelming weight of grief settled on my shoulders. Everywhere I looked, I sensed Kristin's presence. I closed my eyes. It was too, too much.

Fighting tears, I went into the kitchen and called Rob Henrickson. When he didn't answer, I left a message for him to call me. I quickly made a peanut butter and jelly sandwich, grabbed an apple and a hunk of cheese, and returned downstairs. No customers had arrived that morning, but I wanted to be ready, just in case.

As I reviewed the files, I became more and more dismayed by the lack of information. Artistic people weren't always the most careful about details, but I couldn't understand how Kristin could have let things go for so long.

The phone rang. "Treasures," I chirped, making an effort to sound pleasant.

"Is this Kristin Lewis?"

I swallowed hard. "No, this is her partner, Allison Hartwell."

"Oh, well, my name is Doreen Sandler, one of your consigners. I haven't been paid for jewelry that Kristin said was sold before Christmas. When can I expect my check?"

My voice shook as I told her about Kristin and explained that I was working to straighten things out. The conversation ended on a friendly note, but I was mortified. I'd been taught from an early age to be financially responsible.

I dug deeper into the piles of paper on Kristin's desk. The December figures were nowhere to be found. Worrying thoughts circled in my head. I had to do more than prove I could run a business; I had to ensure it was successful enough to support all of Daisy's expenses as well as mine.

Too soon, it was time to pick up Daisy at the school bus stop. My mouth grew dry at the thought of another bout of emotional trauma. I wanted to do things right, but I had no real experience to guide me.

Apprehensive, I walked down the hill and joined the other women at the bus stop. They smiled and nodded at me, but I was sure the *real* mothers there could tell what a fraud I was.

The yellow school bus rolled to a stop. Daisy's sweet face peered out the window at the gathering of women. Her gaze settled on me. I waved and forced a cheery smile. She turned away and headed down the aisle, her little shoulders slumped.

I hurried over to the door of the bus to greet her.

Two girls hopped off the bus steps ahead of her. Then it was Daisy's turn. Staring at me, her eyes filled with tears.

Mouth dry, I took her hand in mine. "Hi, Honey! Have a good day?"

She shook her head, and remained silent. Her round blue eyes studied mine. I put my arm across her. With a shake of her shoulders, she edged away from me. We walked to the gallery side by side, glancing at each other, but saying nothing. As we approached it, she looked up at the apartment. "Mommy's not there?"

I shook my head. "I'm sorry, Daisy. Nothing has changed. Come with me into the gallery. I have a snack for you."

Silently, she followed me inside. After settling her in a chair in the office, I cut up the apple and cheese for her and brought out the coloring book and crayons I'd discovered in a desk drawer. As I set them before her, the bell on the front door tinkled. "Here you go, Daisy. Sit there and I'll check on you in a few minutes."

Excited, I hurried to greet a customer. I was in the midst of making a much-needed sale of an expensive Chihuly-like glass vase when Daisy interrupted me.

"I want a cookie!" she whined, tugging on my sleeve.

"I'm sorry. I don't have any, right now," I said quietly. "Why don't you go back to your coloring book? I'll be there in a minute."

"No! No!" Daisy flailed her arms, slapping at my body, pushing me away. "You can't tell me what to do! You're not my mother!"

"Excuse me. I'll be right back," I told the wide-eyed customer, a pleasant older woman.

Taking Daisy's hand, I led her to my office. *What would my mother say?* Sitting her in a chair, I spoke quietly but firmly. "Daisy, I need you to stay here until you stop fussing. I'm busy with a customer. You can come out front after you've calmed down."

I left her and returned to explain the situation to the customer, praying I hadn't lost the sale. Sympathy saved me, but as I wrapped up the vase, I realized I'd need to hire an afternoon babysitter. At the moment, however, it was out of the question. I couldn't afford it.

When I finally was able to go back into the office, I found Daisy dozing, her head resting on an open page of the coloring book. She hadn't filled in the colors but had, instead, drawn angry Xs across the page. My heart ached for her.

I rubbed her back. "Daisy? Do you want to go upstairs now?"

"I want my Mommy!" she wailed.

I lifted her into my arms and rocked her. She settled

against my chest and I breathed a sigh of relief when she snuggled close.

After a few minutes, she agreed to follow me outside and up the stairs. In the living room, she stared at the door to her mother's room. "I don't like it here anymore."

Glancing at the surroundings, I felt the same way. Kristin's ghost was everywhere. "Tell you what, you can sleep with me tonight, like a sleep-over, right here in the living room. How about that?"

Daisy gave me a dubious look, then bobbed her head in agreement.

She followed like a silent shadow when I went downstairs to lock up the gallery. Even as I cooked a simple meal of baked chicken and salad, she was never far from my side. After dinner, I managed to get her to take her medicine and into a bath, but I sensed how uncomfortable she was in the apartment. We couldn't stay there. Neither of us wanted that.

"Aren't you going to get into your pajamas?" Daisy asked, as we pulled out the sleep sofa.

"I will soon," I promised. I turned off the lights in the living room, careful to keep the hall light on so Daisy wouldn't be frightened.

I settled beside her on the mattress. "I'll stretch out here until you fall asleep."

Daisy lay back against the pillow, holding onto a stuffed bear, staring up at the ceiling. "Is Mommy an angel?" she asked in a little voice that told me so much.

"Yes, I believe she is," I answered, touched by the idea. "I believe she's your very special angel, keeping watch over you."

Daisy was quiet for a moment and turned toward me. Reaching out, she touched my cheek with a finger and whispered, "I wish you were Mommy."

"I know." I took hold of her hand and gave it an

encouraging squeeze. I'd give anything to have Kristin here taking care of her daughter, helping me with the business.

Daisy turned over and within minutes, was asleep.

Later, showered and shampooed, I settled on the sleep sofa next to Daisy, my muscles tight with stress. There were so many things for me to take care of—Daisy, the gallery, living quarters. It was all such a damn mess.

I hadn't been asleep long when Daisy awoke with a cry. Bleary-eyed, I rubbed her back and murmured softly to her until she was breathing deeply again. But sleep was ruined for me, kept at bay by worry.

Morning light was streaming in the window when I awoke. I sat up with a jolt. Daisy was nowhere to be seen.

"Daisy? Where are you?"

She came out of the kitchen, her mouth ringed in something dark. I hurried over to her. "What have you been eating?"

Her eyes gleamed with mischief. "Chocolate. Mommy sometimes lets me have candy in the morning."

I didn't believe a word of it. "Well, you've had enough chocolate this morning. It's late. We've got to get you ready for school."

"I'm not going to school." She gave me a defiant smile.

Blinking in surprise, I stated, "I really think you should."

Her lower lip jutted out. She crossed her arms in front of her. "Why? Why should I? Mommy's not here."

Ahhh, time to put my foot down, set my own rules. Isn't that what my mother would do? "But *I'm* here, Daisy. And I can't prepare a surprise for you if you stay home."

Her eyes lit up. "Surprise? What kind of surprise?"

I smiled. "If I tell you, it won't be a surprise. But I think it's something you'd like. A change from here."

She studied me for a moment. "Is this like a fairy

godmother surprise?"

I shook my head. "It's not magical, but it's something nice."

Daisy put a hand on her hip and narrowed her eyes. "If I go to school, can I have chocolate cookies when I come home?"

Oh, the battle is still on. "We'll see. Maybe one."

"Two."

"Okay, two." I was afraid I'd end up giving her three if the bartering continued. She'd apparently had a lot of practice at this. "Now go dress, while I get breakfast ready."

I got coffee going and took a moment to send an email to Roberta Rosenberg, telling the school psychologist what I was about to do, and then hurried to get dressed myself.

A short while later, standing with the other mothers at the bus stop, I waved good-bye to Daisy. Somber, off her sugar high, she stared out the window at me, wiggling one finger.

Progress.

I hurried back home, made a list of things I'd need to do, and called Rob once more.

Downstairs in the gallery, I continued sorting through papers, working to make sense of them. I'd put everything into Excel files and Quick Books—if only I could get into the damn computer!

I was dusting shelves when I heard someone pull into the parking lot. I watched through the front window as a man got out of a black truck and strolled toward the door. He was tall and lanky, with dark brown hair that hung over his brow. Dressed in jeans and a flannel shirt, he moved in rhythm to his long-legged gait, stepped into the gallery and settled a green-eyed gaze on me. Not exactly handsome, he had an interesting quality about him—square jaw, Roman nose, alert expression.

"Allison?"

At my nod, he walked over to me and held out a hand. "Rob

Henrickson. I got your call. I just heard about Kristin." His eyes grew misty. "I couldn't believe it. She was supposed to call me a couple days ago. Now I understand why she didn't." He pinched the bridge of his nose and drew in a deep breath. "How's Daisy?"

I let out a sigh. "We're trying to get used to the whole idea. You know, my taking care of her."

He studied me blatantly, assessing me in an unblinking manner I found unnerving. "Kristin talked about you all the time. I know she'd be happy you're here for Daisy."

Touched by his words, I turned away so he wouldn't see my fresh tears.

"So you still want the house?" he asked. "I've got the signed contract here, but I could talk the owner of the house out of the lease."

I faced him. "No. Daisy doesn't like being in the apartment. I understand. I see Kristin there, everywhere I look. We'll both be happier in a new place without so many memories. I want to set up Daisy's room in the new place before she comes home from school today. I'm hoping you or someone you know will be able to help me make it happen. It's a special surprise for her."

"Nice idea. I can do it. I'm free until four." He held up a set of keys and jingled them. "I stopped at the real estate office to pick these up. We'd better get started."

"Have you been selling real estate for a long time?"

"Off and on. It fills in my time when I'm not playing in my band. But it's the band that's really important to me."

"Why does the owner want to rent, not sell it?" I asked, closing up the gallery.

An odd look crossed Rob's face. "It belongs to a friend of Lisa's. The two of them think they might want to come back here someday. They're renting a place in Santa Fe, though I heard they're leaving for a long vacation abroad. Catherine's got a lot of money."

"Oh." Now it all made sense. Catherine was the reason Lisa had left Kristin. It had very little to do with her art. I hadn't known Lisa well, but my memories of her weren't pleasant. She was a large, broad-shouldered, loud woman whose air of confidence could sometimes bowl people over. Lisa's interests had always focused on money—having it and spending it. It was no wonder Kristin hadn't been able to keep Lisa content.

As I walked up the hill, the clear, cool air made me happy to have escaped the snowy weather back east. Rob stopped in front of a small yellow Victorian house trimmed in crisp white. It sat like a ray of sunshine on the hillside. A white picket fence marked the roadside boundary of the front lawn. I envisioned climbing pink roses on it in the summer months. At one corner of the house a tower-like structure with many windows added an intriguing dimension. A broad porch swept across the front. I could imagine sitting there on a hot summer day to enjoy the water view below.

"Nice, huh?"

I grinned at Rob. "Even better than the one photo I saw. Let's go inside."

Rob unlocked the front door, and we stepped into a sizeable living room whose main feature was a brick fireplace. A small dining area beyond it led into a modern kitchen with stainless steel appliances. French doors near the eating area opened onto a back deck, which held a wooden Jacuzzi tub. Charmed, I followed Rob upstairs. The master bedroom was roomy enough for a king-sized bed and had a curved window seat that matched the shape of the rounded tower.

I knelt on the cushioned seat and peered out the windows. I loved the sight of the water below, and thought I could see all the way to San Francisco.

"You're happy with it?" Rob asked. He'd showed me two other bedrooms.

"Oh yes! Now I have to make sure Daisy is."

We returned to the gallery.

"Any idea what the computer password might be? I've looked everywhere for a note on it and I've tried every variation of Kristin, Daisy and Lewis I can think of."

A grin spread across Rob's face. "Have you tried Daisy Mae Jones? She was the subject of an old joke that Kristin used to like."

I hurried over to the computer and typed it in. The computer opened up to me. "Thanks, Rob! Any other magical tricks?"

He laughed. "No, but hey, if you need help with the gallery, my girlfriend, Jessie, can probably help out when she's not working at Nordstrom's."

"Thanks, I'll remember that."

Rob helped me take apart Daisy's bed and we loaded it, the mattress and the rest of Daisy's bedroom furniture into his truck and drove it up the hill.

We set everything up in a sweet little room with a sloped ceiling which overlooked the small garden in the back of the house.

"Looks great." Rob stood back with a satisfied smile. "What about your bedroom?"

I took a deep breath. "If you'll help me move my stuff inside, I'll gladly pay you the going rate for your work. I need to empty and return the U-Haul trailer."

Rob shook his head. "Consider it a gift. Something I'm doing for Kristin." His eyes filled. "She's the one who got me the job at the real estate office."

"Surely there's something I can do in return," I protested.

He grinned. "Invite me and Jessie for a home cooked meal

sometime. Kristin used to have us come to her house quite often."

I smiled. "Deal."

I returned to the gallery for my SUV and backed it into the driveway of my house. Rob helped me unload the boxes inside, along with my bed, the mattress, a couple of stuffed chairs, end tables and a love seat from the condo I'd shared with Will.

Wiping the sweat from my brow, I turned to him. "I'll take care of everything else, if you'll help me put together my bed." I gave him a teasing smile. "I'm thinking you've earned a big steak dinner with a nice bottle of wine."

Rob laughed. "No problem. We'll get it done."

After Rob left, I drove to the U-Haul dealer to return the trailer and, worried about being late to pick up Daisy, raced through aggravating traffic to the bus stop. When I arrived, the yellow bus was pulling away from the curb. Daisy was standing in the midst of a group of mothers and children, crying. Her pink backpack lay next to her on the ground.

I got out of the car and ran over to her.

Cindy stepped forward, her lips tight as she glared at me. "You're late." She nodded her head at Daisy. "After all she's gone through recently, the poor thing thought you'd forgotten her."

"Oh, but I hadn't!" I exclaimed. My heart pounded in dismay. "Daisy? I'm sorry if I was a couple of minutes late." I knelt before her, feeling like a criminal instead of a woman so tired I could hardly see.

Daisy's face scrunched into angry lines that marred her pretty features. "You weren't here when I got off the bus. You were *supposed* to be here!"

I pressed my lips together. I wasn't *supposed* to be raising an eight-year-old girl! And dammit, I was attempting to make things nice for her, which was why I was a couple of minutes late!

I rose and held out my hand, telling myself not to let the disapproving stares from the other women bother me. "C'mon. I'll drive you up the hill."

Daisy hesitated, then picked up her backpack and took my hand. I could feel the eyes of the other women on me as I turned and led Daisy to the car and helped her into the backseat.

I slid behind the wheel and we took off.

From the backseat, Daisy leaned forward and tapped me on my shoulder. "Where's my surprise? You said if I went to school, you'd have a surprise for me."

I glanced at her in the rear view mirror and smiled. "It's all set for you."

"Hey! Where are we going?" Daisy asked as we passed by the gallery.

"That's part of the surprise." Wait until you see our new place."

I pulled into the driveway and looked at the pretty house with pride.

"This is where we're going to live?" Daisy climbed out of the car and followed me inside. "What're all these boxes for?"

"Those are mine. They came from the trailer behind my car."

Daisy frowned. "Where are my things?"

I smiled. "Come on. Follow me."

My heart beating with anticipation, I led her up the stairs. Rob and I had worked hard to set it up exactly like her old room, including placing her stuffed animals on the bed just so.

At the doorway to her room, I cried, "Surprise!"

Daisy's eyes widened. "This is my new bedroom?"

"Yes! Come see out the window. There's a tree outside. We

can put a birdfeeder there so you can watch the birds."

"I hate it! And I hate you!" Daisy cried. She ran out of the room. The thump of her shoes on the stairs echoed in angry beats.

Shocked, I collapsed on the bed and lowered my head. Tears misted my vision. I sat for a while, breathing in and out slowly, trying to decide what to do.

"Allie?"

I turned.

Daisy tiptoed toward me, concern written on her face.

Sighing, I held out my arms. "Come here."

She sidled up to me. I put an arm around her shoulder. "Daisy, I know you're not happy that your Mommy is gone. There's nothing I can do about it. You're not used to having me for a new Mom and I'm not used to taking care of a little girl. We'll have to do the best we can. You and me. Understand?"

Uh-huh," Daisy muttered.

"Take a look around the room. Is everything right?"

Daisy climbed up on the bed and pawed through the mound of toys resting on her pillows. "Where's Susie? She's my favorite doll."

"She's not there?" I gritted my teeth, hoping Daisy wouldn't have a meltdown. I didn't think I could handle it.

"I'll double check the apartment tomorrow. She must be there. Okay?"

Daisy's lips trembled. "Okay."

She jumped down from the bed. "Can I have my chocolate cookies now? All three of them?"

"Two."

Life with Daisy was like riding an emotional roller coaster.

CHAPTER FOUR

After Daisy finally went to sleep, I unpacked my boxes. It felt odd to see my barely used wedding gifts in an entirely new setting. I'd been so hopeful at the beginning of my marriage, thinking it would be forever. That hope was quickly erased when I discovered the evening business meetings Will attended were not with his boss, like he'd told me, but with one of his old girlfriends.

Once the divorce was final and I'd had a few sessions with a marriage counselor, I understood Will was a player and probably always would be. I'd already heard he was cheating on the girl he'd told me was perfect for him.

Sighing, I put the last of my things away in the kitchen cupboards.

The next few days passed in a blur. An autopsy on Kristin confirmed the doctor's diagnosis of a brain aneurysm and then, according to her wishes, she was cremated.

I sorted through her papers, searching for her will. After signing our partnership agreement, she'd told me she was going to rewrite it. I thought she had, but in typical fashion, Kristin must have let it slide. There was no evidence of one.

I worked long hours to install a computerized bookkeeping and inventory system. Then I input all the information from the prior three years into it, painstakingly sorting through receipts and papers Kristin had thrown into expandable files. I thought about the task of going through the apartment, clearing out Kristin's things, but the idea tore my insides to shreds.

When I could no longer avoid doing it, I posted a sign on the door of the gallery, asking customers to honk for service. Slowly, I climbed the stairs to the apartment. Tears built inside me. Until now, death had been a stranger to me. To have it appear so suddenly, with such terrible consequences, made me feel so vulnerable. I stood at the threshold of the apartment and closed my eyes, praying for strength. When I opened them, I moved with determination to Kristin's bedroom. I looked at all the clothes in her closet. They were so like her—brightly colored, slightly funky. I collapsed on the bed, filled with grief. Nearby, I picked up a forgotten teddy bear, a white one with a pink bow, and hugged it to me.

"Kristin?" I whispered, "I'm going to do my best, but if you can hear me, please guide me. I have no freaking idea what I'm doing."

I picked up a doll that was hiding on the closet floor and straightened its rumpled blond hair. It unexpectedly wailed "Ma-a-ma-a-a", its eerie cry filling the room like a half-sung song. I thought of all that Kristin and Daisy had lost and burst into tears, wondering how I could ever make things right for that little girl.

I drove myself to complete clearing the apartment. After several days, undoing the apartment, working at the gallery and taking care of Daisy, I was ready to collapse from sheer exhaustion. To ward off some of the stress I was feeling, I started running again, like I used to do in Maine.

Each morning, as soon as I got Daisy on the school bus and before the gallery opened, I ran for a couple of miles. It was a good way to get to know the town. Sarita's population was nestled in houses amid the rolling land that abutted the waters of Richardson Bay. Narrow paved roads wove gently back and forth along the slopes like a lazy snake uncoiling for a sunny stretch.

I pounded along the winding surfaces, extending my muscles, enjoying the crisp, salty tang of the air that prickled my nose in satisfying breaths. Upon occasion, I made my way down the hillside to the center of town, where a number of stores clustered around a small marina, like ducklings waiting to dive in for a swim.

One morning, I sat on a large, wooden deck overhanging the water outside a small coffee shop. I relaxed with a hot latte, lost in thought. A man's voice interrupted my musings.

"Mind if I take one of these chairs?"

I gazed into light blue eyes that reminded me of the Maine sky on a sunny, summer day. "Go ahead. Nobody's joining me."

He frowned. "I saw your picture in the paper. You're Kristin Lewis' partner, aren't you?"

"Uh ... yes ..."

"Wanna join us? My friends and I are talking about the upcoming wine festival. We can use everyone's input."

The winning smile that spread across his Hollywood handsome face filled me with warmth. I turned to the group and recognized a few storeowners who'd recently introduced themselves to me. Pleased to be included, I rose to my feet. "Thanks. I'd like that."

He held out his hand. "Blake Whiting. From Silver Goose Winery."

I shook hands with him. "Allison Hartwell."

His gaze wandered over me in appreciation. And suddenly I knew who he was—the man I'd seen in the convertible the first day I drove into Sarita. I smiled. He proved once again to be an example of California's beautiful people. Not that I'd ever mention it to him.

"Blake, darling. You ready to go on with the meeting?"

Janelle Martin, co-owner of Gifts Galore, waved us over.

When Blake turned his attention to the empty chair, Janelle's dark eyes shot me a "keep away" warning.

I calmly followed Blake over to the table where Janelle sat. She'd have no competition from me. I had no intention of getting involved with any man at this point in my life. Not with all my commitments to my business and to Daisy. And after the damage Will had done to me, it would take a very special man to gain my interest.

"This is Allison Hartwell, from Treasures, Kristin Lewis's gallery," Blake said to the others, after we both sat down.

I looked around at the circle of faces. They murmured their names and uttered their condolences.

"We need to do something to remember Kristin, make her a part of this celebration," said the owner of the book store.

"I second that. Let's work something out."

Murmurs of approval followed. I smiled, touched by their thoughts.

"Okay, let's get down to business," said Blake.

I leaned forward, curious to hear more about a wine festival. It was so...so...California.

"Each year we have a wine festival in the middle of February for Valentine's Day. The whole idea is to feature red wine and chocolate," Blake explained. "It's a great combination."

"Sounds wonderful." Chocolate and I were old buddies.

"I want to find a way to include all the businesses in Sarita in the celebration this year, not just a few," said Janelle. "Businesses away from the harbor complained they were not included last year. I want this year to be the best ever." She tossed her long brown hair behind her ear with the flick of her hand and gave Blake a broad smile.

I sat back and listened as they discussed coordinating different events during the entire weekend.

"Instead of hosting wine tastings in the town hall," I suggested, "why don't you offer general tickets to tastings and have those located in different businesses, either after hours or during business hours?"

Janelle's eyes widened. "We could have a walking tour of the town, with assorted wines at different places. We'd give people a map and allow businesses to advertise in it."

"And come up with specific books and other gifts for sale at each location," offered the owner of the local book store.

"Do you mean exhibit items from other businesses at each stop?" I asked.

My excitement grew at the thought of having some of *Treasure's* offerings displayed in waterside locations. I couldn't help smiling as I envisioned a whole new way of marketing, a way in which every business could showcase samples of their wares throughout the town. I'd become worried about Treasures being off the main drag. And with Daisy to support, my concern had grown.

"I'll take charge of making the walking map and assembling blurbs from each participating business." I was well aware I'd have to move quickly to have everything done in time. But it was too good an opportunity to pass up.

"I'll coordinate wine choices with the other wineries and then get together with you to make up a sequence of tasting events," said Blake.

Janelle offered to coordinate the store events with Blake, and the other eight people at the table agreed to handle the other aspects of the festival.

We talked for some time, genuinely excited about the prospect of making the event even bigger than it had been in the past. By the time we concluded our meeting, the sky had clouded over and it looked like rain.

I huddled in my jacket, anxious to be on my way. Waving

good-bye to everyone, I started to trot toward home.

"Wait!" said Blake. "I'll drive you."

Tempted as I was for the ride, I shook my head. "No, thanks. I need the exercise." I still needed to shake off the memory of Daisy crying this morning because I couldn't brush her hair the *right* way.

Blake waved to me and walked over to his silver Mercedes convertible parked in the large lot by the marina. I headed up the hill toward home, my mind whirling with plans for the festival.

Blake drove up beside me and lowered his car window. "I know it sounds corny as hell, but haven't we met before? I swear I know you."

I stopped and laughed, thinking it was a line, and realized he was serious. "You may have seen me, but we've never met. I came here from Maine."

He shrugged. "Maybe I've seen pictures of you at Kristin's house." My surprise must have shown because he added, "Kristin and I go back a long way. I'm one of the first people she met in California after she left the University of Maine." He shook his head. "She was a great person and way too young to die."

My mind spun. "Were you in the wine business when you met her?"

"Just getting started. The winery has been open ten years next June. It's done really well."

I smiled. "I couldn't help but wonder about the name. Why Silver Goose instead of Golden Goose Winery?"

Blake chuckled. "Everyone asks me that. I thought it was bad karma to name it Golden Goose. Silver Goose has a nice ring to it, don't you think?"

"I do. It's interesting."

"Okay, I'd better go. See you later." He took off, and I

continued up the hill to my house on Water Way, thinking about Blake. His blond hair and tanned skin in this winter month seemed fresh and healthy, and there was a rugged look to him I found undeniably attractive. Kristin seemed to have many friends, but few as outstanding as he. Why, I wondered, hadn't she ever mentioned him to me? God! I missed her so much!

That afternoon I stood at the bus stop, several minutes early. I'd vowed to never be late again. The bus arrived and several boys got off, pushing and shoving each other amid loud whoops of laughter. Smiling shyly, a young girl climbed down off the bus next and ran to her mother's outstretched arms. I waited anxiously for Daisy.

Then I saw her. Her blond hair looked like a halo around her sweet face as she made her way toward the front of the bus. Descending the bus steps, she searched through the small crowd of waiting women. When she noticed me, her lips curved and she ran over to me.

I felt a tug of tenderness as I put my arms around her. We walked up the hill, hand in hand. "Guess who's coming to dinner?"

She grinned. "Who?"

"Jessie and Rob. You remember them, don't you?"

Daisy smiled. "Yes! They're Mommy's friends. Rob carries me on his shoulders." She did a little skip.

I gave her hand a squeeze. Overall, she was having a good day. Not all days were.

Shortly after six, Rob and his girlfriend arrived. Tall, with dark hair and brown eyes that sparkled with intelligence, Jessie Ives exuded an air of excitement about her that was in perfect contrast to Rob's laid-back manner. I liked her right away.

Rob did the honors of grilling the beef filets I'd splurged

on. Daisy hung out on the deck with him, watching his every move. I made a salad and finished off the twice-baked potatoes, chatting comfortably in the kitchen with Jessie.

"So how's it going?" Jessie asked.

I shook my head. "I don't know how Kristin did it. One minute everything's fine; the next, it's a crisis. It's that I'm not used to kids, you know? I want her to be happy."

Jessie placed a hand on my shoulder. "Relax. You're doing fine." She cleared her throat. "Rob told me you might need help with the gallery. I'd like to apply for the job. I'm working in San Francisco at Nordstrom's. They're a great company, but I'd love to be able to move to this area. Be closer to him."

I smiled. "Things are really tight. But with the wine festival coming up, I'm definitely going to need help. "

"Great." She pulled a business card out of her purse and handed it to me. I was impressed she was so organized.

Dinner was pleasant. Even Daisy seemed to enjoy it. She cuddled close to Rob, looking like a fluffy white kitten with her flyaway curls and snub pink nose.

Jessie noticed my watchful gaze and smiled. "Kids and dogs love Rob. It's one of the things I love about him."

At the end of the meal, Rob checked his watch and stood. "Hate to eat and run and all that, but gotta go. We've got a gig coming up in Berkeley and we need to rehearse. 'Should be a good show."

Daisy's eyes filled. She clung to his arm. "I don't want you to go."

"Sorry, sugar." He ruffled her curls. "Like I said, I have to leave."

Daisy threw herself down on the floor. She flailed her arms in rhythm to her feet, pounding an angry tattoo on the floor.

I let out a long sigh. "Sorry. Along with everything else, she must be overtired. We didn't get much sleep last night."

"No problem." Jessie gave me a sympathetic look. "We'll let ourselves out."

I decided to ignore Daisy and start on the dishes. Within minutes, Daisy stopped her tantrum, got to her feet and came over to me. Wrapping her arms around my waist, she leaned her head against me. I rubbed her back. I understood better now that Daisy's emotions were sometimes too difficult for her to handle. The psychologist had explained Daisy was the type of child who magnified every emotion, which was one reason she was on mild medication.

After she was asleep, an idea came to me. I picked up the phone and called Jessie. "Can you meet me at Treasures first thing tomorrow morning?"

"Sure thing," she said, and we hung up. I hoped I hadn't been wrong about her.

The next morning, Jessie met me at the gallery. "Is this about a job?" Excitement shone in her eyes.

"Yes. Would you be comfortable taking over Kristin's apartment in exchange for part of your salary? Money is tight for me, but you could have the apartment rent free as some of your pay. You mentioned wanting to move here."

Jessie's eyes widened and grew moist. "It would be perfect for me. And, Allison, I think Kristin would be happy to have a friend live there, someone she knew."

A sigh of relief escaped me. If Jessie lived in the apartment, it might help all of us to deal with the reality of Kristin being gone. And, God knew, I needed Jessie's help.

Jessie and I were standing outside the gallery, discussing the logistics of clearing out the apartment, when Dawson Smith pulled up in his truck.

"Thought I'd stop by to see how things are going." He drew a hand through his gray curls. "I still can't believe Kristin's gone. She was so young..." His voice drifted off in painful silence. "It's such a shame! It makes you wonder why. You know?"

"I keep thinking I'll wake up and realize this whole thing has been a bad dream," I commiserated. "Then Daisy runs into my room or throws a temper tantrum and I know it's all too real."

He studied me thoughtfully. "You've got a real challenge ahead of you."

I attempted a smile, but the weight of worry stopped me. I'd gone from being a carefree single woman hoping to expand her world to a worried businesswoman with the care of an eight-year-old I was still trying to understand. And so far, I wasn't doing all that well.

Dawson clapped a hand on my shoulder. "Anything I can do to help? What about a service for Kristin?"

I took a moment to gather myself. My feelings were still unbearably raw. A memorial service seemed so final.

"Blake Whiting called to tell me the committee working on the wine festival thought it would be appropriate to hold a memorial service for Kristin on the Thursday before the celebrations begin. They want to dedicate the festival to her and use part of the proceeds from the sales to establish an art scholarship in her name at the local high school."

Jessie agreed. "I think she'd like that."

"I'd be willing to auction off one of my best pieces of work," Dawson offered.

"Oh, that would be lovely," I gushed. "Kristin would be so pleased. Maybe I can talk some of our other artists into doing the same."

"Well, I'd better go." He turned and climbed back into the truck. "I've got a meeting to attend. Let me know if I can do anything else."

As we watched him drive off, Jessie said, "I guess he and

Kristin were real close."

"Long-time friends," I concurred, and couldn't help wondering if that friendship included the making of a little girl. My thoughts turned to Blake. He had the same blue eyes as Daisy.

"What do you know about Blake Whiting?" I asked Jessie.

"Blake? He works hard. He's made Silver Goose Winery into something really special. Janelle Martin has had her eye on him for a long time, but I don't think he's serious about her. Why? Did you fall for those rugged looks of his?"

"I'm not interested in any relationships." Under different circumstances, his blue eyes and the smile that crept across his face on a regular basis might have tempted me, but it was way too soon for me to put my faith in another man. In the end, they were all alike.

CHAPTER FIVE

With Jessie on board and working in the gallery, I was able to complete clearing out Kristin's apartment. Rob rounded up the guys from his band to help us carry out the furniture we were selling. We placed it, along with the rest of the items for sale from Kristin's apartment, in a corner of Treasures parking lot. Sadness washed over me at the sight of Kristin's life reduced to a pile of things that had no meaning for anyone else. The most valuable items had been saved for Daisy's future, but it seemed such a small legacy from her very vibrant mother.

On the day of the sale, early shoppers pulled into the parking lot, eager for bargains. It hurt to see people pawing through Kristin's things. She should be alive, I kept thinking, as the pile of things for sale grew smaller.

The next day, Jessie settled into the apartment. The sound of her movements above the gallery and the addition of her rambunctious cat to the scene gave all of us some comfort. Life did go on, even after disasters. Aching with grief, each footstep above me seemed a benediction from Kristin, telling me it was all right to think of other things, to become involved in the plans for the wine festival, to laugh at some of Daisy's antics.

Jessie helped me more and more. While I prepared materials for the festival, she worked on an advertising program. She agreed that due to our location, we needed to be more aggressive about letting people know where we were. To spruce up the gallery, we decided to order an assortment of inexpensive items relating to Valentine's Day.

I was busy rearranging the merchandise on shelves when I heard a low voice call out, "Allison?"

Startled, I whipped around, and came face to face with Blake Whiting.

"Hey! It looks great!" He scanned the room. "A big difference."

"Thanks. I've made a lot of subtle changes to the gallery—rearranging things, changing some of the lighting, adding some new merchandise for variety. So, what's up?"

His expression sobered. "The wine committee and some of her other friends have come up with suggestions for Kristin's memorial service."

The brightness left the room. The service would be the final step in accepting Kristin's death. I looked down, fighting the tears that threatened.

"I've got all that stuff in my office."

I ushered him into the back office and offered him a chair, hoping he hadn't noticed my raw emotional state. "Coffee? I have some made."

"Great." He smiled. "I need another jolt of caffeine."

I laughed. "This might do it for you. In college, Kristin always complained my coffee was way too strong."

Then, I was weeping. I hid my face in my hands, but couldn't block the sound of my gut-wrenching sobs.

Blake's arms came around me. I leaned into him, needing someone, anyone, to understand how devastated I was by Kristin's death and the frightening changes in my life.

"I'm sorry, Allison. I really am," he murmured, patting my back. "It's gotta be hard on you, with Daisy and all."

His tenderness made me cry even harder. He reached for the Kleenex on my desk and handed me a tissue. He grabbed another and dabbed at his shirt.

"Oh, no! You're all wet!" I stepped back. "I'm sorry. I don't know what got into me."

He reached out and gently cupped my cheek. "It's all right, Allison. Believe me, I understand. We all miss her."

I looked up into his blue eyes. Seeing his sympathy, I fought to keep from crying again. After my demeaning experiences with Will, I was touched beyond words by his kindness.

"Want me to come back another day?" he asked, concern etched on his face.

I shook my head. "Time is running out. We'd better take care of it now." I forced a smile. "Besides, the coffee should be about perfect for you. Nice and strong. I'll be right back."

I dodged into the bathroom to press a cold towel against my swollen face, shocked by the haggard young woman who stared back at me. I couldn't look worse. My honey-colored hair, streaked with blond, hung loose and lank. My normally green eyes were gray with grief, and lack of sleep had left dark stains of color under them. Worry had etched a few subtle lines across my forehead. I'd barely combed my hair.

Following a night of bad dreams, it had been another rough morning. Daisy had screamed at me, saying she was going to run away and find her mother. I patted my eyes, wiped my nose and straightened my shoulders. It was one of the lowest times of my life, but I couldn't completely break down. A little girl was counting on me.

I emerged from the bathroom, poured two mugs full of coffee and entered the office with renewed purpose.

Blake eyed me carefully as I handed him his coffee. "Better?"

"I think so. I'm sorry I broke down in front of you. It's just that..."

Blake took hold of my hand and gave it a quick squeeze. "You don't have to explain, Allison."

Grateful for his empathy, I drew a deep breath,. “Thanks. Now, I guess we’d better discuss the plans. I want it to be a wonderful tribute to Kristin and all she’s done in her life.”

“Both Dawson Smith and Rob Henrickson have offered to speak about her.” Blake looked to me for approval.

“That would be nice.”

He suggested a number of Kristin’s favorite songs for the service. Some I never knew she liked. I realized I didn’t know all that much about Kristin’s life after college. Years had passed with the usual number of quick conversations, emails and notes between us, but until I came to California, I wasn’t aware of the small details of her everyday life.

“Has Daisy’s father been notified of the service?” Blake asked.

I blinked in surprise. “Her father? Do you know who he is?”

He shook his head. “No. Don’t you?”

“Unh, unh. Kristin never told me, and I haven’t been able to find a single thing about him in her personal papers.”

Blake shrugged. “Odd, but she must have wanted it that way.”

“She refused to tell anyone,” I said sadly.

After Blake left the gallery, the thought nagged at me. Who in hell *was* Daisy’s father?

Plans for the wine festival came together nicely. Optimistic for the future of Treasures, I walked the streets of Sarita, going from one shop to another. Their quaint wooden buildings hugged the marina, more like charming little Victorian cottages than the small retail centers they were.

I stopped for a moment, drinking in the beauty of the town, inhaling the sea air, and just relaxing briefly. Sarita, with its charisma, pleasant weather and nearness to San Francisco, was everything I'd hoped to find in a new place to live. If only Kristin were still here to share it with Daisy and me. Blinking back tears, I continued on my way, thinking of the fragile thread of life and how much I missed her.

Late morning, I returned to the gallery, and went to work on a large mock-up of the map we'd hand out to visitors. Mary Woods, at the local print shop, had agreed to print it for her actual cost, if she could put her advertising brochures in all the shops.

The door bells chimed as I was putting the finishing touches on the mock-up. I looked up, surprised to see Blake again.

He grinned, sending goose pimples racing down my back. His appreciative gaze stayed on me as he approached. Unexpected desire curled inside me, surprising me with its intensity.

"Hi, there. How's it going?" he said. "Things better today?"

"I'm okay. Thanks," I willed away the heat in my cheeks and held up the map. "This is almost ready for Mary; she's going to print them this afternoon. And, guess what? The Book Nook and Mario's restaurant have each agreed to display a painting from Treasures."

"Great. I've got a deal for you too. How about hosting one of the wine tastings? I want to pour Silver Goose Reserve Merlot and it needs a classy place like this to showcase it."

"That's a wonderful idea!" Having a tasting in Treasures would be a great way to bring people into the gallery.

A crooked smile appeared on Blake's face. "I'll be here Friday afternoon to set things up. See you then." He turned to go.

"Blake?" I called out to him. "Thanks for the other day."

Our eyes met and lingered. We'd been attracted to each other from the beginning, but I couldn't, wouldn't, succumb to the feelings he stirred inside me. With all I had going on in my life, it would only lead to another disaster.

He gave me a small salute, and left.

Watching him stride back to his car, I wondered why a guy like him had never married, and recalled the way Janelle Martin had silently warned me away. No doubt they were a pair. If things were different, I might give in to my feelings and challenge her. That smile of his could melt anyone's intentions.

Raindrops slid down the windows in tearful tracks the day of the memorial service. The cold and rainy weather matched my bleak mood. There were times I still railed at Fate and all she'd handed me and how she'd hurt an innocent little girl who fought the changes we were forced to make.

I made myself smile as I knelt before Daisy. "In church, you'll hear music and some of her friends telling stories about your Mommy."

"Stories like Cinderella?" she asked, her sweet face wrinkled with the effort of understanding.

I gave her a hug. "True stories about how wonderful Mommy was. You'll see. I'll be right beside you."

She nodded solemnly and took my hand. "You're my godmother. Mommy said so."

"Yes," I responded softly, wondering at my innocence when I'd so readily accepted that role.

We arrived at the church and were seated at the front of the sanctuary. Daisy squirmed in the wooden pew beside me. I didn't blame her. Waiting for the memorial service to begin, I was as restless as she. Soft guitar music filled the air. The strains of *Amazing Grace* soothed me, allowing me to concentrate my thoughts on my past friendship with Kristin.

The interior of the church, painted a soft yellow, spoke volumes in its simplicity. The plain white, wooden pulpit stood in front, above me. I likened it to a spiritual lighthouse—a symbol of help to guide me through the rough waters I faced. The golden cross mounted on the wall behind the pulpit made a simple but dramatic statement. My gaze kept returning to the comfort of it.

Jessie and Rob appeared beside me, and I relaxed as they slid into the pew with us. Jessie leaned over and whispered in my ear, "You'll never guess who's here. She must have heard about Kristin."

Suspicion forming, I quirked an eyebrow at Jessie. "Lisa?" My stomach knotted at the thought of her boldly showing up. We'd had no contact and I was still upset about what she'd done to Kristin.

Jessie looked at me grimly. "She's in the back with Catherine, talking to a few people. And, Allison, she told me she's anxious to see Daisy. I'm not sure what that means, but I don't like it."

My mouth turned dry. I didn't know what it meant either. I wanted nothing to do with that woman and didn't want her anywhere near Daisy.

I heard Lisa's whispered "hello" as she slid in the pew behind me. I acknowledged her with a nod of my head, telling myself to be calm and to give attention to the moment.

Daisy moved closer to me and took my hand. I glanced down at her. Fear marred her features. Sliding my arm around Daisy's thin shoulders, I murmured, "It's okay," praying it was true.

David Watson, the minister of the church, rose from his chair beside the pulpit and cleared his throat. The room became quiet.

"We've gathered here today to celebrate the memory of one

of our own. Kristin Lewis was an active member of our community ..."

"Kristin Lewis? That's Mommy!" Daisy interrupted in a loud whisper, causing a few titters of nervous laughter.

The minister looked down at Daisy and smiled. "And, yes, she was a mother, too."

He finished speaking, and the sound of music brought me to my feet. I opened my hymnal and stood with the rest of the congregation. The solemn Amen at the end of the hymn gave me hope that things would be fine.

I felt a tap on my shoulder and turned to face Lisa.

"Don't leave without talking to me." She tilted her head in Daisy's direction.

I tried to focus on the rest of the service, but anxiety gnawed at my insides like a sharp-clawed cat. What was going on with Lisa?

Rob stood in front of the audience, his guitar in hand. He spoke about his friendship with Kristin and how they'd supported each other through tough times in a new location. Then he played Bach's cantata, *Sheep May Safely Graze*.

My vision grew misty. Everyone around me dabbed at their eyes, too.

"I miss Mommy." Sobbing softly, Daisy leaned against me. I rubbed her back, wishing I could take her hurt away.

Dawson spoke about Kristin's integrity and her genuine concern for the state of the arts in town. He then announced the formation of a scholarship fund in her name for a deserving high school art student.

After the final hymn had been sung and David had given the benediction, I took Daisy's hand and led her from the church.

Outside, a number of people came up to me and spoke about Kristin and how sad it was that she'd left a beautiful, young daughter behind. I smiled, though I kept darting glances at Lisa, who was approaching me with a determined stride. An attractive, well-dressed woman, who I assumed was Catherine, followed behind her.

They stood in front of me. The woman with Lisa smiled and held out her hand. "I'm Catherine Wilkins. We haven't met, though we've talked on the phone about the house you're renting from me. I'm glad you find it a nice place to live. Lisa and I are going to Europe for a month or so, but if you need anything while we're away, leave me a message on my cell and I'll get back to you."

"Thank you." I wondered what this pleasant, well-spoken woman found in Lisa. In our previous telephone conversations, I'd found Catherine to be bright, thoughtful and kind.

Lisa leaned down in front of Daisy and gave her a smile.

Wide-eyed, Daisy stepped back and moved behind me.

Lisa tugged on Daisy's hand, drawing her out. "Hi, kiddo! Remember me? Mommy's very best friend in the world? Remember?"

Daisy shot me an uncertain look. Her lips quivered.

"How about coming to live with me? Mommy would like that."

Daisy's eyes rounded. "No! You can't make me!" She grabbed my hand and began to cry in earnest, glancing from Lisa to me.

People standing near us turned, casting looks of concern.

"Leave her alone," I told Lisa, my voice shaking with rage. "Don't you see how you're scaring her?"

"Okay, I'm leaving. For now." Lisa rose to her feet and glared at me. "But, Allison, there are things you don't know. Daisy should be living with me. I'll be in touch with you when I get back from Europe." Lisa walked away.

Trembling, I picked up Daisy and rocked her in my arms.

Rob came over to me. “What was that all about?”

I shook my head. “I don’t know. But, Rob, I’m scared. Lisa says she wants Daisy to live with her. It’s upset both Daisy and me.”

“Aw, Lisa’s always been like a charging bull with her weird ideas. Don’t worry about her. C’mon, we’d better go eat.” He put an arm around my shoulder. “The ladies are waiting for you.”

A special buffet dinner, put on by the women’s community committee, had been set up inside the church’s social hall. As upset as I was about the confrontation with Lisa, I couldn’t disappoint the people at the church who’d worked so hard to make a nice reception. I held Daisy’s hand, and we walked inside.

Throughout the meal, I kept a close eye on Daisy. She seemed overly quiet. The day had been a strain on her. At seven o’clock, I left the dinner with Daisy, hardly able to keep my eyes open, emotionally exhausted. Daisy, poor thing, looked as wiped out as I felt.

At home, I turned on the television, settled Daisy on the couch and went to look for the special teddy bear she took to bed every night—the brown one with the torn ear. There would be trouble if I didn’t find it. I got down on my hands and knees beside Daisy’s bed, and discovered it hiding behind the pink dust ruffle we’d taken from her old bedroom. Heaving a sigh of relief, I pulled it out and carried it into the living room.

Daisy held out her arms for the bear and looked up at me with big blue eyes. “Am I going to live with Lisa?” Her eyes filled, and tears ran down her cheeks. “I don’t wanna live with her.”

I sat beside Daisy and took her in my arms. “I don’t know

why Lisa said that, but I'm going to do everything I can to keep that from happening, Daisy. I promise."

She stared at me and I wondered once again who her father was. If we could find out, this whole mess between Lisa and me could be resolved.

I stroked Daisy's back until she became interested in the television program and then went into the kitchen to fix myself a cup of soothing hot tea.

When I returned to the living room, Daisy had fallen asleep. Her long eyelashes curled against her smooth, rosy cheeks like fine silken threads spun by angels. Awash with tenderness, I gazed down at her. Whose child was she?

CHAPTER SIX

The sun peeked through early clouds, greeting me with a round, yellow smile. The weather man had promised clearing skies and spectacular weather for our wine festival, which was scheduled for tomorrow. This time, he was right.

I hurried Daisy through her morning routines, making sure she finished her juice and toast. I had so much to do.

"Time to go to the bus!" I chirped.

She frowned. "What if I don't want to go to school?"

I held back my impatience. "What if I want you to? C'mon, silly girl! You love school!" I tickled her. She laughed as I helped her on with her coat and handed her the pink backpack. We hurried down to the bus stop. Daisy climbed up the steps of the bus without hesitation, and I let out a sigh of relief. A good morning.

I waved good-bye to her and hurried back to the gallery to rearrange things for the crowd I hoped would come to Treasures to taste Blake's wines.

Late that afternoon, Blake arrived, followed by one of his staff in a large silver van with Silver Goose Wineries painted in dark red on the side.

"Hey, there! Looks like we're going to have a nice day tomorrow! Things all set?"

His grin made me feel like a star-struck teen. I returned his smile, looping a lock of freshly shampooed hair behind my ear. Daisy had greeted me with a hug when I'd picked her up this afternoon. Now, she was upstairs with Jessie, probably chasing the poor cat.

Blake introduced me to Stu Richards, one of his young assistants. He and Blake set up a long table at one end of the gallery and spread a crisp, white linen tablecloth on it. They stacked plastic crates of small, tasting glasses behind it and placed a number of bottles of wine in a cooler under the table.

Stu turned to Blake. “Need me for anything else?”

Blake shook his head. “Be here by nine o’clock in the morning. Okay?”

Stu gave him a wave of his hand and left with the truck.

“Where’s Daisy?” Blake asked me.

“Upstairs with Jessie. It’s worked out well. Daisy understands Jessie lives there now, along with her cat, Pounce.” I smiled. “She and the cat have a love-hate relationship.”

Blake grinned. “Like most couples, I suppose.”

His remark made me wonder about him. I told myself I was merely curious, even as I admired his broad shoulders, narrow waist and the way his pants outlined his long legs and...and everything.

“As long as we have some time together, how about sharing a taste of the wine?” Blake lifted a bottle off the table. “It’s what we in the business call a significant, robust merlot, a perfect companion to the bittersweet chocolate we’ll offer with it. Why don’t I tell you about it, then you’ll be able to answer any questions your customers might have.”

“Sounds wonderful. I haven’t had a chance to sit down all day. It’s so pleasant, let’s go around to the back of the house and sit in the garden.”

“Great. Let me grab the wine and the opener. You get the glasses.”

I eagerly flipped over the “open” sign in the window and locked the front door. I couldn’t remember the last time I’d had a few quiet moments with a man. Especially a good-looking, pleasant man like Blake.

I entered the backyard, and was once again struck by the size of it. With all my time spent on Daisy and in the gallery, I hadn't paid much attention to the open space, but I saw it now with a fresh, admiring eye. Sometimes it was hard for me to believe I was the new owner of such an extensive property.

I headed toward the Adirondack chairs placed near the small studio Lisa had used in the past and gratefully took a seat. The sun, beginning its downward journey to the edge of the horizon, spread fingers of orange and pink across the darkening sky. Its colors added a warm touch to the cool air. I leaned back against the chair and let out a sigh of pleasure.

Blake joined me, lowered himself in the other chair and stretched out his long legs in front of him. "Nice." He indicated the yard with a wave of his hand. "I'd forgotten how large the lot is."

"Someday I'll do something with it. I don't know what."

"You've got plenty of room to add onto the building."

"Hmmm. I may want to think about that sometime."

"Okay, are you ready for a brief class in wine tasting?" Blake winked at me with those powerful blue eyes of his and my body responded with a jolt of heat.

He opened the bottle of wine and I forced myself to pay attention as he explained that decanting the wine earlier would have helped it open up and develop enhanced flavors.

"How did you learn so much about wine?"

"Reading and working and learning from others," he answered, grinning. "I could never have come so far without my winemaker's assistance. Ted Newton has been kicking around Napa for a long time. He's a very talented guy. There's a whole lot of science that goes into winemaking. I'm more the marketing guy."

Observing his strong facial features and his smile that drew you in with its warmth, I could imagine how easily he could market almost anything.

He swirled the wine in his glass and lifted it to his nose. “Nice bouquet. Hmmm. Some berry, maybe some other fruit and a tiny touch of pepper. It should be very good with the chocolate.”

Following his example, I lifted the glass to my nose and inhaled. At first I couldn’t detect any distinct aroma, but when I sniffed it again, I swore I smelled cherries.

Blake took a small sip of wine and rolled his eyes. “Yes. This is great. Take a taste and tell me if you like it.”

I took a small sip and let the wine roll around in my mouth and down my throat, like he’d done. “Wonderful.” I wasn’t a connoisseur, but I knew good wine when I tasted it. This was like swallowing satin.

Satisfaction filled his smile. “It’s one of our best. Wait until you taste it with this imported chocolate.” He handed me a small square of dark chocolate. “We brought a whole box of it for tomorrow.”

I savored the chocolate as it melted in my mouth, teasing my taste buds with its bitter sweetness. It made me want to wiggle my toes with pleasure.

“Now take a sip of the wine,” Blake coached.

I took a taste. “Yum! It’s delicious!”

“Glad you like it. Silver Goose is promoting the whole concept of chocolate and red wine together. The flavor is intense. Smart, Sensual, Satisfying.” He leaned back in his chair, took a sip of wine, and studied me, his eyes warming to a summer blue.

“So, how’s it going?” His smile disappeared. “I saw the confrontation you had with Lisa at the church. I’ve never liked her. What’s going on?”

Tensing at the memory of our confrontation, I blurted, “I

don't like her, either. She told Daisy that she should come and live with her."

"What? That's crazy. Lisa isn't exactly what I'd call the mothering type. And anyone can tell that Daisy doesn't like her."

"Lisa's gone to Europe for a couple of weeks, but I've talked to a few other people about this. Now I'm looking for a lawyer. She told me there were things I didn't know. I can't imagine what they would be, but I've got to play it smart."

Blake's furrowed. He leaned forward. "I've got a friend who has a family law practice. You might want to discuss it with him. He deals with all kinds of sticky issues like this. I'll email you his information."

I brightened. "Thanks. I'd love it. Lisa said she'd be in touch when she gets back and I want to use these weeks to get prepared."

We sipped wine in silence for a few moments. After being so busy and so worried about everything, it felt good to sit quietly. The tense muscles in my shoulders loosened. I closed my eyes, grateful for the quiet time.

"Allison?"

I turned to Blake with a lazy smile.

His eyes linked with mine, sending silent messages. "I'd ... uh ... I'd like to have you come out to Silver Goose for a private tour. There's a lot I want to show you."

It sounded like such a line I almost laughed, until I saw how serious he was. A spark of interest flew from him to me and back again. I'd missed feeling that kind of chemistry with a man. Especially with a man as sexy as Blake, who was staring at me as if I were one of his pieces of chocolate.

Unable to resist, I said, "I'd like to visit very much."

"Hi, Allie!" cried Daisy, running toward me, shattering the special moment.

The sensual energy between Blake and me evaporated. But I couldn't deny what I'd felt.

Promptly at nine o'clock the next morning, Stu pulled up in front of the gallery in the Silver Goose van. Two girls wearing white Silver Goose T-shirts and black slacks accompanied him.

I went out to greet them. "Good morning! Glad to see you here on time!"

"Annie and Claire are going to help serve," Stu explained, introducing me to the young women who were obviously sisters.

I helped them organize their area and placed a cardboard sign with a huge number 10 on it outside the gallery. Visitors would find us by following the map.

Jessie checked on the babysitter for Daisy upstairs, and we stood by, waiting anxiously for our first customers to arrive. Numbers tripping in my mind, I swallowed hard. We needed a big boost in sales.

A short time later, I thrilled to the sight of a foursome walking toward us, maps in hand. I hurried inside behind the counter near the cash register and nervously rearranged the new, heart jewelry we'd ordered.

The first group of shoppers left, bearing purchases, and another group arrived. It stayed that way all morning.

By afternoon, the shop was jammed with people who'd heard about us. My growling stomach reminded me I hadn't eaten lunch. I went over to the tasting table and helped myself to a piece of dark chocolate.

"Eating on the job?"

At the sound of Blake's voice, I twisted around. He smiled down at me. The light in his eyes caught my breath. It was crazy. He made me feel like the Cinderella princess Daisy was always talking about.

I laughed as he shook a mocking finger at me. "I didn't see you come in. We've been so busy I haven't had time to eat."

He grinned. "All the stores are reporting the same thing. I've just come from the coffee shop. We figure this festival has broken every attendance record. The band is playing on the deck next to the marina and it's a mob scene. The walking map has helped move people out to *all* the stores, not only the ones down there."

"Jessie and I dragged chairs from out back and put them here in front because so many people were sitting on the curb, talking and drinking the wine."

"Ah, here you are, Blake," said Janelle, interrupting us. "I called after you, but you left my store before I could hand you these sandwiches for Jessie and Allison."

The smile she gave Blake was wide, but when he turned to a customer to explain why red wine and chocolate make a good pairing, Janelle's smile disappeared in a cold glare that reminded me of brisk wintery winds back east.

"Thanks for the sandwiches." I walked away, wondering what claim, if any, Janelle had on Blake.

Later, I asked Jessie about it.

She gave me a penetrating look. "He's a hot one, isn't he? Janelle isn't the only one who thinks so. But Blake's been hurt pretty bad in the past. The winery struggled in the beginning, and before he could get it on a much firmer foundation, his long-time girlfriend left him without so much as a good-bye. She was all appearance and no substance. I heard she even took the puppy she'd given him for his birthday. Ever since, he's been unwilling to commit to anyone. Now that he's made a ton of money on the winery, several women, including Janelle Martin, would like to get hold of him and his big bucks.

But that makes him even more leery."

"Is he serious about her?" I asked,

Jessie shook her head. "She'd like him to be, but I don't think so."

Knowing a little of his background, I felt more comfortable about my growing interest in him. Realistically, nothing could come of it. How could it, with our past experiences and all the responsibilities I faced?

As the festival wound down, Blake approached me. "Good day, wasn't it? How about coming out to the winery tomorrow? I've promised to do a wrap-up report for the wine festival committee. I thought you could take a look at it for me, give me some input. Then I could show you around a bit." He grinned, and a magnetic pull flashed through me.

"Besides," he continued, his eyes twinkling, "I have a business proposition to discuss with you."

I hesitated, intrigued and concerned at the same time. "I don't know how I can...I've got Daisy to worry about..."

"No, she doesn't," Jessie piped up, giving me an innocent smile. "I'll watch Daisy. No problem. In fact, I've promised her a sleepover tomorrow night."

Blake's eyebrows lifted. "Well, then?"

Feeling surprisingly giddy, I grinned. "What time?"

"How about five?"

"Okay, see you then."

All eyes were drawn to him as he moved away through the lingering crowd. A magical force seemed to emanate from him, attracting every female's attention. But he seemed not to notice.

"Wow!" said Jessie. "There was no way I'd let you turn down an invitation like that. I saw the way he smiled at you."

A nervous laugh escaped me. I wondered how it would feel to be in his arms, and if his lips were as tasty as they looked.

"Stop, Pounce, stop!"

Daisy chased Jessie's cat across the lawn. Reminding myself I had no time for such foolishness, I shook off captivating thoughts of Blake.

Jessie elbowed me in the side. "Now I know why you wanted to find out about Janelle. Guess we have our answer, don't we?"

I held up a hand in protest. "Don't misunderstand me. I'm sure this is only a business thing for him and I'm simply pleased to have some adult time away from Daisy."

Jessie cocked an eyebrow at me. "Right."

Jessie and I collapsed in the back office and sipped the remainder of an open bottle of the Silver Goose merlot. Everybody had left and the festival had closed down.

"It's the best sales day we've ever had," I said happily. A number of new items were gone, and I'd even been able to sell a few clunkers that had been in the gallery for too long.

"The comments I heard about the gallery were great. I think the changes you've made have definitely increased its appeal."

"I don't know what I would do without your help." I poured Jessie another glass of wine.

"I love working here, with you. It feels right. You know?"

"Any chance you'd consider me a real partner?"

Surprise made me pause. "It's something we can think about." The idea of sharing some of my responsibilities was tantalizing, but I wouldn't do anything without discussing it with my sister, Samantha. She was the one with the business and law degrees.

###

I helped Daisy dress and then let her watch Sunday cartoons while I took a quick shower.

"Time to go!" I called to Daisy. "It's late! We've got to hurry to the gallery."

"No-o-o-o!" Daisy glared at me. Her lower lip jutted out in defiance. "I don't want to go. I want to stay here."

"C'mon, honey," I cajoled. "We have to leave now. We're already late," I kept my tone pleasant, though her high-pitched, whiny voice drilled into me. I held out my hand.

"No-o-o-o!" Daisy's face turned an angry red. Her continued screeches stung my ears like the whine of a hornet.

"No!" she squealed. "I'm not going! I'm watching cartoons. Mommy lets me."

I swallowed hard and fought for control. My mother would have given Daisy one of her "I told you to do it" glares, but I wasn't my mother, and this wasn't really my child.

"I'm not fooling, Daisy, we have to go. *Now.*" I offered her my hand again, praying my deceptive calm would work.

When she remained seated, I gently removed the television control from Daisy's fingers and pushed the off button. The television picture faded.

Daisy shrieked and threw herself across the couch, kicking at the fluffy pillows so hard a few feathers flew out.

I started to reach for her.

She kicked harder.

I stepped back and watched helplessly. What in hell was I supposed to do now?

Slowly breathing in and out, I struggled to keep calm. "Daisy? I'm going to count to ten and then I want you to stop and take my hand."

"No! No! No! You can't make me!"

"One...Two...Three..."

Daisy stopped kicking and peeked at me from beneath a

pillow she'd placed over her head.

"Four...Five...Six..."

"I don't wanna!"

"Seven...Eight...Nine..."

"Ten!" I moved closer. "Take my hand now, Daisy. We're leaving." I held out my hand once more, forcing myself to keep my expression neutral and my voice firm, even though I wanted to shake her.

Daisy stared at my hand a moment and glanced at me. Sniffling softly, she slowly got to her feet. Her fingers wrapped around mine, and without another word of complaint, she followed me out the door.

Inside, I was quaking. I'd almost lost the battle. Then what would I have done? Good God, one eight-year-old was harder to handle than all the disgruntled customers in the world.

We arrived at the gallery, and business took off. A steady stream of customers wandered in and out, drawn by all the advertising we'd done recently for the wine festival in the local newspapers.

When Jessie arrived at one o'clock to give me a hand, I was more than ready for a break.

She took over the gallery, and I headed down to the coffee shop at the marina with Daisy. It felt good to be outside. Refreshing on-shore breezes caressed my face with cool fingers. Waving her arms in the air for balance, Daisy skipped ahead of me.

We each had a snack, and then we returned to the gallery. I kept busy setting up new displays. The results of participating in the wine festival proved to me that I had to come up with a way to bring in more customers every day. Then, I might be able to make a real success of the business.

Jessie worked on the inventory. She caught me checking my watch and gave me a gentle push.

"Go and enjoy yourself. After all the hours you've been putting in here, as well as taking care of Daisy, you deserve this break. Silver Goose is a lovely place. Blake's made it into a real showcase—for business and pleasure."

"Are you sure you don't need me to stay longer?"

She smiled. "Go ahead, leave. I'll close up the gallery. Daisy and I are going to have fun. Right, Daisy?"

"Jessie's going to sleep in my bed and I'm going to sleep in the sleeping bag she gave me."

"Okay, then." I ruffled Daisy's curls, proud of the steps she was making. I knew now why Kristin had worked so hard with her. The good times were really good. The other times? Devastating, exhausting, mind-numbing battles that wore me to a frazzle.

I hoped I'd have the strength to win the war.

CHAPTER SEVEN

I left the gallery and eagerly climbed the hill to my house. Blake was expecting me at five.

After a deliciously long shower, I fussed with my hair and then stood in front of my closet. I tried on several different outfits and finally selected black slacks paired with a honey brown cashmere sweater my mother had given me for Christmas. I added a funky bead necklace and gold hoops and spritzed a flowery perfume on my wrists and neck. Giving myself a last look in the mirror, I fluffed my hair and took a deep breath. It had been a while since I'd dressed up for a man. My nerves tingled with growing anticipation.

Blake's directions to Silver Goose Winery took me up Route 101. At Petaluma, I headed east on Route 116. Observing the sprawling vineyards off in the distance, I wondered about the business of running a winery. I'd always enjoyed wine but didn't know much about the different varieties. Now, I'd have the perfect reason to learn more. And, I had to admit, the good-looking man behind the Silver Goose Winery was as fascinating as his business. Too bad nothing would come of it.

As I drove past the dairy farms around Petaluma, I mentally compared the landscape to the tall pines and more rugged features of Maine. At the three-mile marker, I looked for a large, black sign with a silver goose on it. I saw it to my left, and turned onto a narrow, paved road.

At the end of the long driveway, signs directed me to a parking lot in front of a two-story barn painted a deep red. A gaggle of geese greeted me with curious stares and honked loudly as they waddled out of the way. I laughed out loud at Blake's official greeters. It seemed so appropriate.

A black lab appeared in the parking lot and barked, herding the geese away in a flurry of feathers and defiant honks. Blake came out of the barn and waved. Dressed in khaki slacks and a black turtleneck sweater that did nothing to hide his appealing shape, Blake appeared the height of casual elegance as he strode toward me.

"Glad you made it. I heard on the news there was a big accident at the intersection of 101 and 116."

"Oh? It must have happened soon after I passed through there."

He waited while I climbed out of the car and took my elbow. "Come on in. I want to show you what we've done." He waved to a workman. "The geese are loose again, Juan. Can you round them up?"

Juan grabbed the collar of the dog, and I followed Blake inside the barn.

The barn's interior was finished with high-quality pine paneling stained a light gray; it would nicely accommodate fine pieces of art, paintings, and sculptures, giving the tasting barn a more upscale atmosphere. The first floor of the large, open building was filled with a colorful array of gift items, all related to wine and food. Large, wooden wine racks of Silver Goose wines lined one whole wall of the store.

Blake stopped and pointed to a balcony above us. "That's what I want you to see. Follow me."

He led me up a wide stairway to the open balcony above. At the top of the stairs, a number of paintings for sale hung on the facing wall.

"Some of our higher-priced wines and gifts are here on this level, along with two big tasting areas. I was thinking Treasures might want to showcase a few items up here.

Eventually, if you wanted, we could do some sort of a cooperative exchange, like we talked about for the wine festival."

I grinned. "Dawson Smith's pieces would work here, and we've ordered a number of metal sculptures from two very different artists. And there's a water colorist I especially like, whose paintings would fit in well, too."

Blake's eyes lit with pleasure. "I knew you'd understand." He threw an arm around my shoulder.

I felt the strength of the muscles beneath his skin. The smell of his spicy, aftershave lotion filled my nose with its masculine scent. At the moment I might have leaned into him, he stepped away.

"Look around. The wine business is more about retail than some would realize. The barn helps showcase our wine and gets people talking about it back home. That's what we need to keep our wine in demand." His eyes focused on mine. "So, it's a deal?"

He held out his hand. The feel of his warm skin against mine was electric. I dropped my hand and took a moment to gather myself. As much as I might be tempted to deny it, there was a connection between us I couldn't ignore. And by the dazed look on his face, I was sure Blake felt it too.

His voice turned husky. "Let's go to the private tasting room in The Manor House."

We walked along a crushed gravel path, away from the barn. In the growing dark, I strained to see the vineyards that marched in straight lines across the rolling hills beside us.

"So, have you called my lawyer friend?" Blake asked.

"Yes, but he's away for a few days. Some sort of family emergency."

"Stick with him. He's good. I'll give him a call."

The house came into full view. I stopped and stared in

amazement, feeling as if I'd been magically transported to France. The stucco house resembled the pictures I'd seen of the small *chateaux* my parents had visited on a recent trip to Europe.

"Nice, huh?" A look of pride crossed his face.

"Very nice, indeed."

He grinned. "We hold social functions here quite often—weddings, private dinners, and all. It's another way to earn money and to showcase our wines. Some vintners have little bed-and-breakfast inns on their property. I didn't want to do that."

Blake led me up wide marble stairs to the main entrance. The massive, carved-wood, double doors opened easily. I stood with him inside an immense foyer and admired the gold-toned tile floor, made even richer with Oriental rugs. A huge, crystal chandelier cast soft light on antique, wooden tables, gilt-edged mirrors, and carved wooden chairs stationed around the room.

"It's beautiful."

"Come with me." He held out his hand.

I took it, following him from one room to another, awed by the grandeur, but distracted by the heat of his fingers around mine. We arrived at what he called the back of the house and stood in the middle of a large commercial kitchen.

"Is this where you cook?" I asked.

He laughed. "Me? Not at all. I'd go crazy living in a place like this. My house is farther down the road, away from all this touristy stuff."

His words made me feel more comfortable. As beautiful as this house was, it didn't give off vibe of being a real home.

"I've set up a flight of red wines for you to taste in the library. Most of the wine is from Silver Goose, but I've got some others from places like Chalk Hill and Los Carneros."

The library was one of the cozier rooms. I sat in a smooth, brown-leather, wing-back chair by the fireplace. A fire glowed a warm orange, sending a woodsy scent into the room. As I watched Blake pour red wine into our glasses, I could almost imagine what life on this high scale would be like. My parents were comfortable financially, but I'd always been made to work for what I got and to save a portion of it. And even though Will came from a wealthy family, our brief life together had been surprisingly spartan.

"To your new life in California." With a smile, Blake handed me a glass of wine.

His bright blue gaze settled on me. My pulse jumped at the sexual interest I observed in him. I glanced away and then back again.

Blake smiled at me. "Let's get to the art of tasting a fine wine." He held his glass up to the light, swirling the wine inside gingerly.

"Look at this color. A beautiful, clear, ruby red." He sniffed the wine and rolled his eyes with appreciation. "M-m-m-m. A bit of pepper maybe? Or maybe berry."

I swirled the wine in my glass, emulating him, praying I wouldn't spill it. I held it to my nose and inhaled. Surprisingly, I smelled berries and, yes, maybe a bit of pepper, too.

"There are many aromas associated with each one," Blake explained. "I enjoy discovering what we at the vineyard call the bouquet of each wine."

He took a small sip, opened his mouth a bit, and swallowed. His smile told me he liked it. "Sometimes it helps to get a real sense of the wine by allowing some air into your mouth while the wine sits on your tongue."

In the past, I'd sipped wine without giving much thought to it. I'd heard something about white wine and fish, red wine and beef, but that was the extent of my knowledge. I took a small sip of wine, opened my mouth for air, coughed, and gasped for air.

Blake jumped up from his chair and patted me on the back. I struggled to swallow without spitting out the red liquid or dribbling it down my chin.

"You okay?" He continued to rub my back in circles.

I nodded and finally managed to say, "Went down the wrong way."

Feeling like a total social boor, I sipped again. This time, the wine was like red velvet as it slid down my throat.

"A nice pinot noir, huh?" said Blake, seated once more.

"Truthfully, it's the best I've ever had."

He grinned. "Good. It's a good year for us."

"I have a lot to learn about wine."

"It'll be my pleasure to teach you all about it." His lips curved again, and I couldn't help wondering what they'd taste like.

After I finished the tiny taste of pinot noir, Blake offered me a small piece of bread. "To cleanse the palate," he explained. "Next, I've got a nice zinfandel for you to taste."

I tried to concentrate as Blake took his time to explain some of the differences in wines and their years to me. We'd tasted several wines, when I checked my watch. Shocked, I jumped to my feet.

"I didn't know it was so late. I'm sorry but I've got to leave. Tomorrow is another busy day." I gave him an apologetic look. "Daisy is going to present a talk on dogs for her show-and-tell project, and Jessie and I are going to do a complete inventory."

Disappointment showed on Blake's face, but he graciously rose to his feet. "How about a cup of coffee? First, let's check the news to make sure the roads are okay. I'd hate for you to get stuck half-way home."

Blake slid open a door of an armoire in the corner of the room, exposing a flat-screen television inside. As he leaned over to adjust the picture, I admired his muscular frame. He was the whole package.

A picture of an accident filled the screen of the local television station. A fuel truck had collided with a pickup, flipped and spilled its contents all over the road. "The clean-up crews expect to have the area cleared and the road re-opened by tomorrow morning," the broadcaster announced.

Stunned, I barely listened as a reporter interviewed the driver who had, by some miracle, escaped injury.

Blake turned to me. "Looks like you're better off staying here. I've got a guest room down at my house. I can put you up for the night."

"Or I could sleep here on the couch." I willed the fire in my cheeks to go away.

Blake laughed softly. "It's a lot more comfortable at my house."

At his amusement, I wished the floor would give way beneath me. I was acting like a virginal fourteen-year-old, not the sophisticated woman I preferred to think I was.

He took my arm. "Let's go down to my place. My days start early, too."

Outside, Blake helped me into his truck. He hesitated by the passenger door and leaned toward me.

I held my breath, waiting for his kiss.

He closed the door, and I was left wondering if I'd imagined the whole scenario as Blake climbed behind the driver's wheel. He pulled into the driveway of what appeared to be a simple, one-story ranch with stained clapboard siding.

"Here we are, far enough away from the tasting barn and The Manor House for privacy."

I swallowed nervously, got out of the car and followed him

to the front porch. Clear glass panels on either side of the dark brown door allowed me a quick glimpse inside. Soft light illuminated a flagstone entryway, extending a warm greeting.

Blake opened the door and I stepped inside. My breath caught. The wall of glass on the far side of the living room gave the room an openness I hadn't expected.

"Can't see much at night until you go out onto the deck," Blake said. "The stars are quite a sight."

He walked over to the sliding doors and opened them, beckoning me to follow him outside. Walking to him, I eyed the huge stone fireplace on one wall of the living room and the leather couches in front of it. It was definitely a guy's kind of place, but it had a sense of homey comfort too.

Outside, I wrapped my arms around myself and stood at the railing. The large deck hung over a grass carpet of lawn that eventually met a meadow beyond it. The scent of rich soil and growing things filled my nostrils. Bright stars winked at me from the indigo sky.

"Look!" I pointed to a familiar constellation. "There's Orion."

Blake's brows lifted.

I grinned. "I was a Girl Scout."

He let out a belly laugh. "I should have known." Still smiling, he reached out and caressed my cheek with his broad hand. His gaze held mine. "I'd like to get to know you, Allison Hartwell." He leaned down and placed his lips on mine.

My heartbeat quickened. Desire wove through me, making my body feel liquid. The clean, manly aroma of him wafted around us, and I inhaled. It had been such a long time since I'd been with any man, and I'd missed it. Common sense forced me to take a couple steps back. "Blake, I'm flattered, I really am, but I've only been alone a year and I've got Daisy to take care of now ..." My voice trailed away.

Blake's steady gaze unnerved me. I looked away, swallowing hard, embarrassed by my outburst.

"Allison?"

I looked up at him.

"When you're ready to take a chance again, I'd like to be able to prove to you that it might be worth taking it with me."

At the tenderness in his voice, my vision blurred. With my emotions in such turmoil, I couldn't find the right words to respond.

"C'mon," he said. "We'd better get settled for the night."

Blake led me to the guest room. "Make yourself comfortable. I keep a supply of toothpaste and toothbrushes for overnight guests. There might be a nightshirt in the closet." He paused, giving me a look that sent longing through me. "See you in the morning."

He left and I glanced around the room, surprised at the shade of pink on the walls. I walked over to the closet, opened it and let out a gasp. The closet was half-full of women's clothing. I stared at them, dismayed to find several pieces so daring they could only be called cheesy. And there was one item I'd seen before. On Janelle.

I caught my lip with my teeth. I obviously wasn't the only woman who'd slept in this room recently. In fact, from the variety of styles and sizes, I'd guess there were many. I froze at the thought of being one of them.

Climbing into bed, wearing a shirt from the closet over my panties, I couldn't hide my disappointment. I'd been made a fool before; I wouldn't let it happen again.

A shrill ringing sound brought me out of a restless sleep and onto my feet. I weaved groggily, struggling to get my bearings. It took me a few seconds to realize it was some sort of alarm. I grabbed my purse and ran into the hall.

Blake hurried toward me, wearing just boxers. "Sorry. It's

the security alarm. It's been acting up lately."

I took a deep breath, hanging onto the door jamb, feeling weak as the adrenaline left my body.

"You all right?" Blake took hold of my arm.

I inhaled the scent of him and observed his virile bare chest. With his tousled hair and whiskery chin, he was a magnificent man. Anyone would be lucky to have him.

He wrapped his arms around me and drew me close.

I was tempted, so tempted. But I couldn't play his game. I was a one-lover person. He was not.

"Allison?"

I forced myself away from him. "I can't." I wished things were different.

He stared at me for several seconds and then turned away. As he did, I couldn't help noticing how tempted he'd been too.

I sat groggy-eyed in Blake's kitchen. The report for the festival committee that had brought me out to Silver Goose lay on the table with my few suggestions written across it. I yawned and stretched, and wondered how much sleep I'd gotten, if any. After I'd returned to bed, I'd tossed and turned. Blake had brought out a mix of feelings in me. No wonder so many women were attracted to him. He was a ladies' man, exactly like my ex.

Blake entered the kitchen from outside, bringing a burst of cold February air in with him. "Hey! Good morning! How'd you sleep?"

"Fine," I lied. He'd never know how tormented I'd been by images of him with other women. "I've gone over the figures you wanted me to look at. I'm thrilled we collected over three thousand dollars for Kristin's scholarship. But, Blake, I need to go home. Now."

His eyes widened at the firm tone of my voice. “Okay. I’ll drive you back to your car.”

“Thanks.” I avoided his gaze and followed him out the door.

We drove in silence.

Blake pulled up beside my SUV and turned to me. “I’d like to see you again.”

I tensed. No doubt this was how all his relationships started. “I’ll be bringing out a number of things from the gallery to showcase in the tasting barn. Thanks, again. It’s a great idea.”

He smiled, a little sadly I thought, and took my hand. “I meant what I told you last night. When you’re ready I’ll be here.”

I climbed out of his truck and into my car. He stood by while I started the engine and took off. In my rearview mirror, I saw Blake standing in the parking lot, watching me until I went around a curve in the road. Then, and only then, did I let out the sigh of disappointment that had been tormenting my insides.

CHAPTER EIGHT

When I entered the gallery, Jessie was in the store, dusting,

"Hey!" She gave me a worried look. "You okay? You didn't answer when I called early this morning. You got my message about Daisy?"

"Yes, thanks."

Jessie gave me a scrutinizing look. "So, where were you?"

I couldn't help the heat that crept to my cheeks. "It's a long story, but you know the accident up the highway? It blocked the road and I couldn't get home."

Jessie's lips spread into a wide grin. "And?"

"And nothing. Blake put me up in his guest room and that was that."

Jessie stared at me. "Something bothering you?"

"Well... Blake seems like the kind of guy who strings women along, loves 'em and leaves 'em."

Jessie shook her head. "Allison, I've known Blake a long time. He's not that way at all. He might not be ready to make a commitment to marry, but he isn't fickle."

"That's not the impression I got. There were all sorts of women's clothing in the guest room."

Jessie's brows arched in surprise. "Really? I thought he'd cleared everything out."

"What do you mean?"

"After his girlfriend left, his sister lived with him for a while," Jessie explained. "She was a mess—into drugs and everything else. He tried to help her, but she ran away when he laid down the law about the drugs. Nobody's heard from her since. He keeps hoping she'll come back, but I doubt it. He doesn't talk about it, but it's a sad story."

"That's too bad." I knew what it was like to be betrayed. My thoughts flew to his sister. Even if most of the clothes belonged to her, I couldn't dismiss seeing Janelle's blouse.

"No matter what, I'm off men and dating for a while. I've got Daisy to think of and we've got a business to run. I'm going to investigate an idea for new business, but, first, let me tell you about Blake's business proposal."

I described the plan for showcasing a few of our pieces in the tasting barn.

Jessie clapped her hands. "Great! I love it!"

"I thought a couple of Dawson Smith's pieces would show well there."

"Glenda Grissom might let us use a couple of her metal sculpture pieces there, too," said Jessie. "The extra publicity might make up for the late payment on her sale."

"Good idea." I started to make a list of artists who might be interested in Blake's proposal. Later, I dialed Dawson. He picked up the phone on the first ring, and I explained how Blake's project would work.

"Will you do it?" I asked.

"Yes! It's a great idea, but only if I get a say in what goes where."

"No problem."

"I'll come in later today and we can make a selection. I know it's important to you, Allison, or you wouldn't ask. And it will be a good thing for me."

"Thanks. I'll make sure you'll be pleased." I hung up, thrilled with his participation, and quickly called Glenda.

###

Dawson stuck his head into the shop. “Am I too late?”

I smiled. “Not at all. It’s been a quiet day. I welcome the company.”

He looked around. “Where’s Daisy?”

“Still at school.” I checked my watch. “She should be home soon. Jessie’s picking her up at the bus stop.”

His dark gaze focused on me, and lingered. “She doing okay?”

I shrugged, not wanting to talk about the constant struggles between us that flared and fled with surprising speed. “Some days are easier than others. Underneath it all, she’s a loving child. Sometimes that makes up for everything else.”

He gave me an encouraging pat on the shoulder. “I know how difficult this has been for you.”

I gave him a weak smile. Attempting to raise Daisy was the hardest thing I’d ever done. I wanted so much to do right by her. And now I had to worry about Lisa taking her away from me. I pushed away my concerns.

“Let me show you the pieces I thought would be best suited for Silver Goose.”

The bronze and silver piece he’d brought in recently was my first choice. “Blake didn’t mention it, but I thought this would be elegant in what he calls The Manor House. I want to ask him about it. If he doesn’t want it there, it’s certainly suitable for the tasting barn.”

“Okay. How about the sunset piece?”

We studied the massive round vase in swirled bright oranges and reds. Its globular shape and coloring resembled a setting sun. Dramatic, it would show well.

“Let’s do both of them,” I said enthusiastically. “A short blurb about the artist will be displayed with each piece, along with the price and a brief note about Treasures.”

As I finished writing up the descriptive information Dawson had given me for the two pieces, Jessie and Daisy came through the door.

"Guess who I found at the bus stop?" Jessie grinned at me.

I opened my arms, and Daisy rushed into them. "I told the kids about dogs." She held up the fluffy white stuffed dog she loved.

"Good for you." I held her close to me, enjoying the feel of her warm, little body against mine. After all the tears, the lost sleep, the total disruption of caring for her, hugging her like this filled me with a tenderness I'd never known.

Over the two days, we assembled the various pieces of art to take to Silver Goose Winery. I put off taking them there. The thought of seeing Blake again made me so uneasy. He stirred up emotions in me I couldn't deny—emotions I wasn't ready to act on. In truth, I was as fragile emotionally as I'd ever been. My sham of a marriage to Will had proved to me how easily I could be fooled into giving my heart away. Better to be safe than sorry, I told myself. Blake Whiting was a man who would end up hurting me. The longer I could avoid him, the better.

A few days later, Jessie came over to me. "Am I going to have to take the things out to Silver Goose myself or are you going to do it like you told me? It wouldn't, by chance, have anything to do with seeing Blake again, would it?"

I avoided her gaze. "I'll do it this afternoon. I promise." I couldn't let my insecurities interfere with business.

At three o'clock, I loaded up my SUV, picked up Daisy at the bus stop and headed for Silver Goose Winery. Warm, almost-spring weather had encouraged more visitors to the area, and the roads were crowded with drivers who had no intention of hurrying along. It took me a full hour of frustration to reach the Silver Goose turnoff. The words I rehearsed to explain why I hadn't returned Blake's phone calls became jumbled inside my head.

I pulled up to the barn, and we got out. The geese I'd seen on my previous visit rushed toward us in a small bunch, greeting us noisily. Daisy took one look at them, shrieked and held her arms up to me.

"Help!" she screamed. "I don't like them!"

I gathered her to me. "It's okay, Daisy. I'm here. They won't hurt you. They just like to make a lot of noise." She calmed down, and I realized I still had a lot to learn. I hadn't even considered she'd be afraid.

Daisy stared wide-eyed at the geese waddling away but still clung to me as I carried her inside.

"Oh, hi, Allison." A young girl wearing a black Silver Goose T-shirt greeted me from behind a counter as we walked inside. "Remember me? Claire? I served wine at Treasures during the wine festival. Can I help you?"

"Oh, hi. I'm looking for Blake."

"He's in his office, upstairs behind the tasting area. Do you know where it is?"

"I do. Thanks. By the way, the geese are out."

"Again?" Claire groaned. "I'll let Juan know. Thanks."

I set Daisy down and took her hand. I led her up the stairs and past a number of people lined up at the long wide bar, sampling wine.

Daisy turned back to watch the crowd. "What are those people doing?"

"They're tasting wine from the grapes the winery has grown." I waved at the bartender, led Daisy down a hallway and knocked on a paneled door marked "Office". Waiting for a response, my heart pounded.

"Come in," called Blake.

Daisy and I stepped into a large space lit in part by two

skylights that caught the warm afternoon sun and spread it in sparkling beams below. Blake, his blond hair reflected in the sunshine, looked especially handsome as he paced back and forth confidently, talking on his cell phone.

"No, no," I heard him say. "The 2010 cab won't be ready to ship by then. Better stick to the 2009. Yeah, I understand. I'll be there."

He hung up the phone with a groan. "Problems. Problems." He turned and stared at me, a challenge in his expression I couldn't ignore.

"Sorry I didn't return your calls. " I desperately wanted to wipe my sweaty hands on my slacks. "Daisy and I have been real busy. Right, Sweetheart?"

Daisy nodded dutifully before turning a wide-eyed gaze on Blake. I watched them study each other, struck by the way their similar blue eyes held.

Blake knelt in front of Daisy. "We've got geese here at the winery. Would you like to see them?"

Daisy shook her head emphatically.

"They greeted us outside, and Daisy is unsure about them," I said, letting Blake know the situation.

He smiled at Daisy. "Then, I bet you'd like to see the new puppies in the barn."

"Puppies?" Daisy's face lit up. "Yes! I want to see them."

"Okay." He rose and turned to me. "You brought the items for display?"

"Yes, and an extra piece from Dawson Smith that I thought might look nice in The Manor House."

"Great, let's take care of it now."

We went downstairs, and after peeking outside to make sure the geese were gone, I led Daisy to the car.

"I want to see the puppies." She tugged on my hand impatiently.

"Claire can take her down to the barn while we take these things out of the car," said Blake.

I glanced at Daisy. "Will you go with Claire to look at the puppies?"

"Okay."

Claire approached, and Daisy dashed toward her. "I want to see the puppies! I want to see the puppies!"

Claire laughed and took hold of her hand, and the two of them headed for the barn.

I realized Blake had arranged this ahead of time so he could speak to me privately. He didn't waste any time getting to the point.

"Is there some reason you haven't returned my calls?" His penetrating gaze made me squirm.

I looked away, took a deep breath and faced him. "I got your messages, but I don't think it's a good idea to date. My life is far too complicated right now. I'm worried I might have to do something about Lisa, and I'm working on an idea to bring in new business to the gallery." I knew how shallow my words sounded, how rude I'd been. I glanced away and back again.

Blake gave me a look that told me he knew there was more to my story, but he let it go. "So what's this about a new idea for business?"

I smiled. "It's something Silver Goose may very well be interested in doing. My sister is coming to visit. I want to talk to her about it first. If she agrees my idea is workable, I'd like to be able to give you a call and talk about it."

"Fair enough."

We unloaded the back of the car and soon had the paintings hung and the metal sculptures placed in the upstairs area of the barn. Dawson's sunset piece was given a place of honor in a glass case at the head of the stairs where everyone would be sure to see it.

"Okay, let's see about the second Dawson Smith piece, the one for The Manor House," said Blake, walking back to the car with me.

I lifted it out of the car and held it up for Blake to see.

"I see what you mean. It's beautiful." He fingered the finish of the huge silver and gold vase. "Let's place it in the front hall."

My gaze traveled from his broad hands to his appealing lips. Heat radiated throughout my body at the thought of what either could do. I turned away, amazed by his effect on me. It was as if my body had been frozen with humiliation for the last year and now melted in a blaze of lust at the mere thought of Blake's hands and lips on me.

On the walk over to The Manor House, I studied Blake out of the corner of my eye. He strolled along beside me, gazing out at the vineyards with an obvious sense of pleasure. I knew he'd worked hard for this and I understood his pride. Everything looked orderly, peaceful and lovely—a mixture of nature and careful planning.

"It's beautiful, Blake."

He turned to me with a smile. "Yeah. It took a hell of a job to get it to this point, but it's working out pretty well. Of course, I have the normal ups and downs of running a place like this. It's not always easy."

"Is The Manor House working out?"

"It's used mostly on weekends, but that'll change as we're able to pull in more business groups."

I stopped and studied the building. In the late afternoon sun, it glowed with a golden color, dominating the rolling landscape like a crowned member of royalty.

We approached it, and I followed Blake up the wide front stairs and through the front entrance. Inside I was struck once again by its elegance. "It's gorgeous. Who decorated it?"

Blake grinned. "I hired a decorator. My Aunt Penny had a whole lot of input, which didn't always make it easy. But I like it."

"Me, too. It's absolutely lovely. How about placing Dawson's piece on that table leading into the library?"

Blake set it on the side table. Gold flecks in the frame of the mirror above it brought out the bronze tones of the vase. I clapped in sheer delight. It would be a marvelous show piece for Dawson and the gallery.

"It's perfect." I rummaged in my purse. "Here's the small plaque that goes with it. Hopefully it will bring both Dawson and Treasures new business."

"Looks nice," Blake said agreeably. "Care for a cup of coffee? During the day there's always a pot on in the back kitchen."

"Sounds good." I recalled the time I'd shared coffee with Blake at Treasures, after bawling in his arms. Today, I was much more in control of myself.

Blake led me into the kitchen and handed me a cup of coffee. I leaned against the counter and took several grateful sips of the hot, strong brew and closed my eyes, letting my body relax. When I opened them, Blake was staring at me thoughtfully.

"You mentioned you were once married. What happened?"

I took a deep breath. I'd been such a fool. To admit it was painful. "It turns out he had a yen for other women. One of them was a woman he used to date. Real smart of me, huh?"

He continued to gaze at me. "It must have really hurt you."

"Uh...yeah...not easy," I replied shakily.

"So that's why you're skittish," Blake said, as if talking to himself. He reached out and gently traced the outline of my cheek. "I'd never hurt you, Allison."

Flustered at the gentleness in his voice, I looked away, willing myself not to blubber like a baby. There was something about Blake that seemed to loosen all my pent-up feelings. I took another steadying breath and fought to ignore the impulse to throw my arms around him.

"Guess I'd better head back and find Daisy."

"Sure." Blake's voice held disappointment.

We stared at each other wordlessly. In spite of myself, I was interested in going out with him. But I wouldn't allow myself to enter into an affair, where I might end up hurt. I'd made one poor choice in love and I wasn't about to move so quickly again.

Blake set his coffee cup in the sink, took my empty one and set it down. "Let's go."

We walked side by side, aware of each other, silent.

At the barn, Daisy was sitting in a pile of hay. A number of black lab puppies romped around her, vying for her attention. She screeched with pleasure as a black puppy licked her cheek with a pink tongue. "It tickles!"

It filled me with joy to see her so happy. "I'm sorry, sweetie, but it's time to go. We've got to get back home. It's a school night."

She stood, clutching the wriggling puppy in her arms. "I don't want to go! I want this puppy. Please, Allie!"

I shook my head. "Sorry, the puppy has to stay with her mommy. She's not ready to leave her." I couldn't deal with a puppy at this point in time.

Daisy wailed the too-familiar cry I'd grown to despise.

Blake squatted in front of Daisy and stroked the puppy's head. "I've got an idea. Why don't I give this puppy to you, but instead of taking her home with you, you let her live with her mother. You can come out and play with her any time Allie can bring you." He looked up for my approval.

Daisy's lips curved.

"That's a great idea." I shot Blake a grateful smile.

Daisy gave the puppy a reluctant kiss good-bye, and I helped place the wiggly little pup back with her anxious mother. "There. Your baby girl is back. All's right with the world now."

A shiver crept across my shoulders.

When would *my* world be all right?

CHAPTER NINE

I walked Daisy to the school bus. Each day was a challenge. When I couldn't seem to get a comb through her hair without a little pulling, she sobbed for her mother. When I made her do something she didn't want to do, she told me she hated me. Hiding my hurt, I worked around these scenes, but it wasn't easy.

I returned to the gallery and walked through the backyard to the little cottage nestled in a corner of the large lot. Peering through the tiny-paned windows, I filled with hope. It was roomier inside than I'd thought. If I could line everything up, my plan might work. I dashed back to the gallery to find the keys.

A well-dressed older woman stood at the front door.

"Can I help you?" I asked.

"I realize you're not open yet, but may I come in and look around?"

"Sure." I wasn't about to turn any business away. I'd go inside the cottage later.

While the woman browsed, I rearranged jewelry in a front case, keeping an eye on her. There was something familiar about her. Had I met her before?

Jessie arrived through the back door of the gallery as the woman pointed to a large oil painting of the sea. "I'd like that painting and the blue Dawson Smith piece over there."

Pretending to act as if we sold four thousand dollars of artwork every day, I hurried over to the pieces. Her eyes alight with excitement, Jessie worked with me to wrap the painting.

We placed the Raku piece, surrounded by bubble wrap, in a sturdy box.

When the woman handed me her credit card, I understood why Jessie had been staring at her. She was Penelope Potter, the actress on a television sitcom I used to watch back in Maine.

"Penelope Potter!" Jessie smiled at her. "That's why you look so familiar. I'm so excited you're here!"

"How did you hear of Treasures?" I asked. *Had she seen one of our new ads?*

"My nephew." Penelope smiled. "He's got a winery not far from here. I bought a place in Sausalito a few years back—a nice little getaway." With her refined features and bright blue eyes, she was even more beautiful in person than on television.

"Nephew? You mean Blake Whiting? Don't tell me you're Blake's Aunt Penny," Jessie blurted out. "Blake's talked about you so often I feel I know you." She held out her hand. "I'm a friend of his. Jessie Ives. And this is Allison Hartwell."

Aunt Penny? I blinked. Blake Whiting was one surprise after another.

Penelope beamed. "Of all my many nieces and nephews, Blake's the most like me—an adventurer, but a hard worker too. Who'd ever have guessed he'd end up in the wine business?" She studied me thoughtfully. "Allison Hartwell? Oh...you're the one who now has that adorable little girl, aren't you? Blake told me all about her. He's given her one of the puppies."

"Daisy and Blake get along very well."

Penelope laughed. "All the little ones in our family seem to gravitate to Blake. I don't know what it is."

But, I knew exactly what it was—that rare magnetism of his that drew everyone to him like an undeniable law of physics.

We helped Penelope carry her packages to her car, and she settled behind the wheel of her Mercedes sedan. "Hope to see you both again. Perhaps, on Saturday?"

I gave her a puzzled look.

She clucked her tongue. "I guess Blake hasn't started calling people yet. Dear boy, he's putting on an impromptu little party for me to celebrate the renewal of my show. I'm sure he'll be in touch. Don't disappoint me. Be sure to come. I like what you girls are doing here."

She took off, and the car disappeared down the road.

Jessie turned to me. "Wow! Penelope Potter. Maybe she'll spread the news about the store to some of her big-spending friends. She didn't blink an eye at the cost of what she bought."

"She made Blake sound perfect."

Jessie gave me a knowing look. "What is it with you and him? Every time his name comes up, you act weird. You're falling for him, aren't you?"

I shrugged.

Jessie waggled a finger at me. "Well, if Blake asks us, I'm going to the party. I wouldn't miss it for the world." She grinned. "I wonder who else will be there?"

"You go. It's probably out for me. My sister Samantha called this morning from the road. She and my cousin Marissa will be here by then. They're driving a whole truckload of stuff for me from home."

Jessie arched an eyebrow. "I don't think that will be a problem."

Jessie phoned as I returned from seeing Daisy off to school and stocking up at the grocery store for my sister's visit.

"You know the party on Saturday? Blake said for you to bring along Marissa and Samantha. He even invited Daisy."

I sucked in my breath. "You accepted for us?"

"Damn right." She hung up the phone before I could utter a word.

Later, Samantha called me at the gallery to tell me she and Marissa had reached Sausalito. I said a quick good-bye to Jessie and hurried home.

Before long, a U-Haul truck ground its way up the hill to my house. Staring in awe at the size of the truck, I waved and directed them into the driveway. In addition to bigger pieces of furniture from the condo Will and I had briefly shared, my mother must have added a pile of her own. She was all about making things nice. We girls loved her for it.

Samantha climbed down from the truck and ran to me. I hugged her hard. She looked great—sobriety was working wonders for her. Marissa came up to the two of us and stood aside shyly. I grinned and pulled her into the circle. About the same height, Samantha and Marissa stood tall and straight, their bodies trim like mine. Whereas I had blondish hair that was streaked with added color, Samantha's hair was a rich dark brown, Marissa's auburn. Both of them had the same grey eyes.

I took them inside and showed them around the downstairs, then, led them to the second floor.

Samantha knelt on the window seat in my bedroom and gazed out at the water. "The view is wonderful." She turned to me with a teasing grin. "Well, maybe not quite as beautiful as Casco Bay."

"You're happy here, considering the circumstances?" Marissa asked.

"It hasn't been easy," I admitted. "Besides having Daisy to care for, I've got my work cut out to make a go of the gallery. But it's not all bad; I've met a lot of interesting people." No way was I going to admit I was scared to death I'd fail in this venture of mine.

We completed the tour of the house and returned to the truck. A male voice called my name.

"Ah, here's one of those interesting people now. Rob Henrickson, Jessie's fiancé, is an old friend of Kristin's. I hired him and a couple of his fellow musicians to unload the truck for us."

Rob strolled toward us, followed by two other men I'd never met. Introductions were made all around and then Rob indicated the truck with a nod of his head. "Is it full?"

"Almost." Samantha rolled up the door of the truck.

We all gaped at the furnishings packed inside. From the looks of it, my mother had thought of everything. The couch from my apartment, a number of wooden chairs, overstuffed chairs, wooden chests and my dining room table were stacked neatly, surrounded by boxes and overflowing plastic bags.

For the next couple of hours, I kept busy running back and forth from inside the house to the back of the truck, determining where I wanted everything placed. In a surprisingly short period of time, the unloading was completed. The unpacking of the boxes was another issue. I'd have to do that over several days, if not weeks.

Amid boxes stacked in the living room, we ate pizza and drank beer and sodas in companionable silence. I was pleased to have guests in my house. It felt like the house-warming I'd never had.

After the guys had gone, Samantha said, "I'm going to walk down to the gallery and introduce myself to Jessie. I'm anxious to meet her."

"I'll go with you," said Marissa. "Five days in that truck has cramped my whole body. I need to move."

"Okay, I'll work here until it's time to pick up Daisy."

They left, and I dug through the boxes, happy to have more

of my personal things around me. Later, on my way to the bus stop to pick up Daisy, I dropped into Treasures. Samantha and Marissa were chatting easily with Jessie.

"Glad you guys have met." I was pleased they seemed so comfortable with one another. "I'm on my way to pick up Daisy."

Samantha held up a hand. "Wait! I want to go with you. I can't wait to meet her."

"Me, too." Marissa looped her arm in mine, and the three of us took off down the hill.

"I can't believe you're a mother now," said Samantha, as we hurried along. "I know it's been a real shock to you."

I nodded, surprised by my anxiety. In spite of Daisy's unpredictable behavior, I wanted Samantha and Marissa to like her.

As we approached, the bus pulled up. I held my breath as Daisy stepped off it, saw me and waved. Eyes bright with curiosity, she ran toward us. "Hi, Allie!" she called happily and keeping an eye on Samantha and Marissa, she threw herself in my arms.

I hugged her to me.

She wiggled out of my arms. "Is this Auntie Sam and Cousin M?" She stared at them with those compelling blue eyes of hers.

"It sure is." Samantha knelt on the ground and held out her arms.

Daisy went right into them. I smiled with a mother's pride as Samantha hugged her and Marissa leaned down and gave Daisy a kiss.

Caught up in the excitement of having visitors, Daisy was unusually chatty as we walked home. And for the rest of the day, she followed her routines without much of a fuss.

That night, after Daisy was finally asleep, the three of us sat in the living room in our pajamas, sipping sodas, chatting and giggling like school girls at a slumber party. It felt so good to have family with me. I'd felt so alone, going through one of the most traumatic periods of my life.

In the morning, Samantha and Marissa went into San Francisco to sightsee. With Daisy in school, I set to work at the gallery. The recent sale to Blake's Aunt Penny, plus a number of other smaller sales, had given me enough money to order a few less-expensive items to round out our inventory.

Jessie and I eagerly leafed through a number of catalogs. A jewelry maker in Santa Barbara did beautiful work in silver and 14-karat gold. Simple in design, interesting with their dangling movement, the earrings were exactly what we needed. We called and placed a rush order in time for Easter, and ordered a variety of bead and stone necklaces from a woman in Texas.

We rearranged things in the store and set up a sale corner. Ours was an eclectic collection of unique items, but we had to keep the inventory changing so our customers would find something new each time they came. We also talked about Samantha drawing up papers for Jessie to become a partner.

Samantha and Marissa picked up Daisy at the bus stop and joined us.

"Have you told them where we're all going tomorrow?" Jessie asked me pointedly, knowing full well I hadn't.

Shooting Jessie a daggered look, I sighed with resignation. Having my sister meet Blake could only mean trouble with a capital T, as in Teasing me to death. "We've been invited to Blake Whiting's Silver Goose Winery, for a reception in honor of Penelope Potter of the TV show, *55 Magnolia Drive.*"

"Really?" Marissa squealed with excitement. "Penelope Potter? I love her!"

Samantha placed her hands on her hips and narrowed her eyes at me. "And why, may I ask, were you keeping this invitation a little secret? You know that's one of my favorite shows."

I covered my embarrassment with a nonchalant shrug. "I dunno ..."

"I do." Jessie stared at me defiantly. "It has something to do with Blake Whiting. I think she's got the hots for him."

"Jessie, that's not fair," I protested.

Samantha's eyes gleamed with mischief. "I guess we'll find out tomorrow, won't we?"

I gulped, as trapped as a doe in the headlights of an onrushing car.

Saturday evening, I drove the three of us out to the winery. Jessie had agreed to follow with Daisy as soon as she came home from a classmate's birthday party. I was quiet behind the wheel, nervous to see Blake again. He made me feel so ... so ... unsettled. What would I do if he came on to me in front of everyone? Part of me wanted him to, the rest of me was terrified he would.

We pulled into the crowded parking lot. Seeing all the cars, I let out a sigh of relief. With so many people, I could hide in the crowd.

"This way." I led Samantha and Marissa down the driveway toward The Manor House.

"She's been here before." Marissa jabbed Samantha with her elbow and gave me a wicked grin.

"Yeah, she certainly knows her way around," teased Samantha, laughing softly at my discomfort.

Blake greeted us at the front door.

At the sight of him, Samantha's eyes widened. She shot me a knowing look, and her lips curved with approval. I prayed she'd keep quiet.

"Hi, Allison." Blake's smile was dazzling.

"Thanks for having us," I replied nervously. "Jessie and I enjoyed meeting your Aunt Penny."

"She thought your gallery was great." His smile made me forget everything else.

"Ahem." Samantha nudged me.

Flustered, I introduced Samantha and Marissa, and we moved inside.

"Hi, there," said Janelle Martin, walking toward us with a confident stride. She placed a possessive hand on Blake's arm. "Come in and make yourselves comfortable. Wine and drinks are being served in the library and there's plenty of food in the dining room."

Janelle was Blake's hostess? My body went numb. Their relationship was much more serious than I'd been led to believe. No doubt, she'd put more clothes in his guest room closet. Or perhaps they'd moved to the master bedroom. My mind awhirl, I drifted into the dining room.

"It's a beautiful house," said Marissa, nibbling on appetizers. "It reminds me of a French country estate."

I nodded, feeling sick as I observed Janelle work the crowd—smiling, directing the waiters, acting the perfect hostess and occasionally flashing triumphant glances at me.

Marissa edged closer. "I can see why you're so attracted to Blake. He's a hottie if I ever saw one. Was that his girlfriend who greeted us?"

"Apparently so," I answered miserably.

Attractive in a navy blazer and tan slacks, Dawson Smith approached us. Glad for the distraction, I introduced him to

Marissa and Samantha.

"Where'd you find the soft drink?" Dawson asked Samantha.

"Come, I'll show you." Samantha smiled at him, and he followed her through the crowd.

Marissa turned to me. "Wow! You're surrounded by gorgeous guys. You're going to love California, if you don't already."

I laughed, but the timing was off. Gorgeous guys were not on my agenda—especially one certain vineyard owner.

Penelope Potter walked into the room wearing a lacy black shawl over a bright purple dress that flowed down around her ankles. People stepped aside as she made her way toward the library in a sweep of color, looking every bit the television star.

I gave her a little wave.

She came right over to me. "Allison! I must tell you how much I like the painting. It's perfect in my house. And the Dawson Smith piece in my foyer is stunning, absolutely stunning."

"Wonderful. Dawson happens to be here. Would you like to meet him?"

"Oh my, yes! Lead me to him."

"First, meet my cousin, Marissa Cole." I watched as Penelope and Marissa exchanged greetings, marveling at the ease with which Marissa handled herself. She'd come a long way since landing on my aunt's doorstep.

I took Penelope's arm and led her to the front parlor where Samantha and Dawson were deep in conversation.

"Dawson Smith! I've been dying to meet you!" Penelope exclaimed, taking his hand in hers. She sounded like the star-struck fans hovering nearby, waiting for a chance to speak to her.

After Penelope left our group, Samantha turned to me.

"I've been bending Dawson's ear about my consulting practice back home. He told me he's set up a trust fund to underwrite art projects. He said I could apply for funding if one of the women I'm helping is doing something involving the arts. Isn't that wonderful?"

"That's terrific." He was a good man.

At that moment, Jessie arrived with Daisy. Every head in the room turned at their entrance into the room. They were a striking pair—Daisy with her golden looks and Jessie with her dark hair and sparkling brown eyes.

"Allie!" Daisy cried.

I held out my arms and she rushed into them. After we'd hugged, Daisy stepped back and announced to the group around us, "Allie is my fairy godmother."

I laughed along with everyone else, though tears stung my eyes. I wished life was so simple.

CHAPTER TEN

Monday morning, I prayed Daisy could be coaxed into eating her breakfast and going to the school bus without any screaming fights. It would be my first real chance to talk to Samantha, Marissa, and Jessie about my new business idea. I couldn't wait to hear what they thought of it.

Samantha helped me, and the morning routine worked better than expected. With Daisy off to school, the four of us settled in the back office of Treasures.

"Samantha, I know how valuable your consulting business is for women starting out in business. I have an idea for expanding my business and need to know if you think it's possible." I took a deep breath. "So, here goes. If we added a series of decks and a large sunroom onto the cottage out back, we could offer wine and sweets." I turned to Jessie. "The wine festival proved there's a need for a place like this. Remember how it was? People hanging around, sipping wine?"

"A crowd ended up sitting in our parking lot, just for a place to relax and talk."

I clutched my hands in a nervous knot. "I've drawn up a list of things that need to be addressed, but, Sam, you're the expert. I need you to help me write up a business plan and financial projections to present to investors."

Sam gave me a thoughtful look. "Intriguing, but I'd need to know a lot more about it before determining how feasible it is. You're going to need a lot more capital to pull something like this off. Liquor licenses, construction, advertising, compliance with zoning regulations, all those are costly."

Goose pimples danced across my body. Samantha hadn't pooh-poohed the idea. "I've even got a name for our new venture. 'Sweet Talk'."

"Ooh," said Jessie, "I love the name!"

Pleased, I continued. "In addition to selling wine and chocolates, we could sell a variety of coffees, teas, and baked goods. I bet Swanson's commercial bakery downtown would be willing to provide us with pastries and other sweets."

Jessie sat up straighter. "I know Debbie Swanson. I think she'd be thrilled."

"You like the idea? You really do?"

Jessie grinned. "Sweet Talk? I *love* it! If we get the go-ahead, I want to become a partner like we talked about."

Sam smiled. "Let's work through the idea and come up with the costs involved, making it right for both of you. No doubt, you'll need to go for a bank loan, but the property is good equity. Though the land itself is valuable, we'll need a complete appraisal, including all the improvements."

I stood. "Let's go take a look at the cottage. I've done some poking around and will, of course, get it cleaned up before going to any lenders or investors."

We posted a 'Closed' sign on the front door of the gallery, and I grabbed a notepad and pen. I'd already sketched a few ideas for the outside decking. After we'd walked the width and length of the lot, I unlocked the door to the cottage, and we stepped inside. An unmade cot was tucked into one corner of the large room. Paint rags and an easel sat in the middle of the space beneath a skylight. A number of boxes were stacked in another smaller room. It wouldn't take much to get the place spruced up.

"Is it big enough?" said Jessie, glancing around.

"Big enough to hold a wine bar and a couple of display cases," I replied happily. I'd already spent a lot of time with a tape measure, plotting a layout of the rooms. I envisioned a huge sunroom with skylights and a stone fireplace. I pointed to the doorway.

"A series of French doors could open to layers of wooden decks outside where people could linger and talk."

Samantha indicated the small sink. "Running water is already here. That'll make it easier to put in additional plumbing."

I showed them my rough drawings.

"Who's going to pay for all of this?" Sam asked, bringing me back to reality.

"If Sam comes up with a workable plan and my accountant approves, I'd like to offer to bankroll the project." Marissa gave me a broad smile. "As you know, I've received an unexpected inheritance."

"That's so sweet but I can't let you do it." I hoped Marissa would understand. I didn't want my family to have any risk because of me. I already owed my mother five thousand dollars to pay for the move out here.

"No?" Marissa's look of disappointment was touching.

Sam elbowed me. "You could bring Marissa and others in as limited partners."

Marissa smiled. "Maybe that will work. We'll see."

I gave her a hug. "I'd love it if you and Samantha would look over the project and help us find a good bank to give us a loan."

Marissa turned to Jessie. "She's stubborn, but she's smart. When you've come up with your cost and income projections, you'll know exactly what you're in for. Then, if a bank won't lend you the money, we can talk again about a loan or some other business arrangement. I love the idea and want to be able to help."

Grateful for her support, I gave my newfound cousin

another squeeze. Family meant everything to me.

We spent the rest of the morning huddled in the back office going over facts and figures. The boring numbers took on a new life as we talked about all kinds of possibilities. I'd made a rough sketch of a design for the new space, and already had talked to a salesman at Scott Building Supply. He told me that once I had the architectural plans, he'd do what he'd called a "take off", which meant he would figure out what materials we needed and price the project for us for materials alone.

Samantha and I wrote up a detailed list and budget of items we would need to complete the project, including furniture, refrigerators, microwaves, and other equipment for handling food and drinks.

Jessie and Marissa worked on a list of contractors.

By noon, we were ready for a break.

"If we have a good handle on what the expenses of such a project are," said Samantha, "I can go to a couple of bankers I work with for my business and quiz them on the best approach for financing this." Her concern evident, she searched my face. "Allie, it's a big risk. You could lose the business and the property. Are you ready to take that chance? Pretty gutsy, if you ask me."

I fought panic. What choice did I really have? The gallery wasn't ever going to succeed the way I wanted it to without a means of attracting more customers. I needed to make a decent living from it, enough to make at least a reasonable future for Daisy and me.

"I think it's the only way out of merely making ends meet in the gallery business. Maybe it's time I took a chance on something like this. My God, I worked at the same job for three boring years because I didn't want to go for any other job interviews." Though I sounded sure, my stomach clenched at the thought of failing.

"Yeah, I know you hated that job," commiserated Samantha. She turned to Jessie. "How about you? You said you wanted to be a partner in this if the numbers add up and the project is a go. Are you ready to take on a huge risk like this?"

Jessie clutched her fingers together. "I have to wait and see what you come up with but I've got a gut feeling it'll work. And then, yes, I'm in. I'd already talked to my father about going into the gallery with Allie."

"Okay, then. I'll take copies of all the information back with me and work on it at home."

I wrapped my arms around my sister. For all the teasing she gave me, she was the best.

I kept up a stream of useless chatter as I drove Samantha and Marissa to the airport. Sadness tugged at me.

At the airport, we shared quick embraces. I wanted to cling to them, tell them they couldn't go, that I needed them too much. Helplessly I watched them roll their suitcases through the automatic doors. They turned back, and I waved forlornly, overwhelmed by all that lay ahead. Samantha had agreed the gallery was in jeopardy unless we could improve sales; Lisa was due back from her trip and would continue to fight me for Daisy, and I was about to take a big business risk that could prove to be either a major success or a failure.

At the gallery, Jessie gave me a bright smile. The customer with her was holding one of Dawson Smith's vases in his arms. A good sign.

I dropped off my purse at my desk and stared at the note attached to my phone. "Call Blake."

I brushed aside my ambivalence and lifted the phone. I wouldn't let personal concerns rule. Blake Whiting didn't know it yet but he was an important part of my business plan.

He answered on the third ring. "Glad you called me back. Are you available for dinner tomorrow night? Strictly business, of course."

"As a matter of fact, I am," I answered sweetly, well aware my prompt response wasn't at all what he expected. But I needed to talk to him about Sweet Talk.

"Oh, well then," he stumbled, caught off guard by my quick acceptance, "is six o'clock too early?"

"No, that's fine. I'll be ready. Any idea where we're going?"

"Yes," he said cryptically. "See you tomorrow."

I couldn't help laughing as I hung up the phone. It had been a perfect standoff.

For the rest of the day, whenever we weren't busy with customers, Jessie and I discussed plans for Sweet Talk.

After I tucked Daisy into bed that night, I read all I could about chocolate.

Jessie took the following day off to do some personal errands. Left alone in the gallery, I thought of how much I'd come to depend on her. Fate, I thought whimsically, had been cruel to take Kristin away but had attempted to compensate by giving me Jessie.

I closed the gallery at five and led Daisy up the stairs to Jessie's apartment. "You going to be all right with Auntie Jessie?"

Daisy nodded solemnly. "Tomorrow we can go see the puppies? Right?"

"Yes, I promise." I'd keep my part of the bargain, though it bothered me to be trapped into making frequent trips to Silver Goose Winery. But, if I could convince Blake to buy into my plan, an evening off in exchange for a visit to Silver Goose would be well worth it.

At home, I pulled a basic black sleeveless dress out of the

closet, took a quick shower, and studied myself in the mirror. The gaunt look following Kristin's death had disappeared, though the strain of keeping things on an even keel still showed in the worry lines that appeared between my eyes. I disregarded them and brushed mascara on my lashes, spread a glossy red color on my lips and slipped on the black dress. A red print Gucci scarf my mother had given me added the perfect touch for any restaurant he might have in mind.

The doorbell rang, and I ran to greet him.

Blake gave me an admiring stare. "You look great." His gaze traveled from my flushed cheeks to the tips of my toes and back again. "Ready? I've got the perfect place for us."

I smiled. "Are you going to tell me where we're going?"

He shook his head. "Nope. You'll see."

We headed north, chatting about the weather and the fact that it was a drier springtime than most.

"What will that do to the grapes?" I asked.

"We have to irrigate more and watch the sugar content as they grow." He turned to me. "You know, Aunt Penny really likes you, Allison. I do, too."

I frowned. "Blake, let's clear up something. Ours is a business relationship, nothing more. It's only right, considering Janelle..."

His eyebrows shot up. "Janelle? What do you mean?"

"It's perfectly obvious. She served as hostess at your party and made it plain that her real role was more than that." My stomach curled with disappointment all over again.

"Wha-a-at?" Blake pulled the car over to the side of the road so fast I had to clutch the armrest of my door to keep from tumbling against him.

Anger narrowed his lips as he faced me. "Janelle Martin may think there's something serious between us but, believe me, I don't. She was my hostess that night because I hired her to do it. End of story."

Realizing the truth, I felt about two inches tall. "I'm s-s-sorry," I stammered. *He paid her to do that? Like a paid escort?* "I just..."

Blake took a deep breath. "I alone decide who I see for business or otherwise. And I don't like to play games."

"Neither do I."

His steady gaze had me swimming in their blue depths. My heart pounded. He wanted to kiss me. I wanted it too.

He drew me toward him.

I let out a soft yelp.

Startled, we both looked down at the gear shift. "Stupid stick." He reached for me again, and the idling car shifted into reverse with a jolt.

"Whoa!" Blake shifted the car back into park and took a resigned breath. "Damn! This isn't working. Let's go! We've got dinner reservations."

"Where are we going?"

Blake grinned. "To Silver Goose. Where else?"

My jaw dropped. "Wait! That's where we're going to have dinner?"

"Yep. Right at Silver Goose." He winked at me. "This is business, remember? I'm testing a new catering service. I've arranged for them to serve us dinner at The Manor House."

"Oh." I tried to sound excited about the prospect of eating when all I could think of was the kiss that had lingered in the air between us.

He gave my hand a squeeze. "I'd already planned to send them home early when I saw you in that dress."

I laughed, feeling desirable for the first time in a long, long while.

###

At The Manor House, Blake led me into the library. A small table sat beside the fireplace, covered with a starched, white linen table cloth. Crystal water goblets and wine glasses, heavy silverware and gold-rimmed creamy plates gleamed in the firelight.

A waiter, dressed in black pants and a crisp white shirt enclosed at the neck with a black bow tie, appeared at the doorway. “Are you ready to begin?”

“Serve the champagne, then, please leave us alone,” Blake said. The waiter, a man I guessed to be in his mid-fifties, gave us a perceptive smile and bobbed his head politely. He opened the bottle, poured Dom Perignon into two tulip stems, and, after receiving approval from Blake, left the room.

Blake stood by the fireplace next to me and lifted his glass of bubbling liquid.

“To what promises to be an exciting evening.”

I clicked my glass against his. The evening was already the best I’d had in a long time. “To business.”

A look of dismay crossed Blake’s face. “So, back to business, is it? Okay, I need you to rate the service and the food. I’m hiring a new catering service for our functions here at The Manor House. After the party for Aunt Penny, I decided I needed more professional help.”

At my look of surprise, Blake laughed. “Aunt Penny doesn’t like Janelle—as a hostess or otherwise. She told me straight out that I was a damn fool for not going after you.”

“Oh? So she’s the reason...”

Blake shook his head. “No, that’s not the reason I’m attracted to you. Do you have any idea how beautiful you are? And, sweetheart, it’s not only your looks. I see the way you are with Daisy.”

“Oh, but ...”

His lips cut off the rest of my automatic denial. He took the champagne glass from my hand and set it down on the mantel to draw me even closer.

The sound of a clearing throat sent us apart.

"May I pour you more champagne, sir?"

Blake flashed an exasperated look at him. "As bad as the damn gear shift," he mumbled to me.

I laughed and held out my glass to the waiter for more.

The waiter left us alone again. "So tell me what you've been up to," Blake said.

I took a seat on the leather couch and, taking hold of my hand, he sat beside me.

"Remember my telling you I had an idea for expanding business at the gallery?"

He nodded, and I proceeded to lay out the plan for Sweet Talk.

"Very good. How do I fit into all this?"

I caught my lip, pondering how to say this best. I had to make Blake see that it would be worth his while to cooperate with us.

"We're going to have our sweets provided by others. Debbie Swanson has already agreed to provide us with cakes and pastries. I'm investigating chocolates from San Francisco, and we intend to feature a few select wines." I paused. "You mentioned you were coming out with a new cabernet sauvignon and I've already sampled your other varieties. Silver Goose wines are perfect for us. We'd showcase them at Sweet Talk, like you showcase items from Treasures here at the winery. We'd market the wines with maps to the winery itself, offer discounts or whatever else you wanted."

Blake rubbed his chin thoughtfully. "Let me think about it, talk to some of my marketing people. It might work."

"It would strictly be a business deal, with contracts and written agreements between us. My sister is a consultant to small business and she'd insist on it."

"So what do you know about chocolate?" Blake asked.

"I've read quite a bit about it," I responded, grateful for the time I had between Daisy's bedtime and mine to learn about it.

"Cacao seeds are grown in tropical climates, harvested, fermented and dried, then traded on the Coffee, Sugar and Cocoa Exchange to a variety of companies that process the seeds into various chocolate products."

"Whoa! Fermenting cacao seeds? What's that all about?"

I grinned, warming to the subject. "Once the seeds are harvested, the workers scoop them into boxes or put them in piles and cover them with banana leaves. And for the next three to nine days the seeds ferment like fine wine. The pulp around the seeds heats up, activating enzymes and creating compounds that give the seeds their chocolate flavor and their deep, rich, brown color. Interesting, huh?"

"Maybe that's why wine and chocolate go together. Their process is similar."

"I want to make sure we come up with the right wine and chocolate combinations and that Sweet Talk carries only excellent chocolates. I'm looking into a company called Bellano's in San Francisco. They make handmade chocolates with unusual flavors. I'll know what I want when I taste it."

Blake chuckled. "You a chocoholic or something?"

I grinned. "There are very few women around who don't like a taste of chocolate now and then. And men like it too."

"And other things." He drew me close, and as he gazed at me, my heartbeat sprinted. His lips came down on me as sweet as any chocolate I'd ever eaten ...

... and the waiter reappeared to announce the chef was sending the first course in, ready or not.

CHAPTER ELEVEN

As we sat opposite each other at the small dining table in the library, I couldn't keep my eyes from focusing on the strong lines of Blake's jaw, the way his lower lip softened as his mouth moved, or the intense hue of his eyes.

When I could finally tear my attention away from him, I dutifully took a bite and chewed the veal piccata, reminding myself why I was there with him. "Delicious. Honestly, everything so far has been superb."

"Yeah," grumbled Blake, "everything but the service. That's been way too good. We've barely had a moment to ourselves."

I laughed. We'd had many interruptions. I'd heard stories about temperamental chefs. Apparently Francois, holding court in the kitchen of The Manor House, was one of them.

Blake's expression lightened. "It's good to hear you laugh. I know how hard things have been for you."

I sobered. "It hasn't been easy, but Daisy and I are beginning to form a bond. My worst fear is that Lisa will disrupt that, by trying to take her away from me."

Blake frowned. "Kristin never told you who Daisy's father is?"

I shook my head, frustrated by the situation in which I found myself. "The only thing she told me is that she'd done a lot of dating when she first came to California. The father could be anybody. Any ideas?"

He shook his head. "It could be anyone. She and I even went out a few times."

I gasped. The blue of his eyes matched Daisy's.

Blake held up a hand. "I know what you're thinking, but it isn't me. She'd have said something to me. We were good friends."

Despite his denial, I thought again how odd it was that through the years his name hadn't come up in conversations with Kristin.

He took my hand. "If I thought I was Daisy's father, I'd say so. You're going to have to trust me on this."

I nodded, though I had to think about every clue given to me.

"It's probably a good idea to find out what you can about Daisy's father," he continued, "especially if Lisa threatens to take her away. You knew Kristin in college. What do you know about her life out here?"

"That's just it. We communicated about many things but certainly not about the men she dated, especially as she was discovering her true feelings about herself."

"Why don't you ask Jessie for help?"

"Maybe she can fill me in. She and Rob have been friends of Kristin's for some time. I'm running out of time. Lisa should be back from Europe soon."

The waiter removed the dinner plates and brought in small *pots de crème* sitting on white plates piped with a swirly chocolate design.

Determined not to ruin the evening by thoughts of Lisa, I took a taste. It was delicious.

After dinner, Blake left me to talk to the chef. I wandered around the main floor of The Manor House, thinking of our dinner conversation. What if Blake really was Daisy's father? He'd said Kristin would have told him if it was the case, which meant they'd slept together. I stood quietly in the peaceful silence of the room, telling myself not to let that realization affect my growing feelings for him. Perhaps, I told myself, it was time for me to take a personal leap of faith and simply enjoy the present for what it was. As Sam would say, 'take one day at a time.'

Blake found me in the front parlor, studying a watercolor of a vineyard.

His lips brushed a warm, moist greeting on my cheek. I looked up at him and smiled. Yes, I told myself, time I relaxed and simply enjoyed this man who'd fascinated me from the very beginning.

His voice turned husky. "Any chance you can spend the night? Give us time to know each other better?"

"Sorry." My disappointment was sincere. "Daisy's got a doctor's appointment first thing in the morning and I need to be home. But I've promised her we'll come and visit the puppies tomorrow afternoon."

He cupped my face in his strong hands. "I want time alone with you. Soon."

I closed my eyes as his warm lips told me in their special way exactly how much he'd wanted me to stay. How I wished I could.

The next morning was rainy and foggy. After Daisy's doctor's appointment, I dropped her off at school and headed for the gallery. It would, most likely, be a slow day.

My phone rang.

"Got a paper and pencil?" my sister said. "I've got the basic numbers for your project. I emailed them to you around two o'clock this morning. The way I see it, you've got a good chance of making Sweet Talk work with Treasures, provided you keep inventory costs and payroll under control and can sustain your pricing. I know about the sweets. What about the wine?"

"Blake is going to let me know if Silver Goose will cooperate. He liked the idea."

"Blake Whiting? The guy you were all hot for? Ve-e-er-r-ry interesting, sister dear."

"Yeah, well, there might be a problem." I parked the car in the lot of Treasures and turned down the radio.

"Samantha, I have to ask you something, something serious. If you were me, how would you feel if you discovered Blake was Daisy's father?"

I held my breath and waited for her reply. Of all the people in the world, I trusted my older sister to be straight with me.

"You think that's the case?"

"He doesn't think so, but it's possible. Those blue eyes of his are about the same color as Daisy's."

She hesitated. "Well, if he really were her father, it could benefit all of you. He could help take care of her and it would bring you two together. Daisy would be financially secure, which would ease the burden for you. It sounds like a perfect solution to me."

"Yeah, but how would you feel knowing he'd been with Kristin?" I couldn't help the sting of jealousy.

"You're worried about that? Don't be. From what I saw and heard about him, he's the best thing to come along for you in years. Relax, Allison. Take it one day at a time."

I felt a cool calm come over me. Sam always came through for me. "Okay. Hold on! I'm going inside." I made a dash for the gallery, hurried inside to my desk, printed off the email and took pen in hand. "Now, let's go over the numbers."

Jessie came into the gallery as I hung up the phone.

She held up a bridal magazine. "Take a look at this. What do you think?"

I studied the bride's dress she pointed out and let out a sigh. "It's gorgeous. You'd look beautiful in it, Jessie."

"I'm going to find something cheaper, just like it." Her cheeks grew pink with pleasure. "I can't believe Rob actually asked me to marry him after so many years. Not that my mother is pleased about it—she thinks he's way beneath her idea of the perfect man for me."

"How long have you known him?"

Jessie grinned. "Since high school. I was a freshman and he was already in college. He thought I was an idiot when we first met. We started dating off and on the summer after my freshman year in college, eight years ago."

"Did you know Kristin back then?"

"Not well, but I met her through Rob. Daisy was only a baby."

I took a deep breath, knowing I had to ask. "Do you have any idea who Daisy's father is?"

She shook her head. "I've always wondered if it was Dawson Smith."

My jaw dropped. "Dawson Smith? Kristin didn't even know him back then, did she?"

Jessie's eyes rounded. "Why do you say that?"

I shrugged. "Just something about their first meeting, how he helped her when her car broke down."

"True, but that was before Daisy was born. Does it really matter?"

"I hope not."

The next afternoon, Jessie and I were working in the office when an all-too-familiar voice called, "Hello?"

A cold knot formed in my stomach. I jumped to my feet.

Like an apparition from one of my nightmares, Lisa Vaughn marched into the office, carrying a suitcase.

"Sorry it took me so long to get here. Catherine and I had to move some stuff out of one of the bedrooms in her house so we'd have a spare room for Daisy. I've brought a suitcase for

Daisy's things."

My heart dropped to my feet. "What do you mean? Daisy isn't leaving here."

Lisa waggled a finger at me. "I'm Daisy's guardian. That was always the deal between me and Kristin."

Her look of determination shot a wave of queasiness through me. Daisy didn't like Lisa and Lisa clearly didn't like Daisy. It didn't make sense...unless Lisa was after the money set aside for Daisy. "Wait a minute! I ..."

Lisa cut me off. "I've got proof. Look at this." She waved a piece of paper in front of my nose. "It's all here in writing."

"But Kristin told me I was to take care of Daisy if anything happened to her. I'm Daisy's godmother." My mind whirled. "There's nothing in Kristin's files that says you're to take Daisy. I've gone through all of Kristin's private papers, here in the office. You and she broke up, so any agreement between the two of you is void."

Her lip curled. "You wanna bet? This is notarized and legal."

I started toward her, ready to wipe the triumphant grin off her face. Then common sense prevailed.

"You can't take Daisy away from me and everything she knows." I was so angry my voice shook. "She'd be way too upset to cope with a change like that. You have no idea what it's been like, dealing with her."

Lisa's smug expression turned ugly. "I'll go to court, if I have to."

"Go ahead and try, but it won't work." My stomach twisted at the thought of a court battle and what it would do to Daisy.

Lisa's eyes narrowed. "I won't give up, Allison. You'll see. Then you'll be sorry you fought me on this."

I clenched my teeth. I was not about to be bullied by her or anyone else. "You've threatened me, Lisa. Jessie, here, is my witness. If anything bad happens to Daisy, *you're* the one who'll be sorry. Not me."

"I'm calling the police now." Jessie picked up the phone and punched in the number.

"You can't do that," Lisa snapped, reaching for the phone.

Jessie stepped away from her and again punched in numbers on the phone.

"I'm getting a lawyer. We're going to fight you on this, Lisa." I ground the words out between my rigid jaws.

"The police are on their way over," said Jessie, replacing the phone. "They'll be here shortly."

"Fuck!" Lisa waved a fist at me. "It's not over, Allison. My lawyer will be in touch with you." The heels of her shoes sounded an angry beat on the tile floor as she left the room.

My knees shook so badly, I collapsed into a chair. The hatred I'd seen in Lisa's eyes had stunned me. I knew enough about her and the way she operated to understand she wouldn't give up her quest for Daisy. She'd come from a tough, dysfunctional background and would fight by any means to get what she wanted. I'd never liked or trusted her. And no matter how upset I might be by the thought of having to raise Daisy alone, I wouldn't, I couldn't, turn her over to Lisa.

Jessie placed a hand on my shoulder. "I faked the call to the police, but if looks could kill, you'd be dead. Who in hell does she think she's fooling? Lisa doesn't want to take care of Daisy out of the goodness of her heart. She's never even liked her!"

I smacked my desk with my hand. "She's not going to take her away!" Pent up emotions broke out of me in a torrent of tears. I hid my face in my hands and let them flow down my cheeks.

Jessie handed me the box of tissues and rubbed my back. When I finally stopped crying, she gave me a final pat. "I'll help you out whenever I can."

I clasped her hand and squeezed it. "You've been the best friend I could imagine."

"Hang in there."

I prayed I could.

"What are you going to do?" Jessie asked. "I would be sick, absolutely sick, if Lisa got Daisy."

I dabbed at my eyes, gaining strength. "I'm calling my lawyer. He should be back by now. Blake said he'd call him too. I'm going to fight Lisa on this. She's not going to take Daisy away from me!"

I recalled the moment Kristin stood before me, asking me to take care of Daisy. My hands balled into fists of frustration. How could I protect Daisy from a life with Lisa? *Kristin, what have you done to us?*

I left the gallery and stood at the bus stop waiting for Daisy. Thank God I'd alerted the school about Lisa's threat to take Daisy away. They'd promised to keep her safe. Strange, I thought, how quickly life could change. I'd come to California to kick up my heels, have fun and prove to myself that I could run a business successfully. Here I was, in charge of a child, worried about keeping a business afloat, and about to enter a legal fray that was tearing my heart apart.

"Hi, Allie!" Daisy cried cheerfully.

My heart swelled as she raced toward me, her blond curls bouncing. We'd come such a long way, she and I.

"I drawed a picture of my puppy. See?" She held a crayon drawing in her hand and proudly handed it to me.

I studied it, amazed at the accuracy of the black puppy she'd drawn. "Very good, honey."

"I'm going to call her Coalie," she announced happily.

"Let's wait and see if that's all right with Blake, okay?"

A familiar stubborn expression filled Daisy's face. She

clutched the picture to her chest. "Her name is Coalie."

I stared at her in shock. For a fleeting moment, she looked exactly like someone I'd seen.

But who?

Driving into Silver Goose's parking lot, I wondered if the magic of last night's dinner would disappear in the glare of daylight. I parked the car and walked toward the barn with Daisy. Thankfully, no geese appeared.

"Hey, there!"

I stopped and turned around.

A wide grin on his face, Blake strode toward us with purposeful steps. His gaze caught mine, and a warm glow flowed through me. He was as glad to see me as I was to see him.

"Look what I got!" Daisy ran toward him. "It's my puppy!"

He squatted and accepted the picture from her. "That's your puppy all right."

"Her name is Coalie because she's black like coal," said Daisy matter-of-factly.

Blake gave me a wink. "Sounds like a good name to me."

Daisy threw herself into his arms, almost knocking him off-balance. "I knew you'd like it!"

He laughed and, rising, swung her around before setting her down.

Watching them, my breath caught,. I didn't know if Blake was Daisy's father or not, but if he was, Daisy was one lucky girl.

Daisy ran ahead of us toward the barn, shouting, "Coalie! I'm here!"

"You're so good with her," I commented as we walked behind her.

He lifted his shoulders in a noncommittal way. "I like kids—other people's kids. I'm not so sure I want children of my own."

A year ago, I would have heartily agreed with him. Now, I found his words disturbing. "But, what if Daisy..."

Blake held up his hand. "I know what you're going to say, and I've told you already, Daisy isn't mine."

"But..." I began and stopped. There was no point in arguing about it. First things first.

"I'm glad you're here." Blake threw his arm around my shoulders, pulled me close and grinned down at me. The world around me dimmed in the light of his sexy smile.

We entered the barn. Daisy gathered Coalie to her, giving as many kisses as she received. It pleased me to see her so happy, so loving.

"Can you stay for dinner?" Blake asked. "I cook a mean hamburger."

I smiled, pleased with the invitation. "Why not? It sounds good."

I waved at Daisy. "Come on. We're going down to Blake's house for dinner."

"Nooooo!" she howled.

Wondering why everything had to be a battle, I took a deep breath. "Yes," I stated. "Give Coalie a few more hugs and kisses, then we have to go."

"Can I take her with us?"

I shook my head. "No, she's too little. She has to stay with her brothers and sisters."

"But.."

Blake interrupted her. "Have you ever played tetherball? I'll set it up for you."

Seeing the interest on Daisy's face, I moved quickly. "Kiss Coalie good-bye and we'll go see what Blake is talking about."

Daisy looked at Blake.

He winked at her.

She gave him a big smile, set Coalie down, and ran over to him. “Can I play all by myself?”

He ruffled her curls. “Sure. C’mon. Let’s go.”

We all got into my car and I drove to his house, chuckling to myself. I could swear Daisy fluttered an eyelash or two at Blake. Apparently his magnetism worked on everyone.

Blake set up a tetherball for Daisy in his backyard. We watched her punch the ball and race around the pole to hit it again, shrieking with excitement when she was able to turn it in the other direction, like he’d shown her.

While she continued to play, I told Blake about Lisa’s disturbing visit. “I gave your lawyer friend another call, but he was in court. I’m telling you, the whole scene made me sick to my stomach. I can’t let Lisa take Daisy away.” I looked off into the distance, refusing to let any tears fall.

“I’ll give Todd Schaeffer another call myself, explain a little about what’s going on and ask if he’ll see you right away. You need legal advice. Todd is a good lawyer, a good guy, and a family man, himself.”

I heard the concern in Blake’s voice and let out a sigh of relief. I needed all the help I could find.

He leaned toward me and I met him halfway. The warmth of his lips on mine sent a shiver of delight through me. The magnetism between us hadn’t been a fluke at all. The chemistry was there and if I had to grade it, I’d give it an A-plus.

“Hey! What are you two doing?”

I jumped at the sound of Daisy’s voice.

Blake turned to Daisy. “I’m kissing Allie. Any objections?”

Daisy looked solemnly from him to me and shook her head. “When are we going to eat? I’m hungry.”

Blake laughed and tousled her curls. “Grill’s heating up. How does a hamburger sound?”

She smiled up at him, her face aglow. “Can I have lots and lots of ketchup?”

“Sure thing,” he said, amicably.

Observing the two of them, I searched for similarities. Aside from the shape and color of their eyes I could find none. My gaze lingered on Blake. I tried not to be troubled by the thought that he and Kristin had shared a relationship in the past.

Blake checked his watch. “Guess I’d better put those burgers on the grill. Want a beer?”

“Beer? That’s allowed here at Silver Goose?” I teased.

Blake laughed. “On rare occasions.”

Daisy came with me into the kitchen. With its black granite counter tops and white cupboards, it was a masculine version of every woman’s dream kitchen—lots of cupboard and counter space filled with every convenience possible.

Daisy pulled a chair over to the sink and climbed onto it so she could stand beside me as I broke up fresh, crisp romaine for a salad.

“Are we going to live here?” she asked after Blake left the room.

I chuckled. “No, honey. We have our own house.”

“But what about Coalie?”

“Coalie’s staying here, remember?”

Daisy’s lower lip came out. She’d continue to fight me on this. Kristin had given in to her so often that she was used to getting her way. But I couldn’t make a commitment to a dog or anything else until I knew how my battle with Lisa was going to end.

Blake returned to the kitchen with the cooked hamburgers. “Ready?”

Daisy's pout disappeared. Momentarily distracted, she jumped down from the chair.

I gave the salad one last toss in the bowl and sat at the heavy, round, pine table in the kitchen, where we gathered like a regular family. Observing the three of us together, I wished with all my heart that this peaceful moment could last forever.

CHAPTER TWELVE

Todd Schaefer, the attorney Blake recommended, was a heavy-set, pleasant man in his late thirties who'd shaved his head to cover up the fact he was becoming bald. He smiled, and his dark eyes sparkled with intelligence and humor. He accepted my handshake and offered me a seat in his sparsely furnished office. I couldn't help comparing it to my father's plush office in Portland, Maine. But then, I supposed, practicing family law was a far cry, financially, from dealing with corporate law for the paper mill industry.

"Sorry I couldn't get right back to you," said Todd. "I understand you've made several calls. Blake gave me a quick run-down of your situation." He leaned back in his chair. "Why don't you fill me in on the details?"

I explained that Kristin and I had been roommates in college and told how I'd come to California to rescue Treasures. I forced myself to remain calm as I recited the facts of Kristin's death. But reliving the images and emotions of the day, my stomach whirled in sickening circles.

"Okay, let's go back," he said calmly. "So her words to you were 'if anything happens to me, I want you to care for Daisy?'"

I nodded.

"Did she ever put anything to that effect in writing?"

I shook my head. "I haven't been able to find anything like it in her papers. But I'm Daisy's godmother and my guardianship of Daisy was always implied. Lisa Vaughn has a signed, notarized paper giving her guardianship of Daisy."

Tears threatened now. “Kristin and Lisa broke up six months ago. Lisa is living with another woman in Santa Fe. No one thinks Daisy should go to her.”

“Not a good situation, Allison. Let me think.” Todd turned silent, and I could see his mind working.

I glanced at the picture of his family sitting on the scarred credenza behind his desk. A smiling woman was surrounded by four children of varying ages and ethnic backgrounds. Surely, I thought, he’ll be sympathetic to my plight.

Todd cleared his throat. “It doesn’t look good. I have to tell you that up front. Legally, all you have, technically, is hearsay, while Lisa has written documentation of Kristin’s intent. Is there nothing in Kristin’s records to indicate that she wanted you to have the care of Daisy? No letters? No emails?”

I shook my head, wishing I could lie to him. “I’ve looked everywhere.”

“What about the father? Is there someone you can contact? Someone who might be or know Daisy’s father?”

I grimaced. “Kristin never told anyone who he is. She said it was best if she kept it to herself.”

Todd let out a sigh. “I’m sorry, Allison, but without some kind of legal proof that Kristin changed her mind, I don’t think any judge is going to accept your word over Lisa’s documentation.” Todd’s regret was genuine. “Finding the father is the way to go. And, of course, we’ll make a plea that you’re best suited to care for Daisy.”

I curled my hands into fists of frustration. “How am I going to find her father? Everyone tells me it could be anybody she knew. Lisa is only doing this for Kristin’s estate; she doesn’t really care for Daisy. Not like the rest of us.”

The sad expression stamped on Todd’s face frightened me.

“I have to stop her!” I jumped to my feet, ready to take on most anything.

"Okay, okay, I understand. Have a seat and we'll look at other possibilities. You mentioned you've been in touch with the school psychologist. We might find some help there. But even if we can sway a judge that Daisy is happy with you, that piece of paper is hard to fight. Kristin wouldn't tell you who the father is, but do you have any ideas of your own?"

Helpless, I sunk back into my chair. "No. I've asked around but nobody knows, and there are no records of him. Daisy's birth certificate doesn't list a father."

"Any guesses?"

Thinking of Blake, I swallowed hard. "Blake is one guess; another is Dawson Smith."

Todd's eyebrows shot up. "Blake? Dawson Smith? Wow, she traveled in good company."

"Yeah, well, she had a lot of friends."

"It would behoove you to find the father as quickly as possible. With Daisy in school and needing special attention, perhaps Lisa's lawyer would agree to keep her in place here for the rest of the school year. We could offer visitation rights as a means to hold them at bay."

My stomach churned. "Would we have to let Lisa visit with Daisy? It upsets her."

"I have to be able to offer something in return for their cooperation, Allison," he said in a gentle but firm tone I was sure he used at home.

I clamped my jaw together, afraid of what I might say out of frustration.

Todd rose and came around the desk. "I know how improbable it seems, but sometimes miracles do happen. I suppose it's why I stay in this field of law. As heartbreaking as it can be, once in a while things work out. I'm hoping this will be one of those times."

Tears spilled onto my cheeks. I got to my feet and drew a

deep breath. "It's that I never realized I'd fall for an eight-year-old like I have, you know? And I couldn't stand to see her unhappy."

He patted me on the shoulder. "Yeah, I know."

Miserable, I left the office. The only way I could hope to keep Daisy away from Lisa was to find her father. To do that, I had to interfere with people's private lives—something Kristin vowed not to do.

I returned to my house and went up to Daisy's room. The teddy bears and dolls clustered on her bed made my heart ache. I picked up one of the bears and hugged it to me, wondering what I'd do if Daisy was forced to leave me. I'd promised her I'd do everything in my power to keep her from living with Lisa. I realized now, it was an empty promise. The decision was out of my hands.

When I returned to the gallery, Jessie took one look at me and waved me into the back office. "C'mon, you'd better tell me."

I lowered myself into a chair and repeated everything the lawyer had said.

She handed me a cup of coffee. "So, are you going to ask Blake and Dawson for DNA samples?"

"I have no choice. I'll do whatever it takes to keep Lisa from taking Daisy away." I let out a shaky sigh and asked the question that had been haunting me all morning. "Do you think Lisa would make a good mother for Daisy? Am I wrong to feel so strongly about it?"

Jessie pressed her lips together. "I've known Lisa a long time and I've seen how she is with Daisy. I wouldn't let a dog, much less a child, stay with her. She's mean. I've seen her slap Daisy more than once when she got frustrated with her. If it comes to that, I can testify in court."

"Daisy's not an easy child..."

"No, but Lisa makes a difficult situation worse."

Relief helped to ease the knot in my stomach. I hadn't let my ego interfere with what I thought was right for Daisy. The struggle that was about to begin would be worth it.

I was pondering how to approach Dawson Smith, when Blake called. "Before I ask you about your appointment with Todd, I want to tell you and Jessie that my marketing people think Sweet Talk is a great idea. They've been looking for an outlet in the area, away from the vineyard, where some of our products can be showcased. In fact, I'd like to throw in some money for it. Would you consider me an investor?"

My mind worked quickly. It would be a dream come true to have that extra stability. Jessie's money hadn't come in yet.

"R-R-Really?" I stammered. "Hold on! Let me ask Jessie!"

I laid the phone down on the desk and hurried into the front of the gallery, screaming for her.

She jumped down from a step stool. "What's wrong? You okay?"

I flung my arms around her. "Blake agreed to Silver Goose providing the wines for Sweet Talk and, Jessie, he wants to invest in Sweet Talk. Real money!"

Laughing and whirling in a circle, we did a little dance. I jerked to a stop and clasped a hand to my mouth. "Omigod! He's still on the phone in my office."

She laughed and gave me a gentle push. "Go!"

I was still giggling when I picked up the phone. "Are you there?"

"Yep," he replied with good humor. "I take it from all the shouting I heard that your answer is yes?"

"Oh, yes. It's wonderful!" I exclaimed. "And, Blake, it'll do well. You'll see. No matter what it takes, I won't fail. Too much is riding on it."

"My people think it's definitely worth doing. We may use it

as a stepping stone to other things." He paused. "On another note, how did it go with Todd?"

My excitement over Sweet Talk evaporated. I told him everything Todd and I had discussed. "So," I ended, "I'm left with the task of finding Daisy's father."

Blake was silent.

I couldn't avoid the question that hung in the air. "Would you be willing to undergo a DNA test?"

"Me? I've already told you I'm not the father."

"Yes, but..."

"You'll have to trust me on this, Allison." His tone of voice left no doubt he wanted no part of it.

My mouth dropped open. "But Daisy..."

"I'm sure there are others who are much more suitable candidates," Blake said with surprising firmness.

I couldn't hide my disappointment. "But maybe..."

"Sorry, I've got to go. Someone has come into the office for a meeting. Better keep me at the bottom of your list."

Taken aback, I set the buzzing phone down.

"What's the matter?" Jessie asked, coming into the office with the mail.

"Blake refuses to have his DNA tested for Daisy."

"Blake? You asked Blake?"

Jessie's incredulity caught me off guard. "Yes. Why?"

She clucked her tongue. "Remember I told you Blake's girlfriend left him high and dry? She was impatient for the winery to take off, and became pregnant by another man. Blake was forced to take a DNA test to prove it wasn't him. She wanted to make him pay all kinds of money when she realized the winery was taking off. It got a lot of attention in town. He was terribly embarrassed by the whole thing–humiliated actually."

Now I understood. No wonder he was sensitive about it. I

sat in the chair, imagining what secrets I might uncover from Dawson Smith.

Thinking of Daisy's welfare, I resolutely lifted the phone to call him. It rang for some time before a voice message came on, informing me that Dawson was out of the country. I hung up and punched in Todd Schaeffer's number.

Todd listened to my panic, and spoke in his usual calm manner. "Remember, Allison, the wheels of justice turn very slowly. See what else you can learn, and we'll wait for Dawson to return. I'm preparing a letter for Lisa's lawyer now but these things take time. And time is on your side."

Jessie studied me as I hung up the phone. "Better?"

"I think so.". Things weren't as out of control as I thought, but there was plenty to worry about.

Jessie placed a hand on my shoulder. "I know how upset you are but 'take it one day at a time,' like your sister says. "

I forced myself to focus on other things. "Let's rework the figures Samantha gave us. With Blake's investment, we might not need to ask for such a large bank loan."

"I've got a call in to my father regarding my money."

Between waiting on customers, we spent the afternoon working on our budget and perfecting our projections. Jessie had gathered construction quotes for completing the conversion of the cottage. Though they'd once frightened me to a quivering mass of uncertainty, I was slowly becoming used to the high numbers.

At the end of the afternoon, while Daisy colored in her Cinderella book beside me, Jessie and I sat in chairs on the lawn out back, sipping coffee and mulling over details of the deal.

"You're entirely comfortable with this?" I asked her. "If we don't make it, we'll lose everything—the house and gallery, everything. It's scary, I know, but we're not going to do more than squeak by without something like Sweet Talk to improve our income."

Jessie ran a hand through her dark hair and let out a long sigh. "I've never been so terrified and so excited in my life. But no matter what it takes, I want the chance to do it. My father's check should arrive any day."

My lips curved. It's what I'd needed to hear. I'd work myself to a frazzle before I'd allow myself to fail. She obviously felt the same way.

I sprang to my feet. "I'd better help Daisy gather her things. We've got to do her homework."

I loaded Daisy's school bag in the car and helped her inside. On the drive up the hill to the house I'd rented from Catherine, my thoughts turned to her. Did Catherine want Daisy in the life she shared with Lisa? It was a question I intended to ask. Lisa was only half of that partnership.

"Am I an orphan, Allie?"

Daisy's innocent question put a jolting halt to my wandering thoughts. I glanced at her through the rear view mirror. "Why are you asking? Did someone say that today?"

She nodded, and a single tear rolled down her cheek. "I didn't like it. They called Mommy a bad name, too."

My stomach knotted. "Oh, honey, I'm sorry. It's a very important question. Come on inside and we'll talk."

I pulled the car to a stop in the driveway and helped Daisy into the house. My mind raced, seeking the right words. Orphan conjured up all sorts of negative images—images of one being untended and all alone in the world. I didn't want Daisy to ever feel that way. And yet, technically, without knowing who her father was, she *was* an orphan.

I gritted my teeth. Daisy's father was the one person who could help me. Who and where was he? I had to know. An awful thought intruded. *What if Daisy's father was dead and*

I could never find him?

I closed my eyes and whispered a quick prayer for help.

In the kitchen, I pulled Daisy onto my lap and wrapped my arms around her. “So, who called you an orphan?”

“Sarah,” sniffled Daisy.

“Do you know what that means?”

Daisy shrugged.

“An orphan is someone who has no mommy or daddy or anyone else to take care of her. Mommy isn’t here but somewhere you have a Daddy, which means that technically you’re not an orphan. And you’ll never be alone because I and many other people will always be here for you.”

She turned her face into my body and put her arms around me. “I miss Mommy.”

“I do too.” My heart broke at her quiet sobbing. I patted her back. The thought of searching for Daisy’s father terrified me. So many things could go wrong.

Later, after Daisy had finally gone to sleep, Blake called. Relief flooded through me.

“Blake? Jessie told me about your girlfriend and the DNA test...”

“Yeah? Well, I’ve moved on so it’s no big deal.”

I heard the trace of pain in his voice, and tenderness swept over me. I knew what it was like to be hurt, and I silently vowed to do nothing harmful to him.

“How’s Daisy?” he asked. “Have you told her anything about what’s going on?”

“No, I don’t want to alarm her. It’s hard enough for her as it is. Today one of the kids called her an orphan. We talked about it, and she cried and told me she missed her Mommy. It was a pretty hard time for both of us.”

“Any leads on the father?”

I let out a sigh. “I tried to get in touch with Dawson Smith, but he's out of the country. Todd told me not to panic, that the wheels of justice turn slowly. We haven't heard from Lisa, but I can't rest until I know Daisy doesn't have to live with her. "

"Dawson Smith? Yeah, I suppose that makes sense."

"They were close. I found out he even helped Kristin with her finances. If he's the one, it would make things very easy."

"Agreed. Good luck with it. I called to see when you and Jessie can meet to go over our agreement for Sweet Talk."

"Is this only a business call?" I teased.

He chuckled. "Not exactly. I'd like to plan a special evening sometime soon. Just you and me."

My pulse leaped. The memory of his lips on mine filled me with longing. It had all felt so good. "Let me talk to Jessie about watching Daisy, and I'll let you know when I'm free. I'd love it. A visit to the winery sounds wonderful."

"Good." His husky voice was a reminder of the undeniable chemistry between us.

"Back to business. Can we meet at the gallery to discuss the contract?"

"How about first thing tomorrow morning?"

"Sounds good. I'll let Jessie know."

"Thanks, Allison. And let me know about the, uh, evening."

After we hung up, I did a slow dance around the living room, imagining myself in Blake's arms.

I heard a cry from Daisy's room and ran up the stairs. Daisy sat up in bed, her hair tousled, her cheeks flushed.

"What is it, honey?"

"I just wanted to see you."

I hugged her to me. "I'm here, Daisy. I'm here."

Jessie stood beside me in front of the gallery, watching Blake drive off after our meeting.

"Wow!" Jessie gave me a devilish grin. "I thought I was going to burn to death in all that heat!"

"Heat? What are you talking about?"

She jabbed me in the ribs. "Being in the same room with you and Blake is like being set on fire—all those smoldering glances between you."

I could feel my cheeks grow hot.

Jessie laughed. "No wonder you want to have an evening alone with him. The way you are with each other, the two of you should star in some romance novel."

Alarm rang in my head. Were we that obvious? If so, it was too much, too soon. It would be like Will and me all over again.

Jessie threw her arm around my shoulders. "Just teasing, Allison. I'm glad to see you so intrigued with one another, and I'm more than willing to stay with Daisy so you can have some time alone with him. The two of you deserve it."

The tension in my shoulders eased. I could hardly wait.

CHAPTER THIRTEEN

Working with Blake on notes for our financial agreement, I learned how he operated and why he'd been so successful.

Blake crossed off a request to have Silver Goose handle all the orders for uniforms and personalized items. "Remember, we talked about Sweet Talk being a separate operation. You'll have to hire someone to manage all aspects of it. My staff can't be diverted." He said it nicely, but there was an unmistakable firmness to his voice.

"But your store manager knows all the right people. I thought ..."

"She can talk to your manager when the time comes. You've got your hands full with the gallery. I understand you can't do everything, but please don't include my staff."

I swallowed hard. "Jessie and I were hoping you'd let us hire Stu to be our full-time beverage manager. You have someone in that role already."

He took a deep breath, and finally nodded. "Okay. He's a good worker and this would be a nice situation for him. He also knows all our wines and can market them well. Fair enough."

Blake's cell rang. He picked up the call and listened. "I'll be right there. See if you can keep him entertained until I return to the winery. I really need to talk to him." He turned to me. "My lawyer. We've covered everything on the agreement. I've got to go."

I walked him to the front of the gallery. Jessie waved from

behind the counter where she was ringing up a sale. "Samantha said she'd get right on this. If she has any other questions, I'll let you know."

He waved and hurried out to his car, his long legs stretching to quickly cover ground. I paused, enjoying that view of him.

I called Samantha with the details of what we'd discussed. Not only would Blake have shares of the business, Silver Goose would provide all the wines, most of which would come from his winery.

"Has Jessie's money come in?" Samantha asked. "We need that before any partnership papers can be signed. It's important."

I frowned. "I haven't seen it yet." Jessie had told me her father had sent it.

"Allison, this is serious. You tell her to have the money here today. Understand?"

Worry flooded me. Jessie had told me repeatedly it wouldn't be a problem. I also knew that selling stock or whatever her father was doing could take time. But the money was overdue.

"Everything set?" Jessie asked when I returned to the gallery.

I shook my head. "Samantha's worried about your money. I need to have it today."

Jessie's eyes widened. "My father said he'd send it out two days ago. I better call him."

Later, I gathered the mail and placed it on the counter while I rang up a customer. Alone again, I leafed through the stack of brochures and envelopes, looking for the letter Jessie expected. The name of an attorney's office in Santa Fe stared at me from the corner of a smooth, crisp white envelope. I held my breath and ripped it open.

Jonathan Butler, Esquire, had written me on behalf of his client, Lisa Vaughn, regarding guardianship of Daisy Lewis. He stated that without proof otherwise, his client was the legal guardian of Daisy and both he and his client expected arrangements to be made for the transfer immediately, which was to take place in Sarita. He went on to say this matter should be settled quickly and amicably so Daisy could be where she rightfully belonged. Any delay, he warned, would result in a lawsuit. He was awaiting a call and listed his phone numbers.

The words blurred as I struggled to maintain my composure. I gripped the edge of the checkout counter and forced myself to reread the letter I held in my trembling fingers. When I'd finished, I collapsed on the wooden stool behind the counter.

The battle had begun in earnest.

Jessie returned to the gallery from a trip to the FedEx office. Her smile disappeared when she caught sight of me. "Are you okay?"

Wordlessly, I handed her the letter.

Jessie read it and slapped it down on the counter. "The bitch! She knows damn well Daisy's better off with you."

"She's going to take me to court if we don't settle this amicably, as her lawyer puts it."

Unable to sit still, I paced the floor. "Lisa would do anything to get her paws on money, no matter who it hurts. Look what she did to Kristin! She claimed the money she took was hers, but we both know that wasn't true. Lisa doesn't love Daisy. I wonder if she ever loved Kristin. I'm not sure she has it in her to really love anyone."

Jessie's eyes narrowed. "Is she aware Treasures' property is no longer part of Kristin's estate? If she realizes Daisy's trust is not the huge amount she thought, maybe she'll give up."

I doubted it. Fighting the urge to throw up, I placed another call to Todd Schaeffer. He listened carefully as I read the letter over the phone to him. "Fax me a copy and I'll get right on it. In the meantime, Allison, you'd better step up your search for the father. I have sworn statements from the people at school and some of the neighbors, saying what a good mother you are to her, but I'm afraid it won't be enough. And Daisy's too young to make any kind of decision like this for herself."

Feeling as if I were swimming upriver wearing cement shoes, I hung up the phone. Who in hell was Daisy's father? Why had Kristin been so stubborn about not revealing him?

I was still stewing about it when Samantha called me. "I've had a chance to go over the contract between you, Blake and Jessie. It looks fine. You can go ahead and sign it, but not until after Jessie's money comes in. Have you told her that you need her share of money now?"

"Yes, supposedly, it was sent two days ago."

"Hold off on signing until she pays. Hey, you sound down. What's wrong?"

I couldn't hold back my misery. "It's Lisa. She's going to take me to court if I don't give up Daisy." Tears threatened. "Todd Schaeffer, my lawyer, says the school psychologist and others will testify Daisy is comfortable with me, but I really need to find the father."

Samantha clucked her tongue. "I agree with him, Allison. You'd better work on exposing him. I'm going to start digging into Lisa. After all, by leaving Kristin, she left Daisy, too. Good luck, Sis!"

I hung up, scared. The weight of too many things sat on my shoulders.

Jessie walked into the office and waved sales slips at me. "I made three sales! Not big, but still..."

"Good! God knows, we need it. I need to know when you're going to call your father. Samantha brought it up again. She doesn't want me to sign anything until it's here."

Jessie frowned. "I'll go call him now."

She left to go upstairs to the apartment and I took over the cash register. A car pulled into the parking lot, and I turned my attention to the customer heading toward the door.

After making a small sale, I was alone in the gallery once more. I turned to the inventory sheet I maintained at the front desk. All of the consignors had been paid. And with recent sales, we could buy more needed stock. The advertising from the wine festival was beginning to pay off. Some of the tension left my shoulders.

Jessie slowly walked into the gallery. I took a look at her red-rimmed eyes and set down the inventory sheet. "What's the matter?"

She drew a deep breath. "My mother is giving my father a hard time about lending me the money. She says it's inappropriate for her daughter to be involved with a bar." She pounded a fist on the counter. "She's so difficult. Sometimes I almost hate her."

"So he's not giving you the money?" My stomach clenched. All of our plans depended on the money she was bringing to the table.

"He told me to sit tight. He'll call me tomorrow, after he's had a chance to talk to her again." Jessie shook her head sadly. "A lot of my parents' investments were made from money my mother inherited, but not all of it, even though she'd like to think so." Jessie dabbed at her eyes. "Sorry to put you through this, Allison. Why, for once, couldn't she just be happy for me?"

My body turned cold. What in hell would I do if her money didn't come through? I'd been so excited to have her in the business. Now I couldn't think of running it without her. Numbers flashed through my mind. The cost of setting up the wine bar and carrying its expenses until it was well established had carefully been considered in making our plans. If we didn't get her money, we might have to ditch the whole idea.

Groggy from the restless tossing and turning I'd done all night, I decided to talk to Jessie. We had to come up with another idea for funding.

Daisy dawdled at the breakfast table.

"Hurry, honey! You'll miss the school bus." Hearing the sharp tone of my voice, I told myself to calm down.

Daisy lifted her cereal bowl to her lips, and knocked over her glass of orange juice. The liquid puddled on the table and dripped onto the floor in a steady, sticky stream.

Holding back a bad word, I groaned.

"I'm sorry, Allie." Tears filled Daisy's eyes. .

"Aw, honey. It's okay." I grabbed a dish rag, gave her a quick hug and set to work wiping up the mess, checking the clock.

By the time we got things back in order, I knew we'd have to run to the bus stop. I held up Daisy's book bag. "C'mon! Let's make this a race."

She laughed and followed me out the door. Hand in hand, we ran down the hill, catching the bus just before it was ready to pull away.

I helped Daisy onto the bus and stood by, catching my breath.

One of the mothers smiled knowingly. “Bad morning?”

If only she knew.

In the gallery, Jessie was sipping coffee out of one of the new mugs we were sampling. “Good news!”

Relief pounded through me. “Your father agreed to give you the money?”

Jessie shook her head. “No, I haven’t heard from him. But I saw Margaret Atkinson at a church meeting last night and we got talking about Sweet Talk. Before her husband died, they used to own and run the Steak King Restaurant in town. She wants to get back into the business doing something less stressful than running a large restaurant and bar. And she’d love to be our manager.”

“Really? But wait! This job wouldn’t be without stress. Getting this up and running will be anything but easy.” I was unable to remember when I’d last had a decent night of sleep. “And what is she looking for in salary?”

Jessie held up a hand. “It’s all written down in my notes. She has no illusions about the time commitment or the work involved in getting the business started. Here’s her resume. Take a look.”

I reviewed the paperwork Jessie handed me. “If this is real, she’s a godsend. But, Jessie, we can’t do anything until we have the financing in order. And she’s asking for more money than we wanted to pay.”

“I know, but she’s good, and more than that, she’d be reliable.” She checked her watch. “I’m giving my father until noon, then, I’m calling him again.”

I’d just finished a cup of soup when Jessie strolled into the office looking as if she could chew our brick walk. "No answer yet. She's so stubborn. Now my father is worried that if he talks her into it and I fail, she'll make both our lives miserable." Jessie sank onto a chair and let out a sigh. "We're not crazy for doing this, are we?"

"God! I hope not!" But I knew it wouldn't be easy. Running any type of restaurant was tricky business.

"He thinks maybe the weekend will be a good time to settle things," said Jessie, letting out another sigh. "Guess we'll have to wait until Monday to know if he'll come through for me."

My stomach clenched. What choice did we have?

I hurried to get ready for my date with Blake. Jessie arrived at the house with Rob in tow as I finished feeding Daisy her dinner. Her face lit up at the sight of them.

"Rob! Rob!" she cried, running to him, papers in hand. "Look at the picture of my dog, Coalie." She handed him a photograph Blake had given her, along with the drawing she'd made.

He took them from her and studied them. "She sure is pretty. Like you." Rob gave her a growling bear hug,

Daisy's smile spread across her face, and she laughed. Her curly hair framed her face like a circle of light. With her rosy cheeks and bright blue eyes she really was beautiful. Seeing them laughing together, I hoped, as I often did, that I would find her father one day soon. Time was running out.

"Rob and I have something to ask you, Daisy." Jessie squatted beside Daisy and took hold of her hand. Knowing what was coming next, I smiled in anticipation.

"You know Rob and I are going to be married, right? Well, we want you to be our flower girl. Will you do that for us? It's fun! You'll get to dress up and be part of the wedding."

Her eyes alight, Daisy glanced at me. "Can I, Allie? Can I?"

I grinned. "I don't see why not. You'd be perfect for it."

"Can I wear a white dress and veil?"

I laughed. "Not quite yet, but I'm sure Jessie will choose something very special for you."

As Jessie was showing Daisy a picture of the dress she wanted her to wear, the doorbell sounded. Pulse pounding, I hurried to the front door.

Blake stood before me, a grin on his face. For a moment, we simply stared at each other. He wore a red polo shirt and blue jeans and looked well...yummy. I took his hand and led him inside.

Blake greeted Jessie and Rob like the old friends they were.

When I bid her good-bye, Daisy wasn't the least bit upset; she was too busy listening to Jessie talk about the July wedding. After being a couple off and on for many years, Jessie and Rob had decided to be married as soon as possible.

Blake helped me into his car, and we headed north. I sat silently, caught up in conflicting thoughts. I hadn't been sure I'd ever want to marry again, but, being with Blake, I'd experienced feelings I'd never had. Yet, Blake had already told me he wasn't interested in having children. And I intended to fight for Daisy. How would that work?

Blake looked over at me and gave my hand a squeeze. "Worried? Daisy seemed fine. By the way, I looked over the architect's plans for Sweet Talk and have a few suggestions to make with the electrical lighting." His conversational tone drew my focus back to the moment, and I stopped projecting about what may or may not happen in the future.

"Earlier this week, Jessie and I set up an appointment at Seward Financial. We're meeting with Lou Willets at ten on Monday. With Samantha's help we've put together a professional business plan. We need to find out if we're crazy to even think about getting the financing. Until we feel comfortable about it, we'll hold off on signing any contracts."

Blake's brow furrowed. "I thought it was all set."

"I did, too. But Jessie's share of the money isn't certain. Without it, I'm not sure we can swing the deal."

"I know Lou," Blake said. "I can give him a call, if you want."

"No thanks." My reply drew a look of surprise from him. "We want to do this on our own." It was important to me. I wanted to prove women in business could make things happen, that we didn't always need a man to pave the way for us.

"Okay."

Blake pulled into his driveway and turned to me, giving me a hungry look that sent my blood coursing through me.

He reached for me and planted his lips on mine. His slow, thorough kiss drugged me, making me feel languid. He drew me closer and let out a sigh of exasperation. Glancing down at the gear shift between us, he said, "Guess we'd better go inside, huh?"

I laughed, knowing full well one kiss wasn't enough for him, either.

He moved to climb out of the car, and I stopped him, overcome with indecision. "Blake? Let's go slowly. I'm a little confused."

He grinned. "Don't worry. You're not the only one."

Feeling less pressured for something more than some kisses, I breathed a sigh of relief.

Inside Blake pulled a bottle of red wine out of his special kitchen wine cooler. "'Thought we'd grill up some steaks later. That okay with you? Maybe you could fix a salad again. I bought fresh lettuce and other stuff for it."

I slid onto a kitchen bar stool. "'Sounds good."

He opened a bottle of Silver Goose wine, poured it into two large wine glasses, and handed me one. “Here. Try this. It’s the cabernet we’re coming out with. Tell me what you think.”

I swirled the wine in my glass, inhaled its aroma and took a sip. The smooth liquid slid down my throat, leaving a clean finish that spoke of berries and other flavors.

“Delicious,” I murmured. “It’ll be perfect with the flavored chocolates from Bellano’s.”

Obviously pleased, he leaned onto the counter and faced me. “I’m glad we were able to work out details of a deal. Sweet Talk is going to be a thing of the future. I’m sure of it.”

“It’s so, I don’t know...so American,” I added, optimistically, hoping the plans for Sweet Talk hadn’t been an exercise in futility.

He smiled at me, and my uncertainty about him eased. We were completely in tune with one another. This handsome man standing beside me was a friend and about to become a business partner, as well as anything else I might want to imagine. And, right now, I was imagining a lot.

We took our drinks outside on the deck. I took a moment to study the darkening sky, loving the stark outline of rolling hills. The air held a springtime chill that did nothing to erase my lusty thoughts. We huddled around the blaze of the fire pit, sipping wine and sharing tidbits of information from our childhoods.

Blake’s features softened when he told me he and his sister Marlee were the only children in their family. Both of his parents had died by the time he was in his mid-twenties. I could imagine how much he must miss them. My own family meant so much to me.

“They were kind and generous people. They left Marlee and me money—enough money for me that I was able to purchase the winery from which Silver Goose has grown.”

"And Marlee?"

Blake's features turned stony. "That's another story. How about *your* family? What are your parents like?"

I shifted uncomfortably in my chair. "My mother, Adrienne, is wonderful—kind, strong and determined. She's twenty years younger than my father and is able to hold her own with him." I hesitated. "My father, George, is... different. Even though he's over eighty years old, he's still practicing law part-time. He's a big-time lawyer for the paper business in Maine."

I'd been a disappointment to my elderly father, and even now, as an adult, I still could not measure up to his unattainable standards, however sexist they might be. My sister fought against him by attempting to outdo my brother. After my failed marriage, I gave up trying to please him, or so I'd told myself. But his opinion of me still mattered.

"My father's okay," I amended, feeling guilty I didn't sound enthusiastic about him. "It's just a little harder with him. That's all."

Blake's nod of understanding was sympathetic. "Aunt Penny's husband was stern like that. He thought she babied all us nieces and nephews, my sister Marlee included. He never understood how much she wanted children of her own."

I smiled. "I think you're her favorite. She told Jessie and me that the two of you are very much alike."

He grinned. "'Probably so."

I couldn't hold back the next question. "Blake? You once told me you don't want children of your own. Did you really mean that?"

He shrugged. "Yes...I don't know. Maybe I haven't found the right woman yet, but at this stage of my life, I'm not sure that's what I'm after."

"You do understand, don't you, that if I end up with Daisy,

like I want, she's part of any relationship I might have with anyone."

"With my business and all the responsibilities I have, kids aren't at the top of my list of priorities. Know what I mean?"

I took another sip of wine, letting his answer roll around in my mind. At one time, the thought of having children had scared me to death. Now I wanted Daisy and children of my own.

Blake's face wore a tender expression as he leaned down and gently traced the outline of my cheek in a sweet caress. "Let's not think about that right now. We're just getting to know one another."

His lips met mine and his moist, firm mouth demanded a response—a response I was only too willing to give. Troubling thoughts disappeared as my arms encircled his neck, holding him close to me.

He pulled me to my feet, up against him, letting me know how ready he was. I thrilled to his reaction and hugged him closer. He trailed hot kisses down the side of my neck and cupped a breast in his hand, rubbing his thumb gently over the nipple through my sweater.

I gasped with pleasure and molded my body even closer to his, exalting in the ever hardening response I elicited from him. I reached up and kissed him, eager to share in our growing passion.

Breathing heavily, he stepped back and held me at arm's-length, his eyes fixed on mine. His look of tenderness made me melt. He took my hand and drew me inside, to his bedroom.

We stepped through the doorway to his room. With a click of a handheld control, Blake flicked on gas logs sitting in a fireplace facing the large bed that dominated one wall. The flames from the fire sent soft light into the dusky shadows.

Stars shone through the skylight above us. I prayed our lovemaking would be every bit as perfect as the setting.

Blake wrapped his arms around me. “Nice, huh?”

I rested my head against his hard, muscular chest, letting my trembling body speak for me. It had been a long time since I’d made love with a man.

He lifted my chin and spoke softly against my cheek. “You’re beautiful, Allison. I’ve wanted you ever since I first saw you down at the marina.”

Pulse sprinting, I nestled against him, reveling in his words.

He kissed the hollow of my throat, and a soft moan escaped me. At the sound of it, he swooped me up in his arms and lay me down on the soft coverlet of his bed. “I want you so much,” he murmured, settling beside me.

“I want you too.” I reached for him.

We kissed, becoming accustomed to the shape and feel of each other. But soon it was obvious kissing and cuddling were not enough, not when our bodies craved more.

“Take it off,” Blake said in mock gruffness, tugging on my sweater.

I laughed, and he lifted his shirt over his head and unbuckled his pants.

My pulse hammered at the image of his muscular chest and the erection that sprang free as he pulled the zipper of his pants down.

I wiggled out of my jeans, pulled off my sweater and lay back against the pillows, breathless with anticipation.

After dropping the rest of his clothes beside the bed, Blake lay down beside me. I pulled him close to me, needing the feel of his skin against mine. He unfastened the bra hook between my breasts and watched as they fell free, open to his eager inspection.

"Beautiful," he whispered. His lips swirled around my nipples with tantalizing possessiveness and then they sought to discover the rest of me.

I caressed his manhood, loving the hard length of it.

He groaned with pleasure and kissed me, stroking my tongue with his.

Still...it wasn't enough.

With gentle touches, he explored my secret areas, spiraling me toward a greater and greater need. I whimpered when he took a moment to take care of protection, and abandoned myself to the whirl of emotions he created as he kissed and stroked me again. In a way I'd never experienced, I became Blake and he became me as we climbed toward release with a fiery obsession I'd never known.

Later, sated, our breathing slowed. I lay on the bed, pleasantly weak.

He rolled on his side and smiled at me.

I reached out and trailed my fingers down his face. How, I wondered, would it ever work out between us? I was going to fight with everything I had to keep Daisy in my life.

CHAPTER FOURTEEN

I pulled up to Seward Financial and climbed out of the car. Tense, my legs felt like wooden sticks as Jessie and I walked to the front door. The outcome of our meeting with Lou Willits would prove whether or not our planned project was feasible.

Inside the building, a cheery receptionist ushered us into a small conference room. I paced the room, nervously going over the numbers.

Lou Willets rushed into the room with an apologetic smile fifteen agonizing minutes later. "Sorry I'm late. Have a seat and we'll start." He sat opposite of us. "So what did you ladies want to talk to me about?"

We introduced ourselves and I handed him the bound business plan we'd drawn up. He took a moment to leaf through it and sat back in his chair. "So how do you think something like this is going to give the bank a good return on its investment?"

Taking a deep breath, I launched into a presentation of our project, giving as much detail as I could. We couldn't leave anything to chance. We needed approval for a sizeable loan so we could go ahead and hire Jamison Construction to do the work. Jessie's money still hadn't arrived.

Jessie gave him a rundown on her merchandising experience and then I explained about the consulting Samantha had done for us and Blake's involvement.

Lou quietly studied the two of us. "You've got a real heavy hitter supporting the project. That speaks as loudly as anything you've told me. I'll try to push this through the committee. Blake Whiting is well-known to us and a buddy of mine. I'll have a definitive answer for you within a matter of days."

Blake's name meant more than all our planning? Holding in my frustration, I gathered our paperwork, and rose.

Lou smiled and shook my hand. "The scholarship fund for the high school in memory of Kristin Lewis is growing nicely. How's Daisy doing? She's your daughter now, isn't she?"

His innocent question hit me like a punch to the belly. All my gut-wrenching worries burned my stomach like acid. With difficulty, I managed to say, "There are still some legal issues to resolve."

Things were in a nerve wracking state of uncertainty. I'd run an ad in the paper, asking anyone who might have known Kristin Lewis ten years ago to give me a call, cloaking my request with a reference to the scholarship fund. Dawson Smith was not due home for another week, and I'd heard nothing further from Todd Schaeffer, who was awaiting a response from Lisa's lawyer.

He smiled. "Good luck with everything. You've got a lot to think about."

Outside, Jessie turned to me. "Are you okay? You turned white as a ghost when Lou asked you about Daisy."

"Jessie, it was so strange. I felt so afraid for her. What if we can't stop Lisa from taking her?"

Jessie put her arm around me. "We've got to remain upbeat about that and everything else. Steady, girl. You've got a lot of people behind you. I'm circulating a petition from friends and neighbors right now, to show the court how happy Daisy is with you."

"Guess I'd better focus on this project, so I don't go crazy with worry."

###

We returned to the gallery to find a FedEx delivery for Jessie at the door.

Jessie took hold of the envelope and fingered it, giving me a worried look. "My father was to let me know either way. I can't tell if there's a check inside."

My stomach knotted. "Go ahead and open it."

I held my breath as she ripped open the envelope and lifted out a sheet of paper.

She read quickly and breathed a sigh of relief. "He wired the money into my account this morning. And look, he signed the letter, *Love you, Dad.* He did it! Like he promised." Tears splashed onto her cheeks.

I leaned against the door frame, weak with relief.

Jessie swiped at her eyes and gave me a tremulous smile. "Now we can meet with Wayne Jamison."

I gave her a quick hug. "Let's have him go ahead and prepare a contract for the work on Sweet Talk. It looks like the bank loan will go through. If not, we always have Marissa. We need every bit of extra time we can get if we're going to be ready for the summer trade."

Wayne Jamison had converted an old barn outside of town into his offices. Round-bellied and in his fifties, he was a hearty, red-faced man whose every other word began with a capital F. Behind his crude manner was a jovial, capable contractor who'd worked on many projects in the area and who prided himself on getting in and getting out of projects on time. He was exactly what we were looking for. He agreed to look at our architectural plans and come back to us with suggestions and an estimate of cost.

Back at the gallery, I called Todd's office and found he was in court. I left my name, praying my jitters had nothing to do with the eerie feeling that I'd had at the bank.

Sensing my distress, Daisy became uncontrollable. At bath time, Daisy refused to cooperate. When I made her undress, she sat on the bathroom tile floor and screamed, "I hate you!"

Her words, sharp as knives, pierced my heart. I was working so hard at being a good parent. "I'm going to get your nightgown," I told her as calmly as I could. "I'll be right back."

Inside Daisy's room, I sank down on Daisy's bed and let my own tears flow, too exhausted to stop them.

"Allie?" Naked, Daisy stood in the doorway, staring at me.

"What is it, honey?"

She ran over to me and laid her head in my lap. "Sorry."

"Me, too." I rubbed my hand through her soft curls. "Sometimes we have to do things we don't want to do, you know?"

She lifted her face and studied me with those blue eyes of hers. "Okay."

I hugged her. As tough as it was from time to time, Daisy was learning to live with new rules, like the psychologist and her doctor had suggested.

After Daisy was asleep, my mother called. Hearing her familiar voice, I wished I could crawl into the comfort of her lap. My emotions were in turmoil. Mentally and physically, I was worn out.

"Hi! What are you doing up so late?" I asked.

"Just thinking about you. How are things? Daisy doing okay? And how's business?"

"Daisy and I are going to make it, thanks." If I said much more, I'd break down completely. I focused on the less emotional topic of my life. "Good news on the business front. I'm pretty sure we've got a loan for Sweet Talk, and the gallery is starting to pick up more customers."

"Good. Now, more importantly, how are *you* doing,

Allison? I worry about you. You've had a lot to handle."

The concern in my mother's voice brought me to the edge of tears. In her mind, I was still her little girl. And despite my need for independence, it felt so good to know she was there for me. By the time we hung up, I was re-energized. My mother had promised to visit.

At breakfast, I handed Daisy a photograph. "Guess who that is?"

Daisy looked up at me and smiled. She loved guessing games.

"That's my mother. She's coming to visit us sometime soon. She wants to meet you."

"Is she my grandmother?"

"Not exactly."

Daisy's brow wrinkled with concentration. "Oh, I know. She's my fairy grandmother."

I laughed and hugged her to me. "Sure. Why, not?" My mother would be pleased with the title. It suited her.

Work on the project continued. I lined up quotes for landscaping and interior designers while Jessie worked with the print shop to design menus and advertising pieces.

A few days later, Daisy and I were about to eat dinner, when the doorbell rang. Grumbling about solicitation calls, I went to the front door and opened it.

"Surprise!" My mother stood there, looking as beautiful as ever. Her dark hair, streaked with a luscious gray, brought out the color of her green eyes.

I whooped with joy and threw my arms around her.

From behind me, Daisy peered at her. "Is that Grandmother?" Her high piping voice, filled with such eagerness, brought a mist to my eyes. Kristin's own mother had wanted nothing to do with Daisy.

My mother set down her purse and opened her arms. Daisy hesitated for a moment and then threw herself into my mother's embrace.

"It's so, so good to see you," I said, as Daisy wiggled away from her. We kissed, and I hugged her tightly. We'd had our tugs of war in the past, especially during my teen years, but I loved her deeply.

She glanced around and gave me a nod of approval. "Very nice, Allison. You've done well with what you've had."

I grinned. Her words of praise meant a lot. I'd taken bits and pieces of old family things, garage sale items and store bargains and mixed and matched them into an attractive arrangement that beckoned to visitors to come in and sit down. Not fancy like my parent's home, it had a flair that pleased me.

I took her coat. "I'm so surprised to see you. How did you get away?"

"Your father is tied up with a trial in Maine, and I thought it a good time to come see you. You know how grumpy he becomes when these things drag on. Samantha will keep an eye on him for me."

"Grandmother? Can I show you my room?" Daisy tugged on my mother's hand. "It's upstairs. "

My mother smiled at me and allowed herself to be led up the stairway.

I lugged my mother's suitcase to the guest room. As I climbed the stairs, I heard Daisy say, "Grandmother? Am I grandchildren?"

"You certainly are my grandchild," my mother said.

I peeked into the room. Daisy sat in her lap. Watching them together, my heart filled with happiness.

"Mom? We were just about to sit down for dinner.

Spaghetti is one of Daisy's favorites. Come join us."

Daisy jumped out of my mother's lap and faced me, hands on hips. "Not now! I want to show Grandmother all my dolls and animals."

I drew in a deep breath. Daisy was overexcited. This was only the beginning of a scene. "You'll have plenty of time to show her later, Daisy. We need to eat now."

"No-o-o-o!" Daisy threw herself on the floor and kicked.

I signaled my mother to follow me. The scene would only become worse if Daisy had an audience.

On the stairway, my mother turned to me, wide-eyed. "Does this happen often?"

I felt an unexpected urge to protect Daisy from my mother's criticism. "When she's overtired or had too much excitement. It's her way of coping. She'll soon calm down."

My mother clucked her tongue. "No wonder you look so tired, Allison!"

After Daisy had reluctantly gone to bed and my mother and I were alone, I was able to talk to her about the situation with Daisy.

"Does Lisa know what it takes to deal with Daisy?" My mother gave me a worried look. "I've never seen a temper tantrum like the one Daisy pulled tonight. It lasted for over half an hour."

I shook my head. "Believe me, Daisy's had worse. Even though Lisa and Kristin were together, I don't think there was much interaction between Daisy and Lisa. And when there was, apparently Lisa was impatient and sometimes mean. Everyone who knows Lisa agrees she doesn't really love Daisy. My lawyer is working on several angles but it's going to be difficult to fight Lisa's legal document. That's why it's so important for me to find her father. Sometimes, I think I'm going crazy with all that's happening."

"I'm very proud of you, Allison." My mother inspected me with a gaze that missed nothing. "You've had a lot to handle. But Samantha tells me you've met some nice people. Now tell me about this man you recently met."

"Blake Whiting is a great guy..." Memories of making love with Blake made me pause. *How should I describe Blake? A great lover? No-o-o-o. A family man? Not really. A successful businessman? That wouldn't mean that much to my mother who was married to one.*

"So, he's a great guy?" my mother prompted.

I spoke from my heart. "I'm so happy when I'm with him."

My mother beamed at me. "That sounds good. I can't wait to meet him." She stifled a yawn. "But now I better go to bed."

We turned out the lights and walked up the stairs, arm in arm.

Daisy ran over to greet my mother. "Are you coming to the bus stop with Allie and me?"

I handed my mother a mug of coffee and turned to Daisy. "I'll drive all of us down to it, so Grandmother can see the town."

"Okay. C'mon, Grandmother. Let's go."

My mother took a sip of coffee and went for her coat. I smiled as she and Daisy walked hand in hand out to the car.

Daisy was given a good sendoff, and I drove through Sarita, allowing my mother a view of the marina and the cluster of shops surrounding it.

"Charming," she gushed. "Even prettier than the pictures Samantha showed me. No wonder you like the area so much."

After breakfast, I drove my mother to Treasures. My stomach was aflutter as I opened the front door and awaited her reaction.

Taking in the sight, my mother clasped her hands. "Wonderful! I can't get over all you've done here!"

Smiling broadly, Jessie hurried toward us from the back office. "You must be Allison's mother. Hello, Mrs. Hartwell! I'm Jessie." Watching my mother and Jessie hug, I knew how lucky I was. Jessie's mother hadn't even acknowledged her thank you for the start-up loan.

Jessie grabbed my arms. "We just got a call from Lou Willets. The loan committee met on another hurry-up issue and our loan has been approved. We can go ahead with all of our plans for Sweet Talk!"

"Great! Let's call Wayne Jamison with the news. I can't wait for him to begin." I turned to my mother. "Wait until you see the plans!"

I laid out the blueprints on the counter and explained in detail what we had in mind.

"Let's go outside so you can show me." My mother's voice crackled with enthusiasm. "I want to see for myself."

The sun was bright, casting a golden tint on the little cottage that was at the heart of our new construction. A nice omen, I thought, as the heat of the sun warmed my skin. I paced out the size of the decks and indicated how far back the sunroom addition would go.

My mother nodded in agreement. "Your architect did a wonderful job of making the exteriors compatible in size and shape. It'll look as if this whole complex was built at the same time. Very clever."

That afternoon, my mother and I stood at the bus stop, chatting about the plans for Sweet Talk. After the bus rolled to a stop, Daisy surprised me by being one of the first ones off.

"Grandmother," she shouted. "Here I am!" She ran toward

her with outstretched arms.

My mother hugged her close. Daisy turned to me with a little wave. “Hi, Allie!”

I smiled and waved back, happy that my mother was part of Daisy’s world, if only for a short time.

CHAPTER FIFTEEN

Blake invited me, my mother and Daisy to Silver Goose for dinner. As we headed to Silver Goose, Daisy's chatter did nothing to break the unease that had clung to me all day. I hoped my mother and Blake would get along. They both could be outspoken about certain issues.

"Grandmother! Wait until you see Coalie! She licks me all the time. Do you think she'll lick you? Allie says her licks are kisses."

My mother laughed. "I like dogs and I'm sure I'm going to love Coalie." She turned to me. "How long did you say Blake has been in the wine business?"

"About ten years. He started with one small vineyard and has added to it over the years. He has partners and a well-known wine maker. Penelope Potter, the actress, is one of the partners." I grinned. "She's more than an actress to him; she's his Aunt Penny."

My mother's eyebrows shot up with surprise.

"He's worked hard for what he has. Silver Goose is quite a sophisticated operation. The Manor House, which is where functions are held, looks like a French *chateau*, the kind you and Father visited on your last trip to France."

My mother silently absorbed the information.

I pulled into the Silver Goose parking lot, slowing down to show my mother The Manor House in the distance.

"Beautiful," she murmured, continuing to gaze out the window as we drove closer to the tasting barn.

"Blake asked us to meet him here." I stopped the car.

As soon as I stepped out of the car, Blake emerged from the barn, a huge smile on his face. He strode toward us with confidence.

"Blake! Where's Coalie?" Daisy ran toward him. "I want Grandmother to see Coalie!"

He put his arm around her. "She's inside. I'm keeping her with me and her mother." He gave me a meaningful look. The other puppies must have gone to their new homes—something I hadn't warned Daisy about. He came forward and held out a hand. "Mrs. Hartwell, I'm Blake Whiting. Great to meet you."

My mother's expression was a bit star-struck as she shook hands with him. I smiled, recalling how I'd felt at those movie-star looks the first time I saw him. Funny, I didn't even notice it now. It was simply part of who he was.

"C'mon, hurry!" Daisy tugged on my mother's hand impatiently. "Coalie's inside!"

Blake clasped my hand as we followed my mother and Daisy into the barn. He gave me a quizzical look. "You nervous? Your fingers are cold."

I shrugged, unable to tell him how important this meeting was to me. We went directly to Blake's office on the second floor. Pepper, Coalie's mother, rose from a red plaid dog pillow next to Blake's desk and came toward us wagging her tail. Coalie pranced at her side.

Daisy dropped to her knees and hugged the puppy. She laughed at the licks the puppy gave her and turned to me. "Where are the other puppies? I want to show Grandmother."

"The other puppies are at their new homes," I told her in what I hoped was an upbeat manner.

"They left their mommy?" wailed Daisy. "But they need to stay with their mommy!" Her voice rose, warning me she was about to have one of her meltdowns.

I knelt beside her and put my arm around her. "The time

had come for the puppies to go to their new homes, so other children could play with them."

"No-o-o-!" howled Daisy. She threw herself down on the floor.

"We'll meet you outside." I clasped Daisy's hand firmly. "We'll go down to the car so we can talk in private."

Crying, Daisy slapped at my hand as we made our way through the crowd of tourists gathered for a tasting. Several of the women in the group shot me disapproving looks. I sighed. Nothing about Daisy was easy.

Inside the car, I held Daisy until she grew calmer. We talked quietly about mother dogs and their babies. "It's important for each puppy to have a special home of its own, a place where they will know special love."

"But, Allie, I loved them too! I didn't want them to go away."

"Sometimes things like that happen whether we want them to or not."

Daisy's eyes filled. "Like Mommy?"

I nodded and hugged her close. My thoughts strayed to Lisa. Her lawyer still hadn't been in touch with mine. Dawson's return had been delayed but he should be back soon. If he were Daisy's father, the issue of Daisy and me might be easily settled.

I patted Daisy's back. "Ready now?" Blake and my mother emerged from the barn, followed by Pepper and Coalie. Daisy and I got out of the car to greet them.

"Daisy can play with Coalie at The Manor House," Blake said. "Normally I wouldn't allow puppies inside, but I think this is a special occasion. Right, Daisy?"

Patting Pepper, Daisy nodded solemnly.

I mouthed the words "Thank You" and smiled at my mother.

Her lips curved, but the furrow on her brow told me something was wrong. I glanced over at Blake. He stood apart from me, his body tense. Twinges of unease pricked me. What, I wondered, had been said in my absence? My heart froze at the thought of a disagreement.

"The new catering company has prepared a meal for us. I thought dining there would give your mother a chance to see The Manor House." Blake's words sounded so formal they brought another chill to me.

Daisy walked ahead with Blake; I stayed by my mother's side.

"Isn't it beautiful?"

"Yes, indeed. Everything I've seen so far indicates Silver Goose is doing very well."

"Do you like him?" I whispered, unable to wait another second.

"We'll talk later." My mother gave my hand a squeeze, making me wish we'd never accepted Blake's invitation. Something was wrong. Very wrong.

Blake led us into the house and graciously gave us a tour.

"Wonderful," my mother said, admiring everything.

And later, at dinner, my mother listened attentively as Blake told her about the winemaking business. I could hardly choke down a bite of the meal. Behind all the pleasantries, I knew something was bothering my mother. Blake, charming as always, avoided my inquiring gazes. Even Daisy's antics with Coalie did nothing to chase away my worries, though we all laughed softly when Coalie licked Daisy's ear, causing her to shriek with glee.

After dinner, Blake walked us back to my car. I kept glancing at him, trying to determine his feelings but he, like my mother, maintained an affable front. When he finally settled his gaze on me, it was devoid of the smoldering passion

I usually observed in his eyes.

Watching Blake and my mother shake hands, like two adversaries sizing each other up, acid rolled into my stomach.

"Good night, Allison." He gave me a quick hug.

"I'll call you after I get back from taking Mom to the airport."

He gave a quick wave and walked away.

Silence reigned in the car as we headed home. There was so much I wanted to ask my mother, but with Daisy awake in the backseat, I held back my questions.

The moment Daisy's murmurings quieted and she'd fallen asleep, I glanced at my mother. "Okay, Mom, what's going on? You're upset. Why?"

When she turned to me, my mother's expression was full of anguish. "Oh, honey, it's not that I don't see why you wouldn't fall for Blake. He's got it all—good looks, a successful business, manners, everything."

"But?"

"But when I asked him about family and the future, he tried to laugh it off, saying he lives for the present, not the future, and that he was too busy with his work to think about other things. I was shocked that he'd be so blunt about it. From what you told me, I thought he genuinely cared about you. Honey, you've just gone through a bad time with Will. It was devastating for you, really. I'm afraid this man is going to hurt you, too."

Wounded by Blake's response to my mother's questions, I gripped the steering wheel. *Too busy to think of other things? Of me and Daisy?* I remembered the women's clothing in Blake's guest room and wondered if it all belonged to his wayward sister as I was told, or if some of it was leftovers from encounters with other women, like I'd originally thought. Janelle's shirt couldn't be ignored. My God, I was still making dumb mistakes! Blake was a player, like my ex!

My mother patted my arm. "I'm so sorry. I don't mean to upset you. I just don't want you to get hurt again. He couldn't give me any reassurances about how he really feels about you."

A knot formed in my throat. How could I blame her? Why hadn't I trusted my first instincts? I couldn't afford to play a game like this. I wasn't made that way. Like a fool, I'd read too much into our time together. How, I wondered, could I have been so gullible? Was I that desperate for attention?

I cried myself to sleep, forcing my face into the depth of my pillows, so no one would hear me. I'd imagined everything between Blake and me was perfect, but Blake, caught off guard, had let his true feelings show.

I felt like a lost child as Daisy and I bid my mother good-bye at the airport the next morning. We stood and waved long after she'd disappeared into the crowd. When we got back in the car to return to Sarita, Daisy bawled in loud, sobbing gulps. I wanted to join her.

"Is Grandmother going to come back?" Daisy asked after she'd calmed down.

"She wants to return sometime after Sweet Talk opens. Maybe late summer."

I vowed to make my life a success by pouring all my energy into helping Sweet Talk succeed. I wouldn't be sidetracked by Blake and his idea of a casual relationship.

For the remainder of the day, I worked at the gallery, dividing my time between waiting on customers and attempting to appease Daisy's demands, which seemed to grow as I fought to climb out of the doldrums. I wondered, as I often did, how Kristin had kept her cool when the situation with Daisy was so frustrating.

Blake telephoned in the afternoon. "Hi, Allison..."

"I'm sorry, I'm busy with a customer and can't talk," I answered crisply, struggling with the white lie. I needed to be truthful with him, but now was not the time. I had to be much stronger to face him.

Jessie checked in with me a little later. "Are you all right? You look exhausted."

"I couldn't sleep last night. We have so much to do for Sweet Talk."

She grinned. "It's going to be so cool. I can't wait. Everything is coming along nicely. Want to look at the ideas for ads that I drew up last night?"

"No, it's your day off." I pushed her gently toward the door. "Go have fun with Rob."

"All right." She grinned. "We'll go over them in the morning."

A small but steady stream of customers came and went, forcing me to keep my mind on business. Mary Lou Kingsley, who introduced herself as a friend of Penelope Potter, bought a number of things, including a high-priced metal sculpture.

"Penny told me I'd love the gallery and she was right," Mary Lou commented pleasantly.

I smiled at her response. If we could build our customer base with high-end buyers like her, it might mean we'd be able to continue to carry unique, one-of-a-kind items not seen elsewhere along the coast. "How do you know Penny?"

The woman laughed. "She and I go back a long way—we started in show business at the same time. She went on to do well while I married young and decided I'd rather be married to a director than to be a starving star. Guess I never was cut out for all that glamour stuff. Take a look at me." Her grandmotherly curves were wholesome and healthy.

I liked her. In spite of myself, I wanted to know more about Blake's family. "Did you know Penny's family?"

"I knew them very well. Too bad about her sister."

"Penny's sister?"

The woman clucked her tongue, warming to the subject. "Patricia got into drugs. If you ask me, her husband got her started. They ended up dying at a young age. Penny doesn't discuss it much, but one of them died from liver disease and the other from an overdose shortly afterwards. Through the years, their poor kids counted on Penny for stability and plain common sense."

My heart fell. "You mean Blake Whiting and his sister Marlee?"

"Yes. I heard there's trouble with the girl, but the boy has turned out fine. Owns a winery near here."

Long after the woman left with her purchases, my thoughts returned to what I'd learned about Blake. A pretty ugly picture. At an early age, Blake had been abandoned, in a sense, by his parents and then, later, by a girlfriend who turned on him. No wonder he was afraid to put his heart on the line again.

I understood better why Blake couldn't seem to talk about a future with anyone. But I needed the reassurance of someone who would always be there for me—who wouldn't let me down. I was willing to take a chance to have that. Blake apparently wouldn't or couldn't. Blake would hurt me—not because he wanted to, but because he couldn't help feeling the way he did.

That evening, when Blake called to ask if he could stop by, I told him yes. Better to have the confrontation with him behind me then to keep replaying it in my mind.

Daisy was asleep upstairs when Blake arrived. My heart skipped a beat. My brain was telling me to do the right thing by facing the issues, while my heart ached at the thought of ending the relationship.

I stepped away from his kiss. "We've got to talk, Blake. It's important." My voice quivered with nervousness.

"What's going on?" His eyes narrowed. "Does this have something to do with your mother's visit?"

"Among other things. I realize now that we need different things from a growing relationship."

"What do you mean?" Hands on his hips, he glared at me.

"Isn't it true that when my mother asked if you had any thoughts of the future, you laughed and said you only live in the present?"

He frowned. "Yeah, but, so what? What does that have to do with us?"

I swallowed my tears. He'd just confirmed my worries.

"Allison, we're simply dating."

I gulped and nodded. "I realize that, but I've made a terrible mistake. I thought we were moving toward a life with each other. I'm sorry. I'm too vulnerable to be in any kind of relationship that has no future. I'm not that kind of woman."

"This is bullshit," he exploded. "We're getting to know each other, that's all. Don't make it more than it is."

A stab of pain struck the core of me. "I've fallen for you. You have to know that, after our time together. I understand now it isn't like that for you. I'm sorry, but I'm not very good at playing games."

For a minute, he didn't say anything.

I fervently hoped he would argue with me, deny my words, at least say something!

He searched my face. "I see. So long, Allison."

Stunned, I watched him walk away. The minute his car left the driveway, I let out a high-pitched wail of despair. It was over.

CHAPTER SIXTEEN

I woke up Monday morning with swollen eyes and an aching heart. I'd done the right thing to break off with Blake, but I hadn't realized it would hurt so much. To make matters worse, Daisy announced she didn't want to go to school.

"You know you have to go to school," I told her, holding in my impatience. "Besides, your teacher told me that the class is going to make a special trip to the library in town. You don't want to miss out on that, do you?"

She gave me a look out of the corner of her eye. A bargaining chip was about to be played. "Then can I wear the new dress you bought me? The one with the flowers on it?"

I shook my head. "That's too fancy for school. Instead, why don't you pick out one of the flowered T-shirts we bought."

She drew in a deep breath to form a scream.

My head ached already. "Okay, okay." I was too ragged from lack of sleep to fight her on this. If she wanted to look as if she was going to church, so be it. But by darn, I'd see that she wore a coat.

Breakfast was a standoff. Daisy ate most of her egg and a cookie for dessert.

By the time we got to the school bus, she was chatting happily and I was thinking I was a complete failure. But when she waved good-bye cheerily, I told myself to relax. I'd done the best I could with her when all I wanted to do was to go back to bed and hide under the covers.

I stomped into the gallery in a foul mood, hoping the day was about to get better. Then, Todd Schaeffer called.

"I've heard from Lisa's lawyer," he said. "Due to her special needs, Daisy can stay with you through the school year. That's the good news. The bad news is that Lisa wants visitation rights established right away. She's even willing to pay for Daisy to come visit her in Santa Fe. She's asking for a visit the fourth week in May and expects the permanent transition to be made in July, within a couple of weeks after school lets out for the summer."

My heart fell. "But Daisy will be scared making a plane trip alone..."

"Lisa's already thought of that," interjected Todd. "She'll fly here to pick her up and take her back down to New Mexico."

"How do I know she'll let Daisy come back to me?" Every instinct told me Lisa would try to defy the rules. And I'd need time after the visit to make the transition easier for Daisy.

"I wouldn't worry about that if I were you. She's not about to blow the whole thing by breaking the agreement at this point—not when she wants to win guardianship of Daisy. I'll make sure she signs an agreement stating that the child will be returned to you at the agreed upon time."

"Do I *have* to let Daisy go for the visit?" Knowing the answer already, I felt sick to my stomach.

"If you refuse, you could lose her permanently right away." Todd's tone of voice left no question in my mind as to what I was facing. "I'm asking you to put aside your worries for the moment. It's in Daisy's best interest for you to do so."

I hung up the phone, so scared I could taste it.

A few minutes later, Jessie arrived at the gallery with a latte for each of us. Silently I sipped the hot milky liquid, inhaling its pungent aroma. Depression gripped me with fingers of frustration.

"Want to tell me what's going on?" said Jessie. "You look

like hell, and so does Blake. I saw him down at the coffee shop with Janelle Martin. She positively smirked when I said hello."

My insides fisted. "Blake was with Janelle? He didn't waste any time, did he?"

Jessie shot me a baffled look. "What do you mean?"

"I broke it off with Blake last night. He and I have very different goals. Remember how I was worried he'd end up hurting me? Now I know for certain he would. Janelle Martin?" I let out a snort of disgust. "I might have known."

"Don't you think you acted too soon? Blake's really a nice guy."

I held up my hand. I'd been betrayed once before and now this. "He's just my business partner. Nothing more. Dammit! I can't believe he's already seeing Janelle Martin again!"

I fought to control my emotions. "And, Jessie, that's not all. I heard from my lawyer. Daisy has to go visit Lisa in Santa Fe. I know something's going to go wrong."

"Oh, oh. You better tell me all about it."

Giving Jessie the details made the situation seem even more hopeless.

I struggled to set aside my concern for Daisy, like Todd had asked. She was sensitive enough to pick up on any worries I had. But no matter how hard I tried, I couldn't put aside thoughts of Blake and Janelle. I'd foolishly hoped Blake would call and tell me it was all some horrible mistake. With each passing hour of silence, my resolve to have nothing more to do with him strengthened.

My sister called. "Hey, how are things going?"

I told her about Daisy. "And, Sam, I've ended it with Blake. It turns out he has something going on with Janelle after all."

I drew a deep breath, reminding myself the Hartwell women were strong, they didn't need a man to make it through life.

"Are you sure you did the right thing? He seemed nice, and you know how Mom is—she'll fight anyone she thinks would hurt one of her girls. Look how she stood up to Father when you announced you were moving out West."

I listened, but I didn't change my mind. As much as I wished it weren't so, my initial concerns about Blake had been right on. Janelle had quickly spread the word she and Blake would head the committee for the next wine festival. As harmless as that might seem, she made it sound so much more than that. Even Jessie agreed with me.

"Should we try to find a new partner for Sweet Talk? Someone to replace Blake?" Jessie asked one morning.

I set down the newsletter detailing next year's plans for the wine festival shook my head. We needed Silver Goose Winery to be a part of our operation. They had the perfect selection of wines to accompany the chocolates and the hot and cold accompaniments we were testing. I'd do anything to see that Sweet Talk succeeded—even keep Blake as an investor.

The day before construction was to begin on the project, Todd Schaeffer called to tell me that an agreement had been reached with Lisa for visitation with Daisy. As he recounted the various details of the arrangement, I gripped the receiver so tightly my fingers cramped. Lisa would fly to San Francisco to pick up Daisy on the third Saturday of May. Daisy would spend the weekend and the following week with her, then fly back home to get ready for the permanent move.

"Are you sure Daisy will be fine?" My tongue stuck to the dry roof of my mouth. I fought to get the words out.

"Neither her lawyer nor I sense anything amiss." A note of sympathy rang in Todd's voice. "I think it's important for you to be positive about this visit so Daisy will enjoy herself."

"I ... I'll try." I thought it would take an Academy Award-winning performance to do that.

When Daisy came home from school, I left the gallery with her, to set the stage for a nice visit with Lisa. Daisy didn't like change or surprises and would need time to absorb the new plans. I gave her the rundown of the schedule. Her lower lip jutted out. "Why do I have to visit Lisa? I don't want to."

I put my arm around her and drew her close to me, so torn I felt ripped in two. "Your mother and Lisa were very special friends." I swallowed hard. "They loved each other. Your mother wanted you to be able to spend time with Lisa, maybe even have Lisa take care of you."

Daisy's blue eyes widened, then filled. "But I live with you!"

"Yes," I said as calmly as I could. "I'd be happy to have it that way always, but, as my sister says, 'we'll have to take things one day at a time.' Okay?"

She looked at me with such a sad expression I wanted to pull her into my lap and tell her she'd never have to leave me. But I couldn't do that; it would be cruel in the long run. I had no idea what was going to happen to her. Dawson Smith was still not back from wherever he'd gone, and there were no new answers to the questions I'd asked everyone about other men in Kristin's life.

Wayne Jamison and his crew arrived early in the morning, diverting my attention from the restless night I'd spent. My heart pounded with excitement while I stood with Jessie watching them climb out of their trucks and gather their equipment.

"Shouldn't take long, little ladies." Wayne hiked his pants up and puffed out his chest. "It'll take us a couple of days to do the rough framing and put on the roof, then the plumber and electrician can do their stuff before we finish up. Good thing my crew is between big projects. I can put everyone to work on this. It'll be like an old-fashioned barn-raising." He winked at me.

Jessie and I exchanged smiles. No matter how chauvinistic his behavior became toward us, we'd tolerate him. We'd been told he was the best in the business. And the timing was perfect.

Blake arrived a moment later. His hair was sleep rumpled, as if he'd just gotten out of bed. Dark whiskers added shadow to his face. Imagining him making wild, passionate love with Janelle, my stomach churned. I forced a neutral smile.

"Big day for us," said Blake, focusing his attention on Jessie. He waved to Wayne and a couple guys on the crew.

He continued to ignore me as we observed a crew member take up a chain saw and cut through the side of the cottage where French doors would eventually open up onto a deck. At the sight of the new opening, shivers of delight shot through me. My dream was about to become real.

After watching the work for a while, Jessie turned to Blake. "Let's drink a toast to the beginning of Sweet Talk. I put on a fresh pot of coffee. C'mon, Allison."

Walking beside me back to the gallery, Blake gave me several quizzical glances. I tried my best to ignore them. I wasn't about to fall for that unhappy expression on his face. He'd made his position clear, and I had other worries.

Jessie poured coffee for each of us and lifted her mug. "I never thought I'd be a part of such an exciting business. It's going to be a success. I just know it. Here's to Sweet Talk and the three of us! Long may we live!"

"Hear! Hear! To us!" said Blake, gamely.

I drew my gaze away from him, hating the way he made me want him.

"C'mon, Allison. Join the toast to the business!" cried Jessica.

I gave a half-hearted smile and raised my mug in the air. "Here's to Sweet Talk!" The personal partnership I'd envisioned was gone.

The phone sang a lilting note, breaking into the silence of the office. Jessie rose to answer it.

While she was diverted, Blake looked at me with concern. "Are you all right?" he whispered.

I shrugged, and blurted out, "It's Daisy. Lisa has established visitation rights. Daisy leaves for Santa Fe in late May for a visit and then it will become permanent sometime in early July. I'm afraid she'll try one of her tricks and keep Daisy in May."

His eyebrows shot up. "Todd handled this for you? He couldn't get around that legal paper?"

His concern formed a lump in my throat. "He did the best he could."

Blake leaned back in his chair and stared at the ceiling, lost in thought. He turned to me. "What if you and Lisa shared guardianship of Daisy? Would that work?"

I shook my head. "I don't think so. I've got to find her father. That would solve everything. Even if he didn't want to take care of her, he could designate me as her guardian."

"Hey, I'm sorry. Good luck with it." He took a last sip of coffee and rose. "Stu called me from the winery on my way here. He said to tell you he'd be down sometime today. He's as hyped about this project as we are. He wants to see what Wayne and the guys are doing. Too bad I can't stick around."

Blake motioned for me to follow him. "Let's talk outside."

I shook my head and remained seated.

He gave me a shrug and left.

My heart aching, I watched him go. Blake Whiting would remain off limits to me. My life was complicated enough.

The days leading to Daisy's departure sped by. My panic spilled over. I punched in Dawson Smith's number daily, leaving several messages for him.

One evening after Daisy had gone to bed, he called.

"Allison? I just got back from my trip. What's going on? You sounded upset in the messages you left for me. Is everything all right?"

My knees grew weak with relief at the sound of his voice. I sank onto a kitchen chair. Maybe now I could have his help, find out what his relationship with Kristin was, and end this foolishness with Lisa.

"Remember my telling you that Lisa wants custody of Daisy?"

"Yes. It's a crazy idea. Don't tell me she's still serious about it. Lisa has never exhibited the caring kind of attention Daisy needs."

"I'm afraid she doesn't agree with any of us. She's still fighting for custody." I filled him in on my meetings with Todd and Daisy's scheduled visit to Santa Fe. "Todd says finding the father would resolve all the issues. I'm doing my best to find him."

"How are you going to do that?"

I took a deep breath, hoping Dawson would understand what I was asking of him. "I'm asking any male friends of hers if there might have any reason to believe they could be Daisy's father. If so, I need them to agree to have their DNA tested." I swallowed hard. "You've been a good friend of Kristin's for many years. Do you think you should be tested?"

Silence met my question. I squirmed. So far, he was my best chance at finding Daisy's father.

"My God ...," he uttered, and I could hear the wonder in his voice. "Do you think ...?"

"I don't know. Your name has often come up when I've asked Kristin's friends about possibilities."

"I suppose it could be true, but Kristin and I remained great friends. Surely she would have told me. She told me so many other things."

My breath caught. Blake had said the same thing. I couldn't hold back my rising irritation at Kristin's insistence that Daisy's father remain a mystery. It seemed so unfair in light of the present circumstances.

"So, you'll do it?" I asked, pushing for a commitment.

"Yes, I'd like to know, too. Kristin was a very special person in my life. My God, it never occurred to me that in our brief relationship something like this could have happened. I loved her, you know."

I heard the pain in his voice and didn't know what to say.

"I'll go to the doctor's office as soon as possible."

"Thanks, Dawson. If it's true, then Lisa could no longer claim Daisy for her own."

I hung up the phone with mixed emotions. If Dawson was the father, I'd want to be able to work out a plan with him to keep Daisy. It was all such a damn mess.

That night, as I settled in bed, I ruminated about the uncertainty I was facing. In the last two years my whole life had been turned upside down. Now, once more, I had no idea what the future held.

In one of those crazy, nonsensical dreams that bore no semblance to reality, I dreamed of my ex-husband Will. He was Daisy's father and insisted on taking her away from me. I awoke with wet cheeks and lay there, unable to go back to sleep. Eventually, rosy fingers of light streaked the early morning sky.

Daisy tiptoed into my bedroom, rubbing her eyes sleepily, and climbed into bed with me. I pulled her closer. She lay there quietly, as if she knew I needed the comfort of having her near me.

"Do I have to go visit Lisa?" she asked in a small, whiny voice.

Remembering Todd's admonishment, I put my arm around her. "You're going to like Santa Fe. Do you remember Catherine? She'll be there, too."

It was comforting to know that Catherine was in the picture. She appeared to be a kind, sensible person. Daisy would be happy with her, I imagined, trying my best to picture it. Daisy settled beneath the covers and curled up against me. My thoughts turned to Dawson Smith. He would be the perfect father for Daisy.

I was on the phone in the gallery when Dawson walked in. He glanced from me to Daisy, coloring pictures at Jessie's desk. His expression softened.

Daisy's face lit with a bright smile as he squatted beside her and hugged her.

"Look what I did." She held up the picture of a dog she'd colored. "It's like Coalie."

Dawson gave me a questioning look.

I hung up the phone. "Coalie is the black lab Blake has given her," I explained. "She's Daisy's dog but she stays at the winery."

He nodded and accepted the picture Daisy handed him. "Very good."

"You can keep it. I'm going to do another one." Daisy turned back to her coloring.

Dawson rose and faced me. "I've come from the doctor's office. They've got Daisy's sample ready to go. They'll put a rush on mine."

The soft tinkling sound of the bells hanging on the door alerted me to a customer. Dawson followed me out to the front room of the gallery. We talked softly behind the counter while the customer browsed.

"I can't quite grasp the whole idea," Dawson said. "Kristin and I saw each other quite a bit, but even though I was falling in love with her, she wouldn't make a commitment to me. At first, I thought it was the age difference. But after she sorted things out, it was obvious why she couldn't. We remained very close, though."

"You were in love with her?"

"I would have married her, if I could. Funny, but I don't think she ever knew that. I'd been married once before, and I'd turned down a lot of women. Maybe that's what made her think we could be just good friends."

"I know she counted on you for a lot of things," I commented.

"All my life, I found I couldn't count on people when I needed them most. That's why I wanted to make sure Kristin and Daisy could count on me to be there for them."

I looked at Dawson with new respect. "If it turns out that Daisy is your daughter, what will you do?"

"Take her to live with me, of course."

I gulped. I wanted Daisy to know her father, spend time with him, but I didn't want it to mean he'd take her away from me.

"God knows, I can provide her with the best of everything," Dawson continued. "Private school, ponies, cars, whatever she wants."

At the thought of Daisy's empty room, my body broke out

in a nauseating sweat.

"Allison? I know how hard this must be for you. Why don't we get to know each other better? I'm going to go into Sausalito for dinner tomorrow. Care to join me?" Shy hope colored Dawson's cheeks.

I brushed aside mental images of Blake. "That sounds lovely. I'll get Claire to babysit for me."

The smile of delight that crossed Dawson's face filled me with pleasure. He really was a sweet man.

CHAPTER SEVENTEEN

I'd always loved Sausalito's artistic flavor, much more colorfully defined than Sarita's. As we drove south, the setting sun cast a satisfying rosy glow to the sky, reflecting the cheery, upbeat mood inside Dawson's car.

Dawson drove with the speed and confidence of a man who was used to being in control. I observed him out of the corner of my eye. With his full head of gray hair and his trim body, he looked much younger than his years. His hands were broad, his fingers long and contoured. I could easily imagine them transforming a mound of clay into the beautiful ceramic shapes I'd grown to love.

We pulled up to Bertella's, a well-known, classic Italian trattoria. The valet opened my car door and held out his hand. Feeling like a princess, I stepped from the Jaguar. After working so hard performing menial chores on a daily basis, I'd almost forgotten little pleasures like this.

Dawson had told me he often dined here. He'd made a lot of money in the dot com business, and, though he lived a simple life working on his pottery, he was a very wealthy man who could live in any style he chose.

The restaurant was elegant in an understated way. Crisp, creamy linens topped round tables gleaming with heavy silverware and sparkling crystal. Simple, white lilies accented the tables amid the soft flickering glow of candles in crystal holders. We were led to a table in a corner and seated with a flourish by the maitre'd. A waiter immediately approached us and then sent over the wine steward. While Dawson discussed wine choices with him, I looked around the room, admiring the scenery and the people.

"Classic chianti has a special taste of its own," Dawson explained as we sipped our wine. "It's very different from most California wines. The soil and climate differences in Italy make it easy to distinguish."

I thought of Blake and Silver Goose Winery. Their merlot was my favorite.

The evening passed quickly in pleasant chatter. I learned that Dawson had been out of the country to check on renovations to the small farmhouse he owned in Tuscany.

"Dealing with contractors in Italy is a whole other experience," he said during dessert. "If you think Wayne Jamison can be difficult, you ought to meet Antonio. Aside from the language issue, he has his own ideas about what should be done. We tend to get into arguments that involve a lot of sign language, and I don't mean with only one finger."

I laughed. Studying his face, wreathed in smiles, I found myself drawn to him. He was such a likable person.

As we headed for the exit, several people in the restaurant swiveled to watch our departure. Self-conscious, I gazed down at the floor and bumped into Penelope Potter.

"Allison! Dawson! What are you doing here?" she trilled, glancing from one of us to the other.

"Penny! Good to see you again," said Dawson smoothly, while I stood by awkwardly.

She introduced her husband Dennis to us, and we exchanged pleasantries for a minute or so.

"Sorry to be in a rush," Dawson said, "but we've got to go home to the babysitter."

"Oh, yes, Daisy needs you." Penny frowned at me. "Have you seen Blake lately? I haven't been able to reach the dear boy and imagined he was with you."

Dawson turned to me with raised eyebrows.

"I'll probably see him tomorrow. For a business meeting only," I emphasized.

"Come, Penny," Dennis said impatiently. "We're keeping the others waiting."

She followed her husband away from us, but kept glancing back at me, a concerned look crossing her face.

In his car, Dawson turned to me. "Is there something going on with you and Blake?"

I shook my head. "He's my business partner for Sweet Talk, that's all."

Dawson squeezed my hand and gave me a smile. "I'm glad it's nothing more than that."

My return smile faltered. But I told myself if he were Daisy's father, it would be perfect for me to fall in love with him.

Claire greeted us at the door with a finger to her lips. She pointed to Daisy, asleep on the couch. I tiptoed closer and gazed down at her. Dawson came up behind me.

Daisy's long lashes curled against the curve of her cheeks, dark, spidery extensions of protection for her beautiful blue eyes. Her blond hair curled around her head, reminding me of the Hummel figurines my mother favored at Christmas.

"What a cherub." Dawson's voice was full of something I took for pride.

I handed Claire the money I owed her and mouthed a soft thank you. She left with a silent wave.

"I've got to go, too," said Dawson. "I'm doing a firing early tomorrow morning. Thanks for a wonderful evening."

He drew me into his arms.

My heartbeat picked up speed as his lips came down on mine. I willed myself to feel a rush of heat, a thickening of my blood.

When we pulled apart, Dawson looked at me and smiled gently. "I'll call you soon."

I watched him climb into his car and drive away, tracing my lips with a finger, wondering why they seemed so cold.

The next afternoon, I stood amidst the sawdust and other remnants of carpentry, inspecting the work on the cottage.

"Coming along, huh?"

I whirled around.

Blake and Janelle entered the building.

I took an unsteady breath, hating the stab of jealousy that pricked my heart. Janelle's presence seemed to fill the room, making me feel as if the walls were closing in.

Blake acknowledged me with a curt nod. "I'm giving Janelle a quick tour of the place. I want to talk her into having a special evening function here next year to kick off the wine festival."

He moved past me toward the new addition, leaving Janelle behind.

"I've been wondering what the three of you were up to. I insisted Blake show me." She shot me a triumphant smile that I wanted to rip off her face.

Blake rejoined us from the huge sunroom being added onto the back of the building. "It's a good combination— Silver Goose Winery and Treasures."

"Actually, it's a concept I thought of as a result of the wine festival," I said, struggling to be civil.

"You never know what can happen when you're working on the wine festival." Janelle put her arm through Blake's and gave him a brilliant smile. "Right, Blake?"

Blake shrugged and extracted his arm from her embrace. "I'm going to check out the decking."

Janelle watched him leave the building and narrowed her eyes at me. "He told me you broke it off. Don't try to win him back." The venom in her voice startled me. She turned on her heel and followed Blake.

"Allie? Where are you?" Daisy called.

I left the cottage, and she ran toward me. "Jessie says you'd better come. It's busy."

I put my arm around her, and we headed back to the gallery. Inside, my emotions swirled. Seeing Blake with Janelle made me feel sick. God help me, I still loved him.

The next few days were torture, thinking of Daisy with Lisa and imagining Blake with Janelle. I told myself to be strong. The Hartwell women had a long history of overcoming adversity with strength, and this was a test for me.

I sat on the window seat in my bedroom one morning and glumly stared out at the bay, shimmering with light from the rising sun. The water's rhythmic movement reminded me that life would go on, whether I was with Blake or had Daisy with me. Wearily, I stepped into the shower, hoping not to disturb Daisy. She, too, was showing the strain of not knowing what the future would bring.

Jessie and I walked into the cottage at Sweet Talk for a late morning meeting with Wayne Jamison. Blake's eyes met mine. I glanced aside, afraid to let him see how much I cared.

Wayne led us through the construction site, explaining what finishing details would be made and when we could reasonably expect to open Sweet Talk.

"You're doing a great job, Wayne," said Blake. "Memorial Day weekend would be a perfect time to have a soft opening of the place. Think you can do it?"

Wayne winked at me. "'Told the little gals I'd move fast."

My smile was half-hearted.

"Thing is," he continued, "with the real estate mess, we're

so hungry for the business, my guys are willing to work 24/7. Yeah, if we push, we'll have it ready. I've told them it had to be done before then."

"That'd be perfect. The furniture we ordered should be delivered within three weeks," said Jessie.

I attempted to shake off my dejection over Blake. "When I spoke to her yesterday, the decorator told me the window treatments would be ready then, too."

Blake spoke up. "I talked to Stu this morning. He and Margaret Atkinson will be ready to open the operation. We won't have a full-blown opening until we've got the kinks worked out, though. By the way, Janelle found two new waitresses for us."

At the mention of Janelle's name, I pressed my lips together.

Blake checked his watch. "It's almost noon. I've brought a nice bottle of wine to help us celebrate. Only a few more weeks to go before Sweet Talk is up and running."

We gathered on the deck, taking seats on stacks of lumber. Blake slid the cork out of the bottle and poured red wine into the clear plastic glasses he'd brought. He handed us ours and raised his in a salute.

"To Sweet Talk."

"Hear, hear!" Wayne said, and Jessie and I followed suit.

The wine trailed down my throat with a nice smooth sensation.

"Mm-m-m, tastes good," said Jessie. "What is it?"

Blake described the particular characteristics of the blend. I surreptitiously studied him. His strong profile was as appealing as ever. I loved him. It was as simple, as awful, as that.

He turned and stared right at me, and I noticed the dark smudges under his eyes. He held up the wine bottle? "More?"

"Why not?" I held out my glass as if I hadn't a care in the world.

His hand brushed mine as he poured the wine. A jolt of heat raced up my arm. I turned away and drew a deep breath to steady myself. Damn him! He still had the ability to turn me on. I gulped down the wine, and got to my feet.

"I'd better go back to the gallery. I think I heard a car pull in."

Telling myself he'd only hurt me, I all but ran from the cottage. But a small voice in my head burst through my self-justification. *You're a fool, Allison Hartwell.*

Jessie came into the gallery, looked at me and shook her head. "It's stupid, you know, this business between you and Blake."

"What do you mean?"

She put her hands on her hips. "It's perfectly obvious how the two of you feel about each other. The hell with what you think might happen; enjoy what you have together."

I straightened. "You forget one thing. Janelle Martin is now in the picture. Blake made that perfectly clear." I couldn't control the hurt in my voice.

Jessie rolled her eyes. "She found us two waitresses. Does that mean she went to bed with him?"

"Probably," I said, miserable at the thought.

Jessie shook her head. "I don't know who is more stubborn, you or Blake."

It better be me, I thought, or I'm in trouble.

CHAPTER EIGHTEEN

The day I dreaded came faster than I'd feared. I rose early and quietly checked the contents of Daisy's suitcase, making sure she'd taken nothing out of it. Pride had prompted me to iron her shirts and shorts, polish her shoes and fold her underwear carefully. I vowed Lisa would find nothing to criticize about my care of Daisy.

When Daisy awoke, she immediately began to whine, "I don't feel good."

I touched her forehead. No temperature. I rubbed her back but she continued whining. Her nerves were as tautly strung as mine.

Silently cursing the legal system for not taking my side, I continued to rub her back.

Lisa arrived at nine o'clock. I forced myself to greet her pleasantly, but she brushed by me and made a point of looking around.

"Nice stuff. Daisy ready?"

"She's watching television upstairs. I'll get her."

"No, no, I'll do it." Lisa moved past me so quickly I couldn't stop her.

Furious she'd gotten by me, I followed her up the stairs.

Lisa entered my bedroom and lifted Daisy's suitcase. "Hi, kiddo! Ready to go?"

Daisy's eyes widened. She ran into my arms, sobbing." Allie! I don't want to! Please don't make me go with her!"

Lisa turned to me, her face a mask of fury. "What in hell have you been telling her about me?"

I took a deep breath, struggling to rein in my emotions. "I've been helping her become okay with the idea. That's all."

The corner of Lisa's lip lifted in a derisive sneer. "Bullshit." She grabbed Daisy's hand. "C'mon. Stop your crying. You're coming with me."

Daisy's wails hurt my heart.

Lisa held tight to Daisy's hand and turned to me. "Don't call us. You have to give her a chance to get used to me."

"Help, Allie! Help!" Daisy cried, jerking uselessly against Lisa's grip.

On the stair landing, Daisy threw herself down and started kicking.

"No, you don't!" Lisa picked her up and carried her out of the house, kicking and screaming.

I waited inside until I heard Lisa start the car, telling myself not to run after her. If I made Lisa too angry now, she'd never let me remain a part of Daisy's life.

At the sound of the engine's roar, I ran onto the front porch and watched the car travel down the street until it faded from sight. Tears that had been building all morning poured down my cheeks. I collapsed on the front porch steps, sobbing so hard I couldn't catch my breath. A vehicle pulled into the driveway and someone approached me.

"'Thought you might need a friend this morning." Dawson sat beside me and pulled me into his arms.

I leaned into him and cried even harder. When I thought I couldn't possibly shed another tear, I sat up and accepted the handkerchief he handed me.

Dawson's own eyes grew moist. "You think she's going to be all right, Allison?"

"I hope so." I wondered how anyone could be as insensitive to a child as Lisa. "It seems so unfair..."

Dawson shook his head. "I don't understand it. If it turns

out I'm the father, I promise you Lisa will never get her hands on Daisy again."

"You haven't heard yet?"

"Nope, apparently there were a number of emergencies in the lab, whatever the hell that means."

I let out a tremulous sigh. Waiting was the hardest part.

"I saw Wayne Jamison's truck at Treasures. How's the construction going?"

I struggled to muster enough energy to respond. "They expect to be finished in a week or so."

"Why don't you take your mind off Daisy and show me what they've done."

I accepted his hand.

We arrived at Sweet Talk to find the electricians busily unloading boxes of ceiling fans. Inside, three of Wayne's men were installing ceiling molding and tacking baseboards onto the newly painted wall surfaces.

"There you are, little lady," boomed Wayne, approaching me with his usual bluster. "What do you think? Should we add an extra piece of molding at the top? If you ask me, it makes it a little fancier."

Having learned about the financial surprises of remodeling, I gave him a skeptical look. "How much extra does it cost?"

Wayne laughed. "Not much. In fact, I'll even throw it in. How about that?"

"It's a deal." The finishing touches were all-important.

The sunroom, as we called the new addition, was a large room with high, cathedral ceilings and plenty of windows. A stacked-stone fireplace at one end of the room stood proudly and would add warmth at those times when cold fog rolled in off the water.

Dawson fingered the stones as if they were treasured pieces

of fired clay. He smiled his approval. "Handsome. Hard to believe the little cottage could be transformed into something like this." He put his arm around me. "Clever idea, this. I believe Kristin would be very surprised and pleased by what you've done here."

The mere idea of Kristin filled me with sadness, followed by anger. Why hadn't she been more open about Daisy's father? I turned to the man I thought might fit that role.

"We've got to protect Daisy. The legal system doesn't always consider the child. They can't, if they've got legal documentation dictating what has to be done."

"I'll call the doctor's office again when I get home," he promised.

For the rest of the day I threw myself into my work, though I felt numb inside. I rearranged the gallery, went over the books, and ordered new items for our summer trade. At the time of afternoon when I ordinarily met Daisy at the school bus, I paced my office. By now Daisy should be in Santa Fe. Why in hell hadn't Lisa called to tell me they'd arrived safely? It was the least she could do. I shook my head. She'd never think of it. That's why.

Jessie came into the office with a carton of brochures. "I picked these up from the printer. They're beautiful!"

I lifted one out of the box. Against a light merlot color, chocolate-brown letters spelled "Sweet Talk – A Place to Congregate and Enjoy the Treats of Life." Inside was a limited menu of sweets, along with accompanying wine suggestions and a variety of coffees and teas. One whole section of the simple brochure was devoted to the history of Silver Goose Winery, another told the story of Treasures and some of our long-term artists, like Dawson Smith.

"Very nice. Thanks."

"I'm going to meet Rob and a few friends for drinks down

at the wharf. Why don't you join me? With Daisy away, you don't have to worry about being home. Besides, it'll keep your mind off her."

I shrugged. "I might as well." The thought of facing the empty house was depressing.

Jessie gave me a sympathetic look. "Chin up. Daisy will be all right."

I made an attempt to joke. "Lisa won't know what hit her when Daisy throws one of her big temper tantrums."

Jessie chuckled. "It'll serve her right."

I locked up Treasures for the night and decided to walk down to the wharf. I set off briskly, enjoying the warm air. It hardly seemed like I'd been in Sarita only six months. So much had happened in that period of time.

Jessie waved to me from among the crowd clustered in chairs on the deck in front of Reggiano's Italian restaurant. I checked to make sure Blake wasn't among them and moved forward.

Jessie patted a metal chair beside her. "Saved one for you. Rob is going to meet me later. He got stuck with a showing. Some house near Sausalito."

I sat down and stretched my legs, unable to remember the last time I'd been able to relax like this. The waitress, a young niece of the owner, came up to me. "Can I get you something?"

"A glass of pinot noir. From Frog Hollow."

She left, and I grinned at Jessie. "I have to check out the competition."

Jessie elbowed me in the ribs. "You sure it doesn't have anything to do with your split with Blake?"

I laughed. "Not really."

"Good, because here he comes now."

Tensing, I twisted around. He approached us alone, his gaze focused on me. My pulse leapt. No matter what I told myself, I still loved him.

Blake pulled a chair into the circle and sat opposite me.

I made an effort to keep from staring at him.

"Hey, how's it going, Blake? Heard you were a partner in Sweet Talk."

Blake turned to the man whose name I'd forgotten. "Allison, Jessie and I are all involved. It's going to be great. Come see for yourself. The grand opening should be soon."

"Where's Janelle?" asked one of the women in the group.

Blake glanced at me, shifted in his chair, and mumbled, "She had to work late."

The waitress arrived with my wine, and I took a deep sip, foolishly wounded at his response. They were still seeing one another.

Rob arrived, and the atmosphere became more upbeat. A natural with people, he had a way of making everyone feel comfortable. I loved the way he kissed Jessie hello. They were a great couple, warm and affectionate.

"So how's the wedding coming along?" one of the guys teased Rob.

He rolled his eyes. "Between Jessie, her mother and mine, it's going to be what each of them wants. I've been told to shut up and stay out of the way."

Even Jessie laughed as we all chuckled. "C'mon, you guys, it's a big moment. I want it to be perfect. I certainly don't intend to do it again."

Rob held up his hand. "I'm not going through this again either. No way."

I listened to them kid each other. I'd once thought my marriage would be forever, but what had once been sweet and gentle had turned into something ugly and mean.

Blake answered more questions about Sweet Talk. As he spoke, I allowed my thoughts to drift along with the sound of his voice. He was remarkable in many respects, a self-made man who'd done the lowliest jobs to achieve what he had today. Unlike Dawson, his success hadn't come easily or with such great reward. In some respects, I admired him more because of it. I wished he had that same kind of commitment to interpersonal relationships.

"So what do you think, Allison?" Jessie poked me.

I startled. "What?"

She laughed softly. "Stop mooning over Blake."

I took the last sip of wine. "It's been such an emotional day I'm going to head home. That wine has made me sleepy."

Jessie leaned over and whispered, "Coward. He loves you. Look at the way he's staring at you with those blue eyes of his."

I ignored her, said my good-byes and left the wharf, needing to get away. I wanted what I couldn't have, shouldn't have—at least on Blake's terms.

I climbed the hill toward Treasures and my house, weary to the bone. Lisa still hadn't called and probably wouldn't. I told myself Daisy was all right, that no news was good news.

Halfway up the hill, a car swerved onto the side of the road ahead of me. I knew who it was before I even looked up.

"Get in." Blake leaned over and opened the passenger's door, his expression grim.

I hesitated, and climbed in. What better way to clear the air? Nobody, but nobody, was going to make a fool of me by trotting off with another woman the moment I was gone.

We drove in a silence pulsing with unspoken thoughts.

Blake pulled into my driveway and turned to me. "Why don't we cut the crap with all this business about me not being good for you? It's bullshit and you know it."

I drew myself up and glared at him. "If we're talking about crap, let's get real. Why, the moment I was gone, were you back in Janelle's arms?" I couldn't hide the pain in my voice.

Damn him! He hadn't waited one day before Janelle was sharing breakfast with him.

Blake's eyes rounded. "What in hell are you talking about? You think I'm ... I'm ... *fucking* Janelle?"

My lips froze. "Janelle has made that very plain. And the morning after we broke up, Jessie saw you at the coffee shop having breakfast with her. The two of you had probably just rolled out of the sack."

Blake grabbed my shoulder, then flinched when I held up an arm and jerked away from him.

"Omigod! I'm not going to hit you, Allison! Jesus ... I never would."

We stared at each other in horror.

He cupped my chin in his hands. "Look at me. Don't you know how I feel about you? I don't give a damn what Janelle has been saying, nothing is going on between us. What kind of guy do you think I am?"

"You told my mother you were interested only in the present and ... Janelle keeps insinuating ..."

"Damn it! What did you expect me to say to your mother—that I was ready to settle down and had picked you out to be my wife? I don't know if or when I'll be ready for that. All I know is that you're the first person in a very long time that's made me even consider it. You haven't really given *me* a chance, *us* a chance. You made up your mind about me, cut me off and expected me to pretend that what we had didn't matter?"

I stared at him, sorting out my feelings, holding back the defensive words racing in my brain, words that might spin the situation out of control. My body craved his with such intensity I clenched my fists to stop myself from flying into his arms. I drew a deep breath. He'd spoken of a chance to be together. Life was about taking chances wasn't it?

As if he'd read my mind, he spoke to me in a quiet voice. "You took a leap of faith starting up Sweet Talk. You can do it for business, but you can't do it for yourself? Think about it, Allison. You let one guy spoil not only your marriage, but the rest of your life? Is that how you're going to play it?"

"What about Janelle?" I was ready to take a chance, but I had to know what I was up against.

He shook his head and raked his fingers through his blond hair. "I know what it looks like, but I'm telling you, we have nothing going on between us. We're heading the wine festival. That's it. She's got this crazy idea we're going to be a couple, but we're not. Frankly, she doesn't turn me on. Never has. Not like you."

Our eyes met. I could see hurt in his. Had I been too quick to end what had been the most marvelous relationship I'd ever had? Samantha and Jessie had both thought so. My mother had spoken out of concern for me, but she hadn't actually told me to break it off with him.

"Allison? Can't we give it another try?"

I swallowed hard. It was time for me to take a chance.

"Come here." His arms came around me and my whole body relaxed. It felt like home. His lips came down on mine. An electrical charge shot through me and melted my insides. God, I'd missed him.

"I love you," he murmured, so softly I almost didn't hear it. His hands drew circles on my back, increasing in intensity as his kiss deepened. He pulled me closer, and then swore softly when I jerked back from the gear shift.

"Damn that stick. Jeez, I'm going to have to get rid of this car," he said seriously.

Our laughter filled the car. Without warning, I found myself sobbing.

"It isn't that bad. It's time to trade it in," Blake teased.

He nestled me in his arms as best he could.

"It's that I'm so happy," I said between sobs. Everyone had told me I'd judged Blake unfairly. Now, I knew they were right. It had taken a lot of courage for him to come after me.

"C'mon, Allison, let's get out of here."

I opened the car door, eager as he to be inside.

In the dark, quiet interior of the living room, I turned to Blake, free from any worries about him I might have had. I would take a chance with him, like he'd asked.

He took my hand and I followed him upstairs, filled with all the sensations I'd tried to conjure up with Dawson. What Blake and I had between us couldn't be faked.

Later, as we lay side by side, sated and satisfied, I trailed my fingers over the light stubble on his strong jaw and outlined his soft lips.

He grabbed my fingers and kissed them one by one, gazing into my eyes with such tenderness I wondered how I ever could have doubted his feelings for me. My heart filled with such love I couldn't speak.

CHAPTER NINETEEN

I awoke, rolled over and faced Blake. Lying next to him, I was content to watch him breathe in and out rhythmically. His eyelids fluttered and opened.

"There you are," he murmured, and pulled me closer.

I nestled against his broad chest and listened to the steady beat of his heart. Teasing him, I trailed my hand lower and lower.

With a mock roar, he flipped me over on my back. "You ready for more?"

Instead of waiting for an answer, he kissed me. I didn't even have to say a word. He knew how ready I was.

Later, I stumbled out of bed and hit the shower, feeling limp from the workout my body had enjoyed. I dried myself off, walked back into the bedroom and came to a stop. Blake lay atop the sheets sound asleep. Filled with tenderness, I silently finished dressing and tiptoed downstairs to savor a few moments alone.

Outside, I retrieved the newspaper from the front porch and stood there, breathing in the fresh, cool air. Renewed optimism colored my feelings. The sky seemed bluer, the sun brighter. The May morning seemed to hold so much more than the promise of a wonderful late spring day.

Thinking back to my relationship with Will, I decided Blake was right. I'd let my bad experiences with my ex-husband affect new ones. No more, I vowed. Blake had shown me what it was like to feel treasured, and I was not about to give that up.

In the kitchen, I measured out coffee and started the coffee maker. I'd simply enjoy Blake and the day ahead. I had two hours before the gallery opened.

The phone rang. I rushed to answer it.

"Is Blake there?"

I recognized the voice immediately. My own turned icy cold. "Why are you calling here, Janelle?"

"Answer me," she snapped. "Is Blake there?"

"Not that it's any of your business, but, yes, he is."

"That's all I needed to know." The phone buzzed in my ear.

A few minutes later, bare-chested and clad in blue jeans, Blake padded into the kitchen.

"Who was that?"

My lips tightened. "Janelle. She's looking for you. When she found out you were here, she hung up on me."

The pleasant smile on his face disappeared. He slapped the counter with a resounding smack. "Dammit! I've given her no reason to act this way."

I put my arms around him. "Maybe, she's one of those obsessive crazies, like the woman Sharon Stone played in the movie."

He managed a grin. "You'll protect me, won't you?"

"Damn right." I picked up the knife I'd used to slice bagels and waved it in the air.

He laughed, then, became serious. "Maybe I should give up running the wine festival."

"Unh, unh." I shook my head. "By chairing the event, you can tie in promotions for Sweet Talk. We need the exposure."

I poured Blake a cup of coffee. He lowered himself into a seat at the table and silently sipped the hot brew.

"Do what you want about the wine festival,"

He gazed up at me. "No, no, you're right. I'll still head the festival, but I'm going to pull in some other people so it's not only Janelle and me working on it."

"Good." There was something disquieting about Janelle's infatuation with Blake.

Later, after Blake left to go home, I paused at the threshold of Daisy's room. I told myself she was all right. At one time, Kristin had thought so much of Lisa that she'd asked her to take care of Daisy. But then I recalled how easily Lisa had manipulated Kristin and grew concerned all over again.

At the gallery, Jessie kept looking up from her work and grinning at me.

"What?"

"It's nice to see you happy. It's been one helluva ride this year. I'm glad you and Blake are back together."

"Thanks," I said, meaning it with all my heart. She knew how much I'd missed him.

We took a break and went out back. Sarah Hoffman, our decorator, was overseeing installation of the window treatments in Sweet Talk. We'd kept the color theme of various wine tones, using them as accents in the fabric on the windows and the seats of the chairs. The look was both sophisticated and casual.

Sarah waved as we entered the building. "What do you think?"

"It's beautiful," said Jessie, and I agreed.

Margaret Atkinson arrived, her red hair frizzier than usual. "I heard Sarah was doing her stuff here today. 'Couldn't wait to see it."

I smiled. Margaret was going to be great as the manager of Sweet Talk. The hardworking single mother of two teenage boys, she exuded an air of fun and friendliness. But beneath her easy-going manner was a veritable drill sergeant who'd insist on excellent, gracious service for our customers.

My mood upbeat, I left everyone at Sweet Talk to go back

to Treasures. I took a moment to study our displays. Going from case to case, I rearranged items to give them a fresh look. When I'd first seen Treasures, I'd whimsically thought of rainbows. Even now, the colors scattered around the room reminded me of slivers of light from a shimmering crystal.

I sighed with contentment and went into the back office to work on updating the inventory. I'd taken a seat at my desk, when the phone rang. A New Mexico number.

I snatched the phone.

"Okay, where is she?" Lisa's snarling voice sent shock waves roiling through me.

"What are you talking about?" I felt the blood leave my face. The room went fuzzy. "What's wrong? Where's Daisy?"

"As if you didn't know," Lisa snapped. "She's gone. Did you come and get her, like she told me you would?"

I blinked rapidly, confused. "I don't know what you're talking about. What do you mean, she's gone? How long has she been gone?" My hands turned ice cold as her words sunk in. I gripped the phone tighter to keep from dropping it. "Gone where?"

"That's what I want to know. She kept saying you were coming to pick her up. Was that the plan all along?"

The room spun around me. I lowered my head and took deep breaths.

"Godammit! Answer me!" screamed Lisa.

I sat up, feeling weak. "I have no idea where Daisy is. I never promised to come for her. You and I had an agreement …"

"Damn right we did. If you find out anything, let me know. I'll talk to you later."

"Wait! Have you called the police? What have you done to find her? Why didn't you take better care of her?"

"Listen, I've got to go!"

"What do you want me to do?"

"Stay by the phone, in case she calls. And, no, I haven't called the cops yet. Do you think I'm crazy? She'll tell them all kinds of stories. I'll find her on my own. Catherine is out in the car, circling the block, looking for her."

Lisa slammed down the phone.

Holding the buzzing receiver in my hand, my body felt numb. Imagining Daisy injured, or worse, dead, I clutched my torso and rocked back and forth. I staggered from the office.

Jessie stared at me with round eyes. "Allison! What's the matter?"

"It's Daisy. She's gone!" I gasped between gulping breaths.

"Gone? Gone where?"

Unable to hold back the rising bile in my throat, I ran into the bathroom. My darling Daisy was lost. I should have fought the system harder.

Jessie followed me.

After I'd emptied my stomach, she handed me a wet paper towel. "Okay, now tell me. For God's sake, what happened to Daisy?"

I blurted out the story, giving her the few facts I knew. "What am I going to do?"

Jessie clasped and unclasped her hands in a nervous pattern that did nothing to ease my concerns. "Lisa's right. You've got to stay by the phone, in case Daisy or someone else calls. Daisy knows the gallery number by heart. She'll want to hear your voice."

I shook my head. "I can't just sit around, doing nothing. I've got to hop on a plane and go down there."

Jessie placed a hand on my shoulder, keeping me in my seat. "Waiting is the hardest part, but we don't even know how long Daisy's been gone. She could be simply wandering in the neighborhood."

Fighting another attack of nausea, I used the paper towel to wipe my brow. I returned to the office, but couldn't sit still. I paced the room, silently praying Daisy would be all right. Worry formed all kinds of awful scenarios in my mind. She was an innocent child, unaware of the evils of the world. How in the world would she know enough to keep safe on her own?

I thought of Dawson Smith. If he were Daisy's father, as we both suspected, he had a right to know what had happened. I dialed his number. He answered on the first ring.

"Hey!" he said cheerfully. "I was about to call you. 'Thought we could go to dinner."

"Sorry. Not tonight." I fought to keep a grip on my turbulent emotions. "Awful news, Dawson. Lisa called to say Daisy's gone. She thought I'd stolen Daisy away. Apparently Daisy kept saying I would come pick her up."

"Gone? What do you mean, gone?"

I barely kept myself from breaking down. "All I know is that Lisa can't find her. When she called me, Catherine was out in the car, circling the neighborhood. She told me to wait by the phone. It's killing me to have to stay here, doing nothing."

"Hold on, Allison. I'll be there as soon as possible. We're in this together, remember?"

"That's why I called ..."

"I'm on my way!"

I hung up, feeling much better. Maybe this is how it would be in the future, Dawson and me sharing the ups and downs of life with Daisy. A sob caught in my throat. Dear God, was she still alive?

Jessie came into the office. "Do you want me to bring you something, run upstairs for a soda and saltines?"

I shook my head. "Until I know Daisy's safe, I don't think I can even swallow water. I called Dawson, and then left a message for Blake to call me. Dawson's on his way."

"Don't worry. I've got the gallery covered."

I leaned back in my chair and let out a long sigh. When Daisy had been left in my care, I hadn't wanted the unexpected responsibility or the work. We'd slowly formed a bond. I realized now how abandoned she must have felt, being sent off to Santa Fe while I stood by and watched. It broke my heart to think I'd failed her. What would I do if I never got the chance to make it up to her?

The phone rang. My mouth gone dry, I picked it up.

"Allison Hartwell?"

I gulped at the sound of a male voice I didn't know. "Yes?"

"Officer Rodriguez, here. Santa Fe police department."

I sucked in an unsteady breath. It couldn't be good news. Tears stung my eyes.

"Daisy Lewis is here with me," he continued. "Don't worry, she's fine. She says you're her ... um ... fairy godmother and she wants to go home. She refuses to tell us why she's here in Santa Fe. What can you tell us? Do you know her? Is she telling the truth?"

I quietly sobbed. *Thank God, thank God.*

Jessie rushed into the room. Unable to speak, I gave her a thumbs-up sign.

"Ms. Hartwell?"

I sniffed and blew my nose. "Sorry, officer. I'm so glad she's all right. I *am* her godmother and have been her guardian since her mother died in January. Daisy's visiting Lisa Vaughn in Santa Fe. Lisa was a friend of her mother's, and she's fighting for guardianship of her. Please, can I speak to Daisy?"

I waited for him to put her on, hoping I would say the right words and Daisy would understand why I had to send her away.

"Allie?" The sound of Daisy's high voice caused a fresh coating of tears to blur my vision.

"Yes, darling. Are you okay?"

Instead of the sobbing noises I expected from her, Daisy's voice was strong, sure. "I want to come home. I don't like it down here. You won't make me stay, will you?"

"That's something I'll have to work out with Lisa. We had an agreement that you could stay with her for a few days." I'd pull Todd Schaeffer into it if it came to that.

"But, Allie, I love you. I want to come home."

I choked back more tears. "I love you, too, Daisy. I'll do my best to make it happen. Now let me talk to Officer Rodriguez." I struggled to remain calm while I waited for him to come back on the phone.

"Yes, ma'am," he said, coming on the line.

"Where did you find her?" I needed all the details before doing battle with Lisa.

"It was the darndest thing. I was stopped at a red light and Daisy, here, ran over to my car and pounded on the window. I pulled over to talk to her. She told me she wanted to go home, that she was lost. When I asked her where she lived, she said Sarita, California. That threw me for a loop. Then she told me she'd been taken away. You can imagine how I felt. I loaded her in the car and brought her to the central station to research missing children. She's not listed as missing, but it was obvious to me she was real upset. What's the story?"

"A fight for legal guardianship. Her mother is dead and, right now, her father is unknown, but I'm working on that."

"In the meantime, where is she supposed to be?"

Reluctantly, I gave him Lisa's address and phone number. "Officer, will you be sure to file a report on this? I'll need it for my records. And can you keep Daisy there with you at the station until I make a call to Lisa to see if we can work something out between us? It might make things easier."

"Why not?" I could almost see him shrug.

We talked a few minutes longer about Daisy and the situation we were in and I hung up the phone.

"Well?" said Jessie. "I gather Daisy's all right and with the police, but what happened?"

I quickly filled her in on what I knew. "Now I have to convince Lisa to bring Daisy back here. Maybe she'd even be willing to stay in a motel downtown and continue to see Daisy here in Sarita."

Jessie cocked an eyebrow. "Doubtful."

Anger overwhelmed me. "If she's not willing to go along with a change in plans, I'm going there. I don't care what anyone says. I can't let Daisy believe I'm tossing her away, that I don't care about her."

"First things first," said Jessie calmly. "Pull yourself together before calling Lisa or she'll never cooperate."

Jessie left the room, and I leaned back in my chair and stared up at the ceiling. In my present mood, I'd kill any goodwill I might be able to drum up between Lisa and me. The echo of Daisy's sweet voice rang in my head. I couldn't believe her gumption in breaking away from Lisa. I'd expected her to cry and sob hysterically on the phone. Instead, she'd stated very firmly that she wanted to come home. There was more to this child than I'd been led to believe.

With a new sense of purpose, I dialed Lisa's number. She answered right away.

"Daisy's okay. She's at the central police station in Santa Fe. She found a policeman, Officer Rodriquez, and told him she wanted to go home to Sarita."

"Yeah? I bet. What else did you coax her into telling them?"

I clamped my teeth shut, struggling to cool my temper. "Look, Lisa, let's not make this into a battle about us. Let's concentrate on Daisy. Would you consider flying up here with Daisy and doing your visitation in Sarita? Once she becomes used to the idea of spending time with you, she'll be happier. You know how she is about change."

"No, as a matter of fact, I don't," snapped Lisa. "I think this whole scenario is something you cooked up. The kid needs to get her butt back here."

I wanted to scream, but forced myself to speak calmly. "Instead of making Daisy upset by staying in Santa Fe, why don't you rent a room at the Beachcomber Motel here in Sarita and stay with her there. It'll ease her into the new situation. She'll love it. Staying at a motel will be a big treat." I swallowed hard. "I'll even pay for the room, if you want."

Silence met my suggestion. Finally, Lisa said, "Okay, I'll talk it over with Catherine. I'll let you know after I call the police and go down there to pick up Daisy."

I hung up. I'd accomplished something, if not an outright victory. Perhaps Daisy's stubborn streak would work for her this time.

Dawson pulled up in his truck as I stepped out of the gallery. I ran over to him.

"Daisy's all right. I talked to her. She found a policeman, told him she was taken away and wanted to come home to Sarita."

Dawson's eyes widened. "She did that on her own?"

I grinned. "She sounded very grownup on the phone, very sure of herself. I couldn't believe it."

I gave him the rest of the details, leaving nothing out.

When I finished, he shook his head. "I hope Lisa is smart enough to follow your suggestion and come back here to The Beachcomber. If she's patient with Daisy, things will be much easier. I know that, from watching you and Kristin handle her."

An unwelcome thought entered my mind. "What are we going to do if it turns out you're not the father?"

A look of disappointment flashed across Dawson's face, surprising me.

"I've convinced myself that I am," he said. "Funny, isn't it?"

"When will you have the results of the DNA test?"

"I should know tomorrow. The whole thing has been one mix-up after another."

"If it turns out you are the father, we'll ask Lisa to leave early." I fervently hoped that would be the case. Dawson would be a steadying, calming influence on both Daisy and me.

Jessie came to the door of the gallery and waved me over. "Lisa's on the phone."

I rushed inside.

"Okay, you win," she said without preamble. "We'll be on the plane to San Francisco tonight. But no way should you meet us. Jessie has already agreed to do that."

I hid my disappointment. "I'll go ahead and make reservations at the motel."

"One room for Catherine and me; an adjoining one for Daisy," Lisa said, pushing her luck.

Thinking of the extra expense, my lips thinned. "Done." Anything was worth having Daisy close to me.

I hung up the phone and faced Jessie. "You agreed to pick them up at the airport?"

"To quote Lisa, 'there's no way she'd allow you to pick them up'. She doesn't want Daisy to see you, at all."

I let out a sigh. It didn't seem fair to either Daisy or me, but there was nothing I could do about it.

Blake called, and I filled him in on the latest news of Daisy.

"You're right. Daisy needs time to get used to being away from you. She doesn't even like Lisa." At my sound of aggravation, he continued, "Hon, I know how frustrating it is to have to wait on the sidelines, but you have no choice. Why don't you come to my house? It might help take your mind off it."

"How about coming to mine instead?" I needed his strong presence with me.

I rattled around my house restlessly, waiting for Blake to arrive for dinner. Jessie and Rob had left for the airport with a promise to phone as soon as they could. Dawson was at home, awaiting a call from me. I was putting the final touches on a lemon and chicken casserole when Blake came in, bearing a bottle of wine.

"Wanted to see how you like this white wine. Thought we might like to serve it at Sweet Talk. Margaret recommended it to go with the tuna tartare she wants to serve."

I smiled. He was as excited about Sweet Talk as Jessie and I were.

He set the wine bottle down on the table and took me in his arms. His warmth and the softness of his lips loosened the muscles that had grown taut with worry. I cuddled into his embrace.

"Let's leave the wine until later," he murmured. "I've got something much better in mind."

My heart raced at the huskiness that had entered his voice. I reached up and stroked his cheek, loving the feel of its roughness beneath my fingers. We stood smiling at each, knowing perfectly well what pleasures lay ahead.

I turned to leave the room. Blake clasped my hand, drew me back inside the kitchen and pressed me up against the wall, his body firm but comfortable against mine. He cupped my face in his hands, and his lips, soft, yet demanding, met mine. His body conformed to my shape, letting me know with no uncertainty how much he wanted me.

I wrapped my legs around his waist, wanting to be as close to him as possible. We moved in a rhythmic, sexual dance. He paused, breathing heavily, carried me into the living room and set me down on the couch. His face flushed, he unbuckled his pants.

I wriggled out of my clothes and held up my arms, offering myself freely to him.

With a soft groan, he settled on the couch. Lying beside me, he protected himself, and with a smile of satisfaction, continued his loving touches, until neither of us could stand the agony of abstaining any longer.

In the languid period that followed our lovemaking, Blake traced my lips with a finger. "You're wonderful."

My heart opened to him. Will had never said anything like it. His attempts at lovemaking had been quick and sometimes painful.

Blake hugged me to him, giving me comfort. The buzzer for the oven broke into the peaceful silence of the living room with a high-pitched whine that demanded my attention.

Reluctantly, I stirred. "Dinner's ready."

Blake's eyes twinkled with humor. "How about more dessert?"

I laughed, and pushed myself off the couch.

Blake slipped on his pants, and I quickly dressed.

In the kitchen, he poured wine, while I put the finishing touches on the meal. We ate in companionable silence, though my thoughts circled around Daisy's expected arrival. Every so often, I caught Blake staring at me.

He reached over and clasped my hand. "I know how hard this is for you. What can we do to distract ourselves until we hear from Jessie? How about going in the hot tub after dinner?"

"Sounds wonderful." The hot tub on the deck outside the

kitchen was one of the features that had attracted me to the house. Relaxing with Blake in the warm water seemed a perfect way to counter my anxiety.

While I stacked the dishes in the sink, Blake turned on the heater for the hot tub. Upstairs, I undressed, wrapped a towel around me, and grabbed a towel for Blake. Outside, I joined Blake on the deck, grateful for the privacy provided by a number of tall bushes edging the deck. I'd dipped a toe in the water to test the temperature, when the phone rang.

I ran to answer it.

"Hello?" Jessie's voice was unsteady.

Alarmed, I asked, "Is everything all right?"

"Yes," she answered, though she sounded as if she'd been crying. "Daisy burst into tears when she noticed Rob and me, ran right over to us and threw her arms around us. We huddled, just the three of us. It really shook me. After we dropped everyone off at the motel, I told Rob I don't want to wait too long after we're married to have kids of our own."

I heard Rob say something to Jessie in the background, and her teary voice lightened. "Rob says we're going to practice tonight. Daisy is fine and happy to be back in Sarita, even though she's been told she can't see you yet."

Relieved, I gave Blake the news and called Dawson. We agreed we'd talk in the morning after he got the results of the test.

I returned to the deck, ready to relax. Blake's naked body glowed in the moonlight. I mentally traced the outline of it, remembering the feel of him nestled against me.

I let my towel drop and stepped into the swirling, warm water. With a soft groan of pleasure, I settled beneath the surface. Blake moved closer until he and I were nestled together.

I leaned back against him and stared up at the starry sky,

feeling blessed. My darling Daisy was safe and I'd found the man I could love for all time. I gazed up at the twinkling stars. I wasn't sure which star was my lucky one, so I silently thanked them all.

CHAPTER TWENTY

The morning light slanted through my bedroom window, waking me. I reached for Blake and remembered he was gone. He'd left sometime earlier, making the trip back to Silver Goose for a scheduled breakfast meeting. Recalling his tender kisses good-bye, I caressed the pillow that still bore the soft indentation from his head.

Our time alone had been wonderful. I no longer thought myself a failure as a lover. Blake had chased that idea away. He'd also proved to me that we had something special beyond our lovemaking. We'd snuggled in bed, and talked about many things, including my time with Will. I'd never felt so comfortable nor been so open with a man before.

I focused on the day ahead. Hopefully I'd hear good news from Dawson regarding the DNA test—then Lisa would be out of my life.

My thoughts turned to business. The last of the kitchen equipment for Sweet Talk was due to be installed. Freezer, refrigerator, dishwasher, icemaker, refrigerated displays, and ovens would all be ready for use by Saturday when we would open the wine bar for friends and family. It would be our "soft opening" before the doors officially opened, to give us time to train staff and work out the glitches before we welcomed the public at large. I could hardly wait. We'd planned a very special party.

Energized by the idea, I bounded out of bed and headed for the shower. So far, Sweet Talk was everything I'd imagined, and more. The architect had done a superb job of laying out workable space, and Wayne had come through for us. The decorator had designed flexible conversation areas where people could gather to talk and enjoy our food and drink offerings. The fabrics and furniture styles were classic and yet had a uniqueness of design. What had once been a little cottage in the back of Treasures was now a special oasis where our customers could relax.

Excited by the progress from dream to reality, I quickly dressed. I wanted to see as much of the final touches as I could before working in the gallery.

I was at the site, talking with Stu and Margaret, when I noticed Dawson pull into the parking area. I ran over to him, crossing my fingers he'd have good news for me.

He climbed out of his truck. The corners of his mouth drooped uncharacteristically and his normal air of confidence was missing.

"What is it?" I looked into his eyes, seeing his disappointment.

He shook his head. "No way I'm the father. The test was conclusive."

My stomach twisted into a knot. I gave him a quick hug. "I'm so sorry, Dawson. I really am. It would have been such a lucky thing for Daisy in so many ways."

His attempt at even a half-hearted smile tugged at me. I silently raged at Fate.

He shrugged. "I'd convinced myself what I felt for Kristin had produced Daisy. Damned if I know who else was involved."

My body turned cold as the realization struck home. What in hell was I going to do now?

Dawson kicked at the ground, struggling to rein in his emotions.

I gave him another hug. "Maybe someday you'll find

someone like Kristin and have children of your own."

My attempt at comforting him produced another sad shrug of his shoulders. Watching him climb back into his truck, my heart ached for him. In spite of all the exciting things he did and all the money he had, he was a lonely man. I took a deep breath. My stomach clenched in painful squeezes. What was I going to do about Daisy?

"Hey, Allison!" Stu called to me. "Come here. We need your opinion."

"Hold on! I'll be there in a minute." Time, I needed time to focus back on work.

Fighting heartbreak, I joined Stu and Margaret outside of Sweet Talk. Regardless of how devastated I was, I had to make sure Sweet Talk would succeed.

"Come on inside," said Stu. "You can settle something for us. Margaret says we should have the display case facing the door. I say we keep it where the architect sketched it in."

I held up my hand, in mock protest. "You two are the food and beverage experts." Stu was like a younger brother to Margaret. They kidded around and argued, but both were good at their jobs and had come highly recommended. Jessie and I had decided to pretty much leave them to their own choices.

Margaret shook her head. "This is one time I'm not going to give in to Stu. I know I'm right."

Now, with good nature, Stu clapped Margaret on the back. "We'll work it out. Now let's fight about the kitchen area."

She grinned, and I turned and walked out to the deck. The coolness of the morning had diminished with the strength of the sun. I took off my jacket, and gazed at the flowers and low, leafy shrubs softening the edge of the ground-level deck. I closed my eyes and inhaled the salty tang of the nearby bay, thinking how different California was from Maine. When I'd driven almost non-stop from New Hope to Sarita, I'd hoped my life would change. It certainly had.

"Hey, what are you doing?"

I opened my eyes.

Jessie crossed the parking lot, walking toward me.

"I was just thinking. Where have you been?"

Her cheeks grew pink. "I stayed over at Rob's last night."

"Oh, yeah, that's right. Another practice session, huh?"

She laughed, pulled out a deck chair and sat down, her expression serious. "I was really touched by Daisy at the airport last night. She's one brave little girl, a real fighter. Lisa was very upset when Daisy threw herself at us, but it thrilled me. I'll do whatever I can to help you keep Daisy here in Sarita."

I lowered myself into a chair opposite her. "Bad news. Dawson is definitely not the father; he found out for certain this morning. What am I going to do?"

"Keep looking. Don't give up. You have to find Daisy's father so you can keep Lisa out of the picture. That woman is awful with Daisy. I can't see what Kristin ever saw in her."

"Will you ask Rob if he can think of anyone else I should talk to? I'm going to put another notice on the internet."

"Sure. We'll help in any way we can. Guess what? Rob's mother called. The bridal shower her sister is giving me is definitely set for the middle of June. You sure you don't mind staying here at the gallery while Daisy and I fly down to LA?"

I smiled. "Not at all. I know how excited you are about it, and Daisy's thrilled to be part of the wedding."

Jessie let out a sigh. "Good. One of the downsides to owning businesses like Treasures and Sweet Talk is that it's 24/7."

I checked my watch and rose. "Speaking of that, it's time to open the gallery. I'll do it. You can look around Sweet Talk and referee Margaret and Stu."

She laughed. "Okay. After I break them up, I'll be right there."

I unlocked the gallery and switched on the lights. Interesting pieces of art caught my eye and dazzled me with color and shape. From the time my mother first dragged to the Museum of Fine Arts in Boston, I'd loved the arts. A finely crafted piece of work in almost any medium pleased me. I fingered a hand-blown glass bowl, letting my hand trail over its smooth surface. How, I asked myself, could I have stayed so long at the job in Maine just because it was easy? A late-bloomer, my sister would call me, though she was no better than I when it came to finding herself.

Thinking of Samantha, I went into the office and called her. She answered groggily.

"Don't tell me I woke you up," I teased. There was a three-hour time difference.

"It was a late night and I had too much coffee," she groaned.

"You promised you'd fly out here for Sweet Talk's opening for family and friends, but I haven't heard from you. It's only a few days away. Are you going to make it? I really want you to see what we've done."

"Of course I'm going to be there, Silly. I wouldn't miss it for the world!"

"How about Marissa?"

"No can do. She and Brad are going to be in New York at a fundraiser for something or other in Barnham. She just found out about it. She'll call you to apologize for bowing out."

"Sam? Thanks for coming. It means a lot to me."

After I hung up, I called Todd Schaeffer. I informed him of all that had happened. He agreed to call Lisa's lawyer to try and convince him that having Daisy back in Sarita but unable to see me was detrimental to Daisy's welfare and happiness.

"Be patient," he warned me.

I agreed to bide my time until the issue was resolved. I hung up and threw myself into the frenzy of preparing for our party.

The touted Memorial Day Parade and festivities in Sarita carried on as I worked with Margaret and Stu to stock the kitchen and bar. We'd installed a special wine refrigerator for red wines while one of the other refrigerators held the whites. An espresso machine sat on a counter, and the big icemakers we'd bought were busily making cubes.

Jessie stayed in Treasures, compiling information for printed handouts that would describe the characteristics of the wines we were going to feature during the month of June.

But, even as I remained busy with preparations for our party, my thoughts remained on Daisy.

Later, I headed over to Treasures.

Catherine crossed the parking lot on foot, toward me. I eagerly scanned the area, hoping to catch a glimpse of Daisy.

"Sorry. Daisy's back at the motel, watching a movie. Is there some place we can talk? In private?"

"Sure." My stomach sank at her serious tone. It couldn't be good news. She looked as if she'd been crying.

I led her to the back office in Treasures and indicated a chair. "Would you like coffee? Water?"

"I'd love a glass of water. Truth be told, I'm a little nervous."

Nervous? My eyebrows shot up.

"It's not easy to admit to someone you hardly know that you've been a complete fool," Catherine explained. Her eyes welled.

I gave her a sympathetic look and hurried to pour her a glass of water.

Catherine accepted the water, took a sip, and, drawing a deep breath, set her glass down on the desk. "I'm leaving Lisa. She doesn't know it yet. I've decided to wait until Daisy is returned to you Saturday morning before telling her. She'll be upset, but no more upset than I've been with her."

Her hands shook as she took another sip of water. "Lisa is a very determined individual who wants to control everything, regardless of who she hurts. Now that she thinks she's going to have control of Kristin's estate, she doesn't need me or my money any more. Lately her poor treatment of me has been inexcusable. I cannot and will not stay with her."

Surprised, I gave Catherine's hand a squeeze of encouragement. "I'm sorry."

"I should have known better." Catherine let out another sad sigh. "Kristin was very generous, leaving Lisa in charge of all that money."

I stared at her, dumbstruck. "What do you mean? What money?"

"Oh, you know, this house, Treasures, everything."

My heart pounded with dismay. "She doesn't know I own all this property now? The bulk of any estate Kristin might have had at one time was worth a lot of money. But it's now mine, part of the partnership agreement drawn up at the time I bought into the business. Kristin's estate without this property and the business is much, much less. Whatever is left is in trust for Daisy. Whoever ends up with Daisy will basically have no real financial help to support her."

The blood drained from Catherine's face. "Lisa showed me a listing of Kristin's assets. She's been keeping it to herself so when the time comes, she has written proof this is what Kristin wanted for her. You're saying it's all changed? Do you mean to tell me that Lisa's been fighting for Daisy for next to nothing?" Her laugh was bitter. "It would serve her right."

"But Daisy would be hurt by it. You understand I can't let anything bad happen to. I'll fight tooth and nail to keep her from going to Lisa."

"And I'll help you any way I can," said Catherine firmly. "Daisy's a difficult child at times, but has sweet moments."

My pulse racing with hope, I leaned forward. "Has Lisa ever mentioned who Daisy's father might be?"

Catherine shook her head. "We were talking about it the other night. She doesn't know."

The spurt of hope died within me. Another thought struck me. If Catherine left Lisa, I might be without a home.

"What are you going to do, Catherine? Where are you going to go? Do you want your house back?"

"No, as a matter of fact, I was going to ask if you wanted to buy it."

"I can't." My regret was real. "You may have heard about my new venture, Sweet Talk. All my money is tied up in it."

"Sweet Talk? The wine bar everyone is talking about?" Catherine's eyes sparkled. "Interesting. Lisa told me that when she took over the property, she was going to turn the cottage back into a studio, make it available to various artists, and charge them a lot of money for the space."

"She's too late." I couldn't hide my sense of triumph. "C'mon, I'll show you around. We're having a party to celebrate its opening Saturday night. Will you still be around?"

Catherine shook her head. "I'll be back in Santa Fe, closing down the house there. A friend of mine in Tucson has invited me to stay with her while I relocate to that area."

"Lisa doesn't know?"

"She doesn't suspect a thing."

My breath caught with added worry. "Promise you'll see Daisy is safely brought to me before you tell her."

"Oh, I will. I wouldn't do anything that might bring harm to that child."

"It seems so unfair to have Daisy back in Sarita and not be allowed to see her," I complained. My need to see Daisy, to hold her, was stronger than ever.

"That decision is very typical of Lisa's behavior," Catherine said simply, and I understood how difficult life with Lisa could be.

I led Catherine out back.

She stopped and stared, wide-eyed. "I can't believe it! It's adorable!" She gave me a sly grin. "Wait until Lisa sees this!"

I showed Catherine the new addition and explained the theme of our wine bar. "That's why we've done so much decorating in wine tones and chocolate brown."

Jessie emerged from the kitchen and stopped in surprise. "Why, hello, Catherine."

"What nice things you've done here," Catherine said smoothly, erasing the look of unease that had begun to cross Jessie's face. "It's hard to believe that little cottage could turn into something so roomy and so classy."

"If the weather is nice, we can easily seat sixty people." Jessie indicated the multi-layered deck with a sweep of her hand.

Catherine slowly turned in a circle, taking it all in. "It's marvelous." She turned to me and smiled. "Good luck with everything. I'd better hurry back to Lisa and Daisy."

Relieved to know Catherine would help me gain custody of Daisy, I walked her out to the front of the gallery.

Catherine gave me a quick hug. "Don't say a word to Lisa. I don't want her to know a thing."

I looked up to see a car heading right toward us. "Look out!" I grabbed Catherine's arm and pulled her out of harm's way. I turned to the driver, ready to do battle.

The car screeched to a halt. "What are you doing here?" Lisa shouted to Catherine through the open driver's window.

I looked for Daisy, but she wasn't in the car.

Catherine stood her ground. "I'm seeing what the buzz is all about. Sweet Talk is really something." Her voice shook.

"Yeah?" Lisa snarled. "It looked like you were much more interested in Allison than any wine bar. Get in. I'll take you back."

Catherine drew herself up. "I'm going to walk back to the motel. It's only a couple of blocks and I need the exercise."

"That's true," snorted Lisa, staring at her. "Look at you!"

Catherine ignored her and walked out of the parking lot.

"Where's Daisy?" I asked Lisa.

"None of your business!" She waved a hand at the building. "You think you can get away with turning this into some fancy, schmancy place? You'll find it's all been for nothing when I get hold of it."

I backed away from the car. "Get the facts. Have your lawyer get in touch with mine. Now tell me where Daisy is." If Lisa had done anything to harm that little girl I'd kill her with my bare hands.

"Daisy's back at the motel, watching a stupid movie. Now, get out of my way." Lisa gunned the engine and tore out of the parking lot.

Trembling, I stumbled to the door of the gallery and held onto the door jamb. As the flow of adrenaline slowed, my knees turned to jelly. What would Lisa do when she learned the truth about Kristin's estate? She should've figured everything had changed when I bought into the business. Something was wrong. Had greed overridden common sense? Was she spaced out on drugs or alcohol? If so, it would make a case for getting Daisy.

###

Blake arrived as I was locking the door of the gallery for the night. He wrapped his arms around me in a strong embrace. I let out a sigh and leaned against him. He made me feel so safe, so protected.

"Hard day?" he asked, tilting my chin.

"Dawson isn't Daisy's father. He found out this morning. Then I learned Catherine is leaving Lisa." I shook my head. "It's all so crazy."

"I stopped at the motel to check on things for you. Catherine and Daisy were in the pool, laughing and having a good time. I left before they saw me, but everything seemed fine. 'Thought you'd want to know."

I hugged him hard. "You're wonderful! I needed to hear that."

"Let's go to Silver Goose. It'll be our last night alone for a while."

"I don't know ... maybe I'd better stay here."

"Ask Jessie to call Lisa and make sure things are going well. Would that make you feel better about leaving?"

"OK, good idea."

After Jessie assured me Daisy was fine, I packed a few things in a bag, slid into Blake's car, and we headed out of town.

Staring out at the passing scenery, I became lost in thoughts of Lisa. She'd come from a rough background in a small mid-western town. Her uncanny ability to convince people to help her had provided a much nicer lifestyle, but, when times were tough, she became mean and vindictive. As frightening as she could be, I'd fight her for Daisy.

Blake squeezed my hand. "Don't look so worried. Daisy's fine."

"She's become like my own. Funny, how she wormed her way into my heart."

Blake gently swiped my cheek with the tips of his knuckles. "You're a nice lady, Allison Hartwell."

I smiled back at him. I loved him so much.

"What do you think your sister is going to say when she sees us together tomorrow?"

Humor bubbled inside me. "She told me she's going to check you out, see if you're good enough. But I don't care what anyone else says, you'll do."

He laughed, and the small lines of concern that had momentarily marred his brow disappeared. "Along with Aunt Penny, I've invited my sister to the opening tomorrow. I sent her an airline ticket but I don't know if she'll come. Things haven't been easy between us for some time. Not since I kicked her out for her drug use."

My heart went out to him. "I hope she decides to join us. I'd like to meet her."

He didn't say anything, but I noticed his grip tighten on the steering wheel.

Pepper and Coalie greeted us with wagging tails. I knelt to accept Coalie's pink tongue on my cheeks, thinking of Daisy and the way the puppy had helped her through tough times. I had the feeling we'd need her help again.

We settled on the deck with a glass of wine. The setting sun cast golden light on the landscape around us. I sighed with contentment as Blake filled me in on his day. Sharing events of the day was new to me and something I really enjoyed. Will hadn't wanted to discuss most parts of his life—certainly not the details of it.

Later, after dinner and vigorous, satisfying lovemaking, I lay in bed beside Blake. I stroked his naked body, loving the feel of his hard muscles beneath the surface of his skin. His heart still pumped furiously. He'd given us both a workout.

"You've got a silly smile on your face." Blake traced my lips gently with his fingers.

I kissed him deeply, wondering if he knew how happy he made me. The magic we shared was something I'd only dreamed about.

His body instantly reacted to my kiss.

Yep, he knew all right, I thought smugly, and snuggled closer.

CHAPTER TWENTY ONE

I awoke with a smile. Today was Sweet Talk's soft opening. More importantly, I'd have Daisy back with me. I could hardly wait to see her. Blake drove and I arrived home to find the message light on my phone blinking. *Trouble?* Heart pounding, I pushed the button to listen.

At the sound of Lisa's greeting, my stomach clenched.

"Hey, Allison. I'm leaving Sarita earlier than I thought. I'll drop Daisy off at your house at eight instead of ten. You'd better be ready for her."

Excitement swirled through me. I checked my watch. Six-thirty.

Full of questions, I raced upstairs to take a quick shower. I hurried through my grooming routines and rushed to the kitchen to prepare fresh baked cookies—the simple kind you bought and sliced and popped into the oven. Chocolate chip was Daisy's favorite.

Life was funny, I mused, as I set to work. My mother used to make cookies for us kids as a celebration of any major event. Now I was doing it for Daisy. It gave me a warm maternal feeling.

At eight o'clock, I sat on the front porch stairs, feeling like a child on Christmas Eve. The moment Lisa drove into my driveway, I was on my feet, running down the steps.

The car rolled to a stop. Daisy peered at me uncertainly from the backseat.

"Hi, Daisy!" I opened the door and held out my arms to her.

Daisy's face scrunched into a mask of anguish. Silent tears

ran down her cheeks. She pushed past me, running as fast as she could, up the front steps, into the house.

Stunned, I stood staring after her.

"What? No lovey, dovey stuff? I thought you and she were real close." Lisa's smug look cut through me.

I bit my lip, struggling to hold back an angry retort. "Where are Daisy's things? I'll take them inside."

Lisa hauled Daisy's suitcase out of the trunk of the car. "Everything's inside. I didn't have a chance to do laundry. I figured you could do that."

Grabbing hold of the suitcase, I turned to go.

"My lawyer will be in touch with yours." Glaring at me, Lisa slid behind the wheel. "It's not over, you know. I expect her in Santa Fe in July. Then there'll be no more nonsense between us."

I stared at her, not knowing what to say. Her confrontation with Catherine must not have taken place. She left, and luggage in hand, I trudged up the porch stairs and set down the suitcase inside.

"Daisy?"

No answer.

I went into the kitchen and gaped at the scene before me. The cookie plate lay on the floor, broken pieces of it scattered everywhere. Warm cookies were trampled into sugary clumps here and there.

Daisy's wails reached me before I'd even reached the top of the stairway.

Knocking gently, I opened the door to her bedroom. She lay curled on her bed, sobbing noisily.

"Daisy?" I sat down on the edge of her bed. "Honey, what's the matter? It'll be all right. You're home now." I reached over to pat her back.

"No!" She whirled away from my touch and stared at me

with such anger, my breath caught. “You didn’t come for me!” she screamed. “You’re my fairy godmother. You were supposed to come and get me.” She began slapping at me.

I took her hands in mine. “Oh, honey, listen ...”

“Lisa told me you wouldn’t come.” Her voice broke. “She said you didn’t care.”

“But ... but,” I began helplessly. “You know that’s not true. You know I love you very much. I had to let you visit Lisa. The lawyers gave me no choice.”

She shot me a look that told me she didn’t buy the story. “You didn’t even come to the airport. Jessie and Rob came for me, but not you.”

My vision misted. Lisa had done the cruelest thing possible. She’d destroyed Daisy’s faith in me. If she’d been in the same room with us, I would’ve strangled her.

“Daisy, listen to me. No matter what Lisa told you, I love you and want the best for you. You know it’s true—deep down, where your heart is.”

I patted her back. Under my gentle caresses, her body, taut with anger, gradually relaxed.

“Daisy? Will you come closer so I can give you one of my cuddly bear hugs?” I held my breath.

Daisy moved a few inches toward me, enough for me to be able to shift her onto my lap. Her body trembling, she placed her head against my chest and wrapped her arms around me. I rocked her back and forth, murmuring endearments, loving the feel of her in my arms. Her legs extended far beyond my lap, but it didn’t matter. She was my baby come home.

After some time, Daisy squirmed out of my arms. “I want a cookie.”

I smiled. Things were going to be all right.

Daisy and I cleaned up the mess in the kitchen and sat at the table, eating cookies. In bits and pieces, I was able to convince Daisy to tell me about her visit with Lisa. It became clear that although she didn't like Lisa, she thought Catherine was nice. That made me feel better.

"Lisa said I have to visit her again. Do I, Allie?"

Daisy's expression was so worried I decided she had to know the whole truth. I set down my coffee mug.

"A while ago, you asked about your father. We don't know who he is. I'm trying to find him for you. If I do, it might mean you won't have to visit Lisa again. So far I haven't found him, but I won't stop trying."

Daisy patted my hand. "You'll find him. You're my fairy godmother."

"I'll try." My voice was thick with emotion.

Daisy settled in front of the television. Later, I heard the distinctive purr of Blake's car pull into my driveway. Smiling at the plan he and I had concocted earlier, I turned to Daisy. "Blake's here. He has a surprise for you."

A smile spread across her face. Her blue eyes, so like his, shone. She raced toward the front door and opened it.

"Coalie! He brought Coalie!" Daisy shrieked.

The lab puppy bounded up the porch steps. Daisy knelt to let the dog lick her face and looked up at me with a broad grin. "She loves me, Allie. She really does."

Blake leaned over and patted Daisy on the back. "Feel good to be home?"

"Yeah," said Daisy. "Allie made me cookies."

"Got any extras?" he asked me.

I laughed. "Come on inside."

"Allie? Can Coalie come inside, too?" Daisy gave me a hopeful look.

Blake smiled at me, and squatted in front of Daisy. "'Might be a good idea so she can get used to it. She's yours, you know. Now that she's trained, Allie says she can stay here with you."

"Really?" She threw her arms around Blake, knocking him to the porch floor. Wagging her tail, Coalie leapt upon him, licking his face.

Laughing, Blake pushed to his feet. "Guess it was a good decision, huh?"

I glanced at Daisy's shining eyes and grinned.

Blake sat with me in the kitchen while Daisy and Coalie raced through the house. After a quick cup of coffee, he left to go to the airport. He'd offered to pick up Samantha, along with his Aunt Penny, who was flying up from LA.

After he left, Daisy and I walked Coalie down the road to Treasures.

"I want to surprise Jessie," Daisy said, acting more like her old self.

I waited outside the gallery while Daisy went in to say hello. Coalie sat impatiently at my feet, as if she couldn't stand to be away from his young mistress.

Jessie came to the door, holding hands with Daisy, easy affection between them. It made me happy to see them like that, although I wished Daisy understood why Jessie had appeared at the airport instead of me.

"Look, Jessie," said Daisy. "That's my dog, Coalie! Allie says she can stay with me."

Jessie glanced from Daisy to me and patted Coalie on the head. "That's good. That's very good."

Daisy and Coalie raced each other in circles on the lawn.

"How are things going with Sweet Talk?" I asked Jessie. "Tonight's the big night."

Her eyes shone with amusement. "Good. For once, Margaret and Stu are not fighting. No one else is allowed inside the building while they set things up for the party. I listened to the training sessions they're holding for the small staff. It sounded like a college class. Margaret is teaching three waitresses about food choices and procedures, while Stu is grilling the two bartenders on the varietals of grapes at Silver Goose. I wouldn't interrupt them for the world."

I laughed. "We'll walk around the outside so Daisy can see the improvements, then head back home. You're going to close early?"

"Yes. My parents are meeting me here at four. I want them to have a private tour of Sweet Talk before the party starts."

"I'll be anxious to meet them." Though they'd finally given Jessie financial backing, they didn't seem the kind of parents who were interested in the everyday details of her life. They hadn't come to Sarita once since she'd joined the business. In fact, Jessie seemed closer to Rob's parents, who lived farther away.

Back home, I waited eagerly for Samantha to arrive. Two years apart in age, she and I had always been close. Even throughout her years of drinking and being out of control, she'd been careful not to tread too harshly on me. Now that she was sober and stronger than ever, she championed my causes with a fervor I found touching.

"When is she coming?" Daisy whined, sensing my impatience. "I want her to see Coalie."

I checked the kitchen clock. "Any minute now."

I hurried outside in time to see Blake's car pull into the driveway.

Samantha emerged from the backseat of the car and met me halfway across the lawn. With her straight dark hair and willowy figure, she was as beautiful as ever. I loved her like crazy. She laughed as Coalie's tongue licked her fingers and Daisy danced around her.

"That's Coalie. She's my dog," Daisy said proudly.

"I see." Samantha lifted Daisy in her arms and gave her a growling bear hug that made Coalie bark louder.

Grinning, Samantha set Daisy down and held her arms out to me. We rocked back and forth in a hug. She pulled away and studied me, a smirk foreshadowing the teasing I was sure to get.

"Loving looks good on you." Lowering her voice, Samantha added, "I forgot what a hottie Blake is. Whew!"

I glanced at him as he walked toward us, his stride easy as he carried Samantha's suitcase to the porch. The delight in his eyes when his gaze settled on me filled me with joy.

"Allison? Come say hi to Penny."

I walked over to the car, eager to see her again.

Penny opened the front passenger door so I could give her a quick hug. We pulled apart and Penny beamed at me.

"I'll be at the party with bells on. It's all so exciting!"

"See you later." Blake climbed in behind the wheel. "We'll be back here early. I want to meet Jessie's parents."

I knocked on Samantha's bedroom door. "Are you ready?"

"Coming," she called, and opened the door.

She wore a black sheath with a V-neckline that showed enough décolletage to be interesting. Jet black beads sewn along the neckline lit her dark hair and brought out the light in her grey eyes.

"You look beautiful!" I mentally tallied the number of unattached males who would circle her. Now that I'd found the man of my dreams, I hoped she'd be as lucky.

"You don't look so bad yourself. Red is definitely your color." Samantha fingered the silk print top I wore over black silk slacks.

"See me?" Daisy twirled around in front of us. She was wearing the new, blue-print sundress I'd bought for her before she went away.

"You're pretty as a picture." I gave her a hug. "That's the dress we picked out for her to wear to Jessie's bridal shower," I explained to Samantha.

"Very nice." Samantha took hold of Daisy's hand. "C'mon, little girl! Let's go to a party."

Samantha and I strolled down the road, side by side. Daisy ran in circles ahead of us, arms outspread like a bluebird about to take flight.

"How're you doing? You must be pretty excited." Samantha smiled at me.

"It's a dream come true." I was lucky and I knew it. Things had fallen into place quickly. "I've always wanted to run my own business, and Sweet Talk is going to be a wonderful addition to Treasures. I think even Father would be pleased by all I've done."

Samantha threw an arm around my shoulder. "So much has happened to you in such a short time, little sister. I hope it all ends well."

A shiver crossed my shoulders. I pushed aside sudden foreboding when I noticed Blake's car among others in the parking lot. He, Jessie, and I would make Sweet Talk a success.

Margaret and Stu greeted us when we walked through the doors. My gaze swept the room. The waitresses wore tan slacks and burgundy-print shirts with the Sweet Talk logo stitched on the front pocket. Behind the counter, the bartenders wore burgundy polo shirts, looking like over-sized choir boys with their fresh scrubbed looks. Crystal glasses sparkled in the racks above their heads. Decanters were filled with a variety of red wines, ready to be poured. My gaze swung to the large assortment of pastries and chocolate strategically placed on tables and displayed in cases.

"Wow!" A wide grin spread across Samantha's face. She

turned to me, her eyes shining. "Great job! It's gorgeous!"

"Can't you see yourself sitting by the fire on a cold, foggy evening?" I indicated the sun room with a sweep of my hand.

"Yeah, with a Coke in my hand."

We laughed. Samantha had been sober for almost two years.

Jessie approached us with an older couple in tow. "Hey! Meet my parents."

I smiled and held out my hand. "We're pleased to have you here. Hasn't it turned out well?"

The withering look Mrs. Ives gave me caught me off guard. "When Jessie told us about the business," she snapped, "I had no idea she was talking about a bar."

"Now, honey..." Jessie's father said.

She turned to him with a glare. "My father, may he rest in peace, would roll over in his grave if he knew any of the estate was used in such a way. I thought you told me this was going to be some sort of sweet shop."

Jessie's face turned bright red. I gave her a sympathetic grimace. She and her father had downplayed the wine aspect of Sweet Talk. According to Jessie, her straight-laced mother had inherited money from a domineering, strict father who'd raised her to believe she had a duty to follow in his joyless footsteps. Studying her mother's expression of disapproval, I understood better why Jessie had gravitated toward fun-loving Rob.

Mr. Ives flashed me a look of apology and took his wife by the arm. "Let's see about those baked goods."

As her parents walked away, Jessie's shoulders slumped. "She makes everything so damn difficult. Thank God my father is willing to put up with her." Her face brightened as Rob came over to us, carrying Daisy on his shoulders.

"Hi!" Rob gave Jessie a kiss. "I saw your mother from

across the room and figured you might need a little defrosting."

Samantha and I exchanged smiles. For all his casual ways, Rob was a sweet guy who really loved Jessie.

"I told Rob all about Coalie," said Daisy, as he set her down on the floor. "He's going to come see her."

"Yes," Rob confirmed. "I promised I would."

"Have you seen Blake?" I asked.

"He's outside, holding court with Penelope Potter."

"Go ahead." Samantha nudged me. "I'll wander around inside for a while. I noticed Dawson Smith. I want to talk to him about something."

Convivial noise filled the building as guests arrived and greeted one another. Their chatter added to the excitement. Aunt Penny and Blake stood in the center of a circle of admirers who listened attentively as she told about some of the funnier antics on her television show. Blake noticed me and he broke away.

"'Looks like we're getting quite a crowd."

I smiled, as another group of four arrived.

Daisy brushed by us, traces of chocolate in a tell-tale pattern around her mouth. I let out a sigh. "I'd better stop the sugar high or I'll be up all night with her."

I left Blake and wandered through the growing crowd to find Daisy. Most everyone had showed up, but in looking through the gathering I noticed that Janelle hadn't come. I gave a mental shrug. It was just as well. She and I would probably never get along.

In the sunroom, I observed Samantha talking to Dawson. Regret filled me once more that Dawson was not Daisy's father. It would have made things so simple. He was a wonderful person. I studied his animated face from a distance and was struck by how happy he looked, talking to Samantha.

Come to think of it, Samantha looked pretty content, herself.

A commotion at the front door drew my attention away from them. Lisa staggered into the main room, disheveled and wild-eyed.

"Where is she?" she shouted. "That bitch has ruined my life. Come on out, Allison, wherever you are."

The blood drained from my head. Mortified, I swayed on my feet as everyone in the room turned toward me.

Blake quickly moved to Lisa's side and took her by the elbow.

She jerked free of his grasp. "No! I want to see her!"

I broke through the murmuring crowd on trembling legs. "I'm here, Lisa. Follow me outside and we can talk." My voice cracked with fear, but I managed to walk past her, head held high.

I'd almost reached the edge of the deck when she landed on my back, shoving me down on the wooden surface. Her body kept me pinned in place. Stunned, I lay there, trying to catch my breath.

"Get off her," Blake snarled, jerking Lisa off me. Maintaining a firm grip on Lisa, he waved away the spectators who'd followed us outside.

Furious, I scrambled to my feet and straightened my clothes. "What's going on? Why'd you do that?"

"Catherine ... Catherine ... told me ..." Lisa stopped, struggling with her emotions. She sniffed noisily and drew in a deep breath. "She told me you own everything now—everything I shared with Kristin. There's nothing left."

"Jessie and I own it together," I answered firmly. "I bought into the business after you took off with the money. And with Kristin's death, the assets reverted to me."

Lisa narrowed her eyes. "Kristin never forgave me, did she?"

I lifted my shoulders. "I honestly don't know."

Tears flowed down Lisa's cheeks. "And now Catherine is leaving me. It's all *your* fault!"

"My fault?" My nostrils flared. "What are you talking about?"

"You've ruined everything. But I'm still fighting for Daisy. She's one thing you're not taking away from me."

My stomach twisted. I stared into Lisa's glassy drunken eyes. "We'll see about that, won't we?"

Lisa seemed to shrink in size. "What the fuck," she muttered and walked unsteadily away from us.

I almost felt sorry for her.

Blake put his arm around me. "Are you all right?"

I looked down at my ripped pants and leaned into him, bruised and sore. "I'm doing better than my new outfit."

He used a napkin to gently wipe a trace of blood from my cheek. "When she threw you down like that, I wanted to crunch her."

Samantha pushed through the crowd of people still gathered by the open door. "Are you all right, Allie?" She held onto Daisy's hand.

I nodded. Noticing Daisy's tear-streaked face, I knelt on stiff knees to face her. She threw herself into my arms.

"I don't like Lisa."

"It's all right, Daisy," I murmured, as shaken as she. Resolve filled me. This was a time of celebration. I looked up at Blake. "Let's get this party rolling again."

He helped me to my feet.

Samantha put an arm around me. "Bet I can out-dance you tonight."

I laughed, even though it hurt to do so.

CHAPTER TWENTY TWO

The building and decks once more filled with the sounds of happy party-goers enjoying good food, wine and conversations. Music sang out from strategically placed speakers among the greenery outside, helping to lighten the atmosphere.

Aunt Penny approached me. “That dreadful woman was once associated with Kristin, wasn’t she?”

“She thought she was going to take over the estate by having legal guardianship of Daisy.”

“Still no word on the father?”

“Unfortunately, no. But I haven’t given up on finding him.”

She patted me on the back. “Good girl. Go for it.”

She left me, and I wandered over to Jessie.

“Are you okay?” she asked me.

I put on my brightest smile. “Guess I need a piece of chocolate.”

She laughed and went on her way.

Samantha came over to me. “Daisy’s real tired. I’ll take her home. Dawson said he’d drop us off.” The flush of pleasure on Samantha’s face as Dawson joined us made me smile.

“Okay, see you guys later.”

I bent to kiss Daisy goodnight, and straightened in time to observe Dawson reach for Samantha’s hand. Well, I’ll be darned, I thought. Wouldn’t it be nice if those two got together?

By the end of the evening, the party had not only been a success, but the whole concept of Sweet Talk was about to take off. The local papers promised to feature us in their weekend columns after we officially opened. Two television networks, one of them the local Food Channel, said they would call to make arrangements to do special programs on Sweet Talk.

After the last guests left, I thanked Margaret and Stu and the rest of the staff, hugged Jessie goodnight and went to say goodnight to Blake.

"I'll drive you home." He helped Aunt Penny into his car.

Grateful, I climbed into the backseat.

"Janelle didn't make it, I see," said Penny.

I shrugged. "I'm not surprised. She was so angry with Blake and me."

"Too bad Lisa showed up." Blake let out a snort of disgust.

"Dreadful woman," added Penny. "I simply can't imagine little Daisy living with her."

Blake pulled to a stop at my house and got out of the car to give me a hand. My body stiff with pain, I walked slowly to the front door.

He bent down to give me a kiss and I felt the familiar heat of his lips. We reluctantly separated. "See you tomorrow," he said, mindful of Aunt Penny waiting in the car. He winked. "And when we're alone, I'll make up for this lame kiss."

I laughed but my body tingled at the thought.

The ringing of the phone shattered the silence in the dark room where I lay sleeping. My eyes flew open. Heart pounding, I reached for the phone. Middle-of-the-night phone calls were never good.

"H-h-hello?" I sat up, blinking rapidly as Jessie's voice broke through the fog in my brain. "Okay, I'll be right there. First, I'll call Blake." All traces of sleep were gone as I scrambled out of bed and dialed his number.

He mumbled a sleepy hello.

"Blake, this is an emergency," I blurted out. "Jessie called. Someone attempted to set fire to Sweet Talk. We have to get down there right away."

"Christ! Who would do such a thing?" he said, alert now.

"Do you think Lisa returned and tried to get back at us?"

"Maybe so. I'll get dressed and see you there."

I hung up the phone and hastily slipped into jeans and a sweater. Careful not to disturb them, I checked on Daisy and Samantha, still sleeping soundly. Downstairs, I scribbled a note to Samantha and let myself out into the fading night. Stars sparkled in the sky above as I concentrated on making my stiff limbs move as rapidly as possible down the road to Sweet Talk. A fire engine was parked in front of Treasures. I hurried over to it and then ran into the backyard. Jessie rushed over to me and grabbed my hands. "They've discovered gasoline-soaked rags around the perimeter of the decking, but nothing like that inside. Apparently, whoever did this tried to break in, but was afraid to set off the alarm."

"What happened?"

"Thank God, I wasn't sleeping well," she explained. "When I got up for a drink of water, sometime around two o'clock, I saw someone prowling around the Sweet Talk building. I ran onto my deck and hollered down to them. They took off in a hurry. I went downstairs to investigate and smelled gasoline. That's when I called the fire department."

"Did you see who it was?" My stomach turned at the thought of our hard-won investment going up in flames.

"Not clearly. The outdoor lights had turned off. Something must be wrong with the automatic timers."

"Or someone tampered with them."

My thoughts focused on Lisa. I'd first met her when she and Kristin were living with each other, right after Daisy was born. Her manner back then was rough, but not vindictive, not like it was today. She'd had high hopes of becoming a famous artist, someone the world would respect. Years of failing to achieve her dreams had made her angry. Or maybe Catherine's leaving had pushed her over the edge.

Blake drove up. He trotted over to us. "Who do you think would do something like this?"

"My bet is on Lisa."

The sky grew rosy with early morning light. The orange tone it cast around us gave me the eerie sensation of seeing flames lick the sides of Sweet Talk. My breath caught.

Blake reached over and squeezed my hand. "I'm going to talk to the Chief." He strode away, toward the Fire Chief who was deep in discussion with a couple of his men.

"Who do you think did this?" I asked Jessie, wrapping my arms around myself to stop my nervous shivering. "Do you suppose it was Lisa?"

She shook her head. "I don't think so. It was too dark to see well, but it looked like someone smaller."

I blinked in surprise. "If not Lisa, who else would it be?"

Jessie held out her hands in a helpless gesture. "I've racked my brain, trying to figure it out. I can't even guess."

I kicked at the ground with a sneaker. I hated the thought, but had to voice it. "Do you think it could have been Janelle?"

Jessie shrugged. "It doesn't seem like her."

"She was very upset over Blake ..."

"Allison! Jessie! Come here!"

Jessie and I sprinted over to Blake.

He held up an oil-soaked rag and handed it to me. "Isn't this yours?"

I unraveled the bright blue rag. I'd seen it before. But where? All at once, it hit me. I'd worn that shirt once, when I'd unexpectedly stayed overnight at Blake's house, the night a car accident had blocked my way home. I'd retrieved it from among other items of women's clothing in the guestroom closet. "It doesn't belong to me. I borrowed it one night from the guest closet in your house." I handed the shirt back to him. "Is it your sister's? Or Janelle's?"

"Maybe Janelle did this. Has she been to Silver Goose recently?" Jessie gave him a troubled look.

Blake shifted his weight and shot us an uncomfortable glance. "She came out to the house yesterday morning to pick up the things she left when she'd acted as hostess for me. She was really pissed about me and Allison. I guess that's why she never showed up at the party."

Jessie and I looked at each other, wide-eyed. Destroying Sweet Talk was a way to get back at both Blake and me.

Jessie narrowed her eyes, as angry as I'd ever seen her. "Let's confront her right now."

Blake caught hold of her arm. "We have nothing but circumstantial evidence at best. But that shouldn't stop us from doing some investigation on our own."

Jessie let out a defeated breath. "You're right. Besides, I have a feeling Lisa is involved in some way. Janelle seems like such a quiet, nice person; I can't imagine her doing anything like this."

"I wouldn't put it past her." I'd felt truly threatened by her in the past.

Jessie patted me on the back. "Thank God, no real damage was done. Like Blake says, we'll do our own investigation and find the culprit."

"Yes, but whoever did this could try again. We can't let that happen." Sweet Talk was more than a building to me; it was the culmination of a dream.

"We won't allow it to be destroyed." Blake's jaw was set. "Trust me."

I gazed at the rising sun. "I'd better go back to Daisy and Samantha." I hugged Jessie. "Thanks for being here."

"Need a ride?" Blake asked.

"No, thanks. You'd better stay here with Jessie and deal with the fire department."

I left them, eager to flex my tension-taut muscles. I needed some time to myself. I'd had a fright I couldn't shake off. I'd put my heart and soul, my entire future into Sweet Talk. If it failed, I didn't know how I could survive.

Daisy was watching television and Samantha was busy in the kitchen, making coffee when I arrived home. Daisy cried out, ran over and grabbed my legs, clinging to me with her sturdy little arms.

I lifted her tear-streaked face. "What's wrong?"

"Where were you? You weren't here!" she wailed.

"There was a problem down at Sweet Talk. I had to make sure everything was all right." I squeezed her tightly. "Samantha was here with you. I would never leave you all alone." I brushed her damp curls away from her face, well aware how traumatic her visit with Lisa must have been. It angered me all over again. I gave Daisy another reassuring hug and strolled into the kitchen.

Samantha handed me a cup of coffee. "Sit down. You look terrible. What's up?"

I told her the whole story.

"What do the people from the fire department have to say?" Samantha's voice was heavy with concern.

"Blake and Jessie will get a full report, but the consensus among us is that whoever it was couldn't get inside and was afraid to set off any alarms. Personally, I think it was Lisa. There's something so violent about her."

Samantha frowned. "Do you need some kind of ongoing protection? You know, something like a security officer?"

I shrugged. The thought of hiring guards to watch the building had entered my mind, but I hadn't discussed it with the others. "We'll have the lights fixed and maybe install more. It's pretty expensive to pay for guards."

Samantha gave me a little punch in the arm. "Sister, dear, I'm not talking about the buildings. I'm talking about you."

My eyes went wide. "You think she'd come after me?"

"She already did. Remember?"

The coffee that had slid down my throat so easily, churned inside. Had it come to that?

"It's something to talk about, Allie. You may think you're getting rid of me soon, but I'm not leaving here until I know things are all right."

The see-saw of emotions I'd experienced during the last week bubbled out. I embraced her. "I love you, Samantha. I really do. You're the best sister in the whole world."

She hugged me back. "You're my only sister, remember? I'm not ready to lose you."

Fear shot through me as another thought struck. "Do you think Daisy is safe?"

Samantha paused, and I could see her mind working. "The way I see it, this is between you and Lisa. She doesn't really want Daisy. Besides, neither one of us is going to let her out of our sight, right?"

My jaw clenched. I could handle myself if it came to a showdown between Lisa and me. But I didn't want anything bad to happen to Daisy.

I'd just stepped out of the shower when Samantha knocked on the bathroom door. "You'd better come downstairs. We have visitors."

I cracked open the door. "Visitors? Who are you talking about?"

"Blue uniforms. Hurry up and get dressed. They want to

speak to you."

I hastily donned clothes and ran fingers through my wet hair, wondering why the police wanted to talk to me. Had they found some other clue at Sweet Talk?

Hank Harrison and Ginger Wyatt, two deputies I knew through the wine festival, smiled at me perfunctorily.

"I've offered them coffee ..." Samantha said.

"Good idea," I interrupted her. "Let's go onto the back deck where we can have some privacy." I indicated Daisy with a nod of my head. She stared at us and went back to her television show.

The officers followed me into the kitchen and out onto the deck where Blake and I had cavorted in the hot tub not so long ago.

Hank and Ginger politely declined the chairs I indicated. Samantha and I leaned back against the railing, facing them. I felt better with Samantha at my side.

"How well did you know Lisa Vaughn?" Hank asked. "I understand she was an uninvited guest at your party last night."

"That's true." I was uncertain how much I should say.

"What is this about, officer?" Samantha asked. "Has something happened to her?"

"Unfortunately, she was killed in an automobile accident early this morning."

I gasped. "Killed? How? When? Was anyone else hurt?"

"We figured the time was around three o'clock this morning," Ginger said. "A single car crash. She was the only occupant of the car."

"We're attempting to piece together the details of her last hours," interjected Hank. "Everyone in town is talking about the incident at your party last night."

"Do you have any reason to suspect that my sister is

involved in any way?" Samantha's expression was as stern as I'd ever seen.

Hank held up a hand. "No, no, nothing like that. As I said, we simply want to understand her last hours. We would like to know, however, if she was served any alcohol at your party."

My mind was still trying to grasp the idea that Lisa was dead. Numbly, I reviewed the incident at Sweet Talk.

"She was pretty drunk when she arrived at the party. I don't know if any drugs were involved, but she reeked of alcohol. Right after our scuffle, she left. No drinks from Sweet Talk were given to her."

"Was she driving a car when she took off?"

I shook my head. "I don't know. I didn't see her get into one. She simply walked away—a bit unsteadily."

"There are a couple of hours unaccounted for. We think she went back to the motel where she was staying. We do know she was seen there shortly before three o'clock. She didn't make it far."

Dizziness made me queasy.

"I'm sorry, Allison," said Ginger. "I know how difficult this must be for you, after all you went through with her."

I looked at her, feeling so conflicted I could hardly speak. "I never wanted Lisa dead. I only wanted her to let me take care of Daisy, like Kristin asked."

"If you think of anything we should know, be in touch." Hank tipped his hat. "It's simply a matter of making a thorough report. We're in conversation with the Fire Department about the incident last night."

"I'll show you out," said Samantha, leaving me in a daze.

Lisa was dead. Relief mixed with horror. For the moment, I didn't have to worry about Daisy's care. Todd Schaeffer would help see to that. My mind spun again. That wasn't the end of it. My mission to find Daisy's father wasn't over. Not yet. I'd already promised Daisy I'd try to find him. I couldn't go back on that. A promise was a promise.

CHAPTER TWENTY THREE

Blake and Jessie joined me in the office of Treasures to discuss the news of Lisa's accident.

"I can't believe it." Jessie shook her head. "I guess one good thing that came out of it was that Daisy doesn't have to live with her." She turned to me. "And you can give up the hunt for her father."

"It's too late. I'd already spoken to Daisy about finding her father. She's excited about it and is convinced I'll succeed. I can't let her down." I glanced at Blake.

He looked away.

Somehow I had to convince him to have his DNA tested—for Daisy's sake and my own peace of mind.

We discussed and rejected the idea of delaying the official opening of Sweet Talk. There was rapid agreement to temporarily hire a security company to patrol the area, and after setting up a work schedule for the remainder of the week, we ended our meeting.

"We have a couple of hours before we have to open," Jessie said. "Anybody for going down to the dock for coffee and a bit of gossip?"

Blake checked his watch. "Can't. I have to get back to Penny."

I shrugged. "I'll go for a short while. Samantha and Daisy have made plans to take Coalie out to Dawson's place so the dog can run around."

Jessie shot me a mischievous grin. "Samantha and Dawson? Now there's an interesting thought."

I laughed. “You never know.”

Sitting on the dock at the marina, I was well aware of the discreet glances cast our way. Word had filtered through town about Lisa’s fight with me and her subsequent accident early this morning. I wanted to put on a brave face, but I couldn’t hide my distress. I glanced at the filled chairs scattered around the deck.

“Where’s Janelle? She’s usually part of the Sunday morning crowd.”

Jessie pressed her lips together. “I’m going to find out exactly where she was last night. It isn’t like her to miss out on a party.” She took out her cell phone and punched in a number. After a few seconds, Jessie clicked off her phone. “Odd. There’s no answer and no voice mail.”

I left her at the dock and walked toward home, my mind racing. If Janelle had attempted to damage Sweet Talk, I’d have to resolve the issues between us. Who knew what else she might be doing to undermine our hard work.

Samantha, Daisy and Coalie were gone when I arrived home. The house seemed unnaturally quiet. I sat on the front porch, staring at the blue water below me. Everything had turned out so differently from what I’d envisioned. I had two businesses to oversee, not one; a tough little girl to take care of; and a man I adored who gave me no promises for the future. Sitting there, alone, I missed Kristin so much I ached. I longed to see her, to tell her everything, to assure her that I would make sure Daisy was all right.

Sighing heavily, I rose and went inside to get ready for work.

As I was about to close the gallery, Samantha and Daisy walked in.

"Let's relax at Sweet Talk for a while," said Samantha. I knew from the tone of her voice she had something on her mind.

"Sure. Let's go."

Stu greeted us when we walked in.

"How're things going?" I asked, silently counting the number of customers on the nearby deck. Twenty people on a Sunday afternoon wasn't bad for a brand new business.

"It's been okay," he responded, handing us a menu. "Debbie Swanson's Chocolate, Chocolate Wine Bars are a big hit. They go well with either coffee or wine. Myself? I like the Silver Goose cab with them. Wanna try one?"

"Sure." After the busy afternoon I'd had, it sounded perfect. Wine and chocolate. Yum.

Samantha ordered Cokes for her and Daisy, and we took seats in the corner of the sunroom away from everyone else.

Jessie came out of the kitchen, saw us and came right over. "How did we do at Treasures?"

"Great. I sold a watercolor by Beth Sinclair, some assorted pottery, and lots of the new jewelry we got in. We'll have to order more."

Jessie smiled. "We're doing okay here. I'm about ready to leave. Margaret is due any minute." She put her arm around Daisy. "Want to come up to the apartment? I've got some wedding gifts to show you."

Daisy's eyes rounded with pleasure. "Can I, Allie?"

"Sure." I was happy she and Jessie had become so close, sharing the excitement of the wedding.

Daisy skipped happily after Jessie. I turned to Samantha. "Daisy is going to be the flower girl for Jessie and Rob's wedding."

Samantha stared at me. "I wanted to talk to you alone. Dawson and I were talking about Daisy earlier today. He's so disappointed he's not the father. Don't you think it's time to ask Blake to be tested? You said you have to follow through on this, even though Lisa's threat has now disappeared."

"You think Blake's the father, don't you?"

She nodded slowly. "Otherwise, it doesn't make sense for him to refuse to be tested."

I started to defend him, and stopped. In light of the present situation, I agreed with her. It was crucial that Blake cooperate—to be either confirmed or eliminated as Daisy's remaining parent.

Samantha gave me a sly look. "It would be great if he was Daisy's father."

I smiled. It would make life so much simpler.

Soon after we arrived back home, Blake dropped by on his way back from taking Penny to the airport. He waved hello to Samantha and gave me a kiss that told me he couldn't wait to be alone.

"Look what Coalie can do!" said Daisy.

Blake squatted beside Daisy while she showed him how Coalie lifted a paw to be shaken. The dog eagerly licked both of them, wagging her tail in a loud thumping rhythm as if she knew they were talking about her. Studying Blake and Daisy, I noticed once again they shared the same bright blue eyes.

Daisy left us to go down to the lawn to throw a ball for Coalie, and Blake joined Samantha and me, taking over one of the rocking chairs on the porch.

"How was business?" he asked me.

I gave him a rundown of the day.

He grinned. "We'll continue to play off one enterprise with another. Silver Goose can send people your way and Treasures can encourage people to stop by Sweet Talk before they leave. It makes for good synergy."

"I thought the fiasco at the party last night would ruin

business today, but lots of local people came by. Even though we aren't officially open yet, they seem to like what we've done. A few asked about the attempted arson, but we said nothing much about it."

"Good. Let's keep it that way."

Samantha tapped Blake on the shoulder. "I want you to promise me you'll keep Allison safe. I don't want to leave without being assured she'll be protected. Allie mentioned you're going to hire AAA Security to patrol the buildings. What about her? Do you think someone should watch this house?"

Blake's face turned white. He turned to me. "My God! Have you been threatened?"

I shook my head. "Samantha thinks someone might be after me. I'm not worried about myself so much; I want Daisy to be safe."

"Who do you think did this?" Samantha asked, pressing her case. "Is there someone the police should be talking to?"

Blake swiped at his hair and let out a sigh. "I can't think of anyone else."

"Jessie is determined to find out where Janelle was that night. But I've been wondering if it has anything to do with my wanting to find Daisy's father."

"Why would that be an issue?"

I shrugged. "I'm reaching for straws, I guess."

Samantha jumped up. "I'm going to make a pot of coffee. Any takers?"

"I'll have some. Thanks," said Blake.

Left alone with him, I decided to get right to the point. "Blake, I need you to go ahead and have your DNA tested. Now that we know Dawson is not the father, it's important to both Daisy and me to know if you're her father or not."

"I don't know..."

I persisted. "Is there the slightest chance you might be? You and Kristin were very close when she first came to California ..."

He leaned back in his chair and gazed up at the porch ceiling. "There was one time ... yeah, maybe ..."

Disappointment shot through me. I told myself to let it go, that I'd known all along from the way Kristin had kept silent about him that there must have been more than friendship between them. The past is the past, I reminded myself, and hated the sense of betrayal I felt.

"So will you do it?"

Blake studied me. "That's what you really want?"

"Yes. I promised Daisy I'd find him."

Samantha appeared, carrying a tray with three cups of coffee. She glanced at me. "Everything okay?"

I nodded, my emotions struggling for balance. If Blake really were Daisy's father, I wasn't sure how I'd feel about it.

My mind spun one twisted scenario after another as I lay in bed, caught in a tangle of dreams. In one, Janelle triumphantly embraced Blake after he realized how much she loved him. In another, Blake claimed ownership of Daisy and pushed me aside as an unfit mother. In still another, I was trapped inside Sweet Talk while flames burned bright and hot. I whimpered and tossed and turned, lost in an unhappy world of my mind's own making.

"Hey, Sis! What's wrong?"

I jolted upright and stared at my sister in a daze. "What happened?"

"You screamed!" She glanced nervously around the darkened room. "You scared me to death."

I struggled to bring myself fully awake. Drawing in a shaky

breath, I looked up at her. "What am I going to do? I'm so mixed up. I want Blake to be Daisy's father, yet, I don't want to know if he is."

Samantha sat down on the edge of the bed and shook my shoulder. "Snap out of it, Allie. We Hartwell women can face anything as long as it's the truth. What are you afraid of? You don't think Blake loves you? He doesn't have to say a word. The way he looks at you tells a whole story of its own. And, honey, it's a whale of a tale."

I let out a long sigh. "It's that after Will, I won't know what to think if he and Kristin..."

"Stop it, Sis." Samantha shook me again. "This is about Daisy, remember?"

"Remember? How could I forget?" I whispered in an effort to keep from shouting in frustration.

The minute I spoke the words I regretted it. I was healthy and alive while one of my dearest friends was dead, never to see her child grow up, to hear her laughter, to feel her arms hugging her.

"Oh, God ... I'm sorry ..."

Samantha patted me on the back. "It's okay, Allie. It's okay."

But it wouldn't be okay until I had the answers to so many questions.

The next couple of days passed quickly, with little to destroy the fun of having Samantha with Daisy and me. When it came time for her to leave, I filled with sadness. Fatigue, worry, lack of self-confidence and love in bloom made me very fragile. And yet, in some ways, I felt stronger than ever.

She gave me a last hug before slipping into the taxi she'd insisted upon taking to the airport. I watched the cab travel down the road, waving until it was out of sight. As I walked back inside the house, I thought of the days ahead. School was almost out for the year, and then Daisy was off to Los Angeles with Jessie for the bridal shower.

Resigned to the chores of making the house right again, I loaded sheets and towels into the washing machine and grabbed the vacuum cleaner. The sound of the telephone halted my steps. I set down the equipment and lifted the receiver. "Yes?"

"Allison?"

At the sound of the familiar voice, I gasped softly. "Will? What do you want? Why are you calling?"

"I'm in San Francisco, with Liz. We're back together. Can we come and see you? It's important."

I hesitated, wondering how to respond politely.

"I know it may seem a bit awkward, me calling and all, but like I said, it's really important. We're driving out to Sausalito anyway, so we'll come on to Sarita. How about we meet you for lunch?"

No way did I want to have lunch with Willard Jackson III and the old and new love of his life. I paused, wondering how I could avoid it. He was so persistent. "If you insist upon coming, you can meet me at the gallery I own. It's called Treasures."

"Oh, I know all about it. I've caught up with the details of your life. Your mother filled me in."

I hated the smugness of his tone. My mother, bless her, would never be rude to anyone. I could almost hear her cheerfully recite all my recent successes to Will rather than hang up on him.

Resigned to seeing him, I let out a long sigh. "Okay. Meet me at two o'clock."

I hung up and collapsed in a chair.

###

The clock on the wall of the gallery seemed totally unaware of my wish for it to slow down. All too soon, two o'clock approached. When I heard the sound of car doors slamming, I wiped my sweaty hands on my slacks and peered out the window.

Will and Liz stood outside, looking around and talking quietly.

I called good-bye to Jessie, went to the door and stepped outside.

"Hello, Will, Liz." My voice sounded as cold as I felt.

They turned in guilty surprise, as if I'd caught them in the middle of some lewd act. I frowned, wondering for the umpteenth time what had prompted this unexpected visit.

"You're looking well, Allison." As good-looking as ever, Will moved toward me with a smile.

I forced a pleasant smile in return.

"You remember Liz ..."

My voice lowered. "Oh, yes."

We hadn't seen each other in over a year and a half. Before then, I'd only had glimpses of her, but her presence was well known to me. She was everything I was not—small and curvy, dark hair, dark eyes.

"Nice setup," said Will. "Do you want to go inside?"

I shook my head. "Let's walk around to Sweet Talk. It's quiet today. We can talk there."

"Sweet Talk? Oh, yeah, that's the chocolate and wine bar. Your mother told me about that," commented Will.

Walking to the cottage, I studied Will out of the corner of my eye. With his dark eyes and dark brown hair slicked back, he was a handsome man. Only the slight curl of his thin lips reminded me of the cruel person he'd become during his unhappy time with me. Today his smile seemed genuine, his happiness real. I was almost glad for him.

I ushered him and Liz onto the deck and waved at Margaret, who appeared at the door.

"Can I get you anything?" she asked.

I turned to Will. "What will you have? We have a marvelous selection of Silver Goose wines and an array of desserts—any kind, though chocolate is the specialty here."

Will's eyes lit up. "How about a brownie? I'll take that and a glass of wine."

Liz patted her flat stomach. "Just red wine for me."

I placed an order with Margaret and waited until she'd served us before saying, "Why are you here, Will?"

"Liz and I got married at Christmas. She was seven months pregnant." His face became unreadable as he took hold of her hand.

Liz's eyes filled with tears. "There was an accident. I can't have any more children."

"Oh, I'm sorry to hear that." I was genuinely sad for her.

Will's expression softened. "You're nice, Allison. Know that? I told Liz you'd be sympathetic. I'm counting on that."

"What do you mean?" I was uncomfortable at the pleading I read in his eyes.

As if to reassure himself, Will glanced over at Liz. "We really want to have a family and thought maybe you could help."

My eyebrows shot up. "What? You want me to act as a reference for adoption? Is that it?"

He shifted in his chair. "Not exactly." He looked away from me.

Uneasy, I glanced at Liz.

She leaned forward, an intent expression on his face. "What he's trying to say is that we want you to be involved."

"Involved?" My blood pounded as suspicion crawled through me.

"I'd never have chosen you for a wife if I didn't know all your good qualities, Allison. You'd make a perfect mother."

The blood left my face so quickly I gripped the arm rests of my chair. "You mean ..."

I choked. "Are you talking about my being a surrogate mother?"

"You could do it! It would almost be like being married again. See?"

I jumped to my feet, wanting to get away from him as fast as I could. When it came to my feelings, he still had no idea of decency. Outraged, I stared wordlessly at him.

Margaret approached us. "Is everything all right? Can I get you anything else?"

"Take care of them, will you?" I said crisply. "I'm leaving."

"No! Wait, Allison!" Will cried, jumping to his feet. "Can't we at least discuss it?"

Furious, I whirled around. "No, we can't discuss it. Didn't my mother tell you I'm already in a family way?"

The surprise on his face was worth the twisted meaning. I stalked away.

Feeling as if I'd been splashed by mud, I raced back into the gallery. Jessie looked up from rearranging items in a cabinet and stared at me in surprise.

"Where are your guests?"

"Gone, I hope."

Hiding out in the back office, I proceeded to tell her the whole story.

"Oh, honey," said Jessie when I'd finished. "I don't know whether to laugh or cry."

"Neither do I," I said, and promptly burst into tears.

CHAPTER TWENTY FOUR

Blake arrived at my house and I hurried onto my front porch to greet him. He smiled and opened his arms. I rushed into them. Nestled against his chest, I considered him the kindest, most decent man I'd ever met. He had none of the selfish traits I detested in Will.

"Hey! Are you all right?" He lifted my chin and gazed down at me.

"Will, my ex, came to see me this afternoon. He and Liz, his new wife, asked me to become a surrogate mother for them."

Blake's eyes widened with surprise. "You're kidding. Right?"

I shook my head. "I'm afraid not. Ever since they left, I've been stewing about his attitude toward me. He's never really understood my feelings about so many things."

"It still has you pretty upset, huh?"

I puffed out an angry breath. "He has no idea what motherhood is all about. I couldn't make a baby and give it away. I just couldn't."

"Obviously, you told him no."

"Yes. I never want to see or talk to him again."

Daisy came running out of the house toward us. Coalie pranced at her heels. My body filled with pleasure as Daisy threw her arms around my legs. Coalie stood by, barking with excitement. This, I thought, is what motherhood is all about.

"Blake! Come see my new suitcase! I got it for the shower trip!" Daisy tugged on his hand. Laughing, he allowed himself to be led inside.

Later, after Daisy was asleep, I stretched out on the couch beside Blake. He put his arms around me. I leaned into him, inhaling the spicy scent of his aftershave—clean and manly.

"I had my mouth swabbed for the DNA test this afternoon," Blake murmured. "I knew it was important to you."

I pulled back and studied him. "What will you do if Daisy is your daughter?"

He waggled a finger. "I don't think she is, but if so, I'll do the right thing by her."

He planted his lips on mine. His fingers played with the buttons on my shirt. I groaned softly and forced myself to move away from him.

"We can't take the chance," I whispered. "Daisy's been waking up several times in the night. We have to wait until this weekend, when Daisy's in LA."

Blake rose to his feet. "Time I was going, anyway. We've got a problem with the irrigation system. Juan and I have to tackle it first thing tomorrow. It looks like there won't be rain for a while." He let out a sigh. "It's always something."

"Well, you don't have to worry about Sweet Talk. It's in good hands. Margaret and Stu are doing a wonderful job, and business should become even better. Jessie and I are finalizing the new advertising program we discussed."

"Good thing you're on it. We're busier than ever at the winery. More and more bookings are being made at The Manor House. The new chef is great."

"Who's acting as hostess now that Janelle is no longer there?"

"Lucille Carter, Claire's mother." He smiled. "She loves it and the customers really like her."

"Still no word on Janelle?"

Blake shook his head. "Nobody has seen her for several days now."

"Strange, isn't it?"

"Yeah, well, sooner or later we'll find out if she's the one who tried to burn down the wine bar. And when we do, I suggest we take swift action."

"And if it isn't her?"

"My bet is still on Lisa. But we won't let our guard down." He put his arm around me and at the door he gave me a lingering kiss that made me want to beg him to stay.

The next couple of days passed in a flurry of activity. Jessie worked overtime to finalize the advertising campaign, while I unloaded fresh inventory, including a few wine-related gift items we'd decided to display and sell at Sweet Talk.

Claire had agreed to help me with Treasures while Jessie and Daisy were in LA. She was working part-time until Jessie left. I watched her carefully tag the new items. Only eighteen, she'd opted to work while she decided what course of study she wanted to take at a state college. Bright and mature for her age, she was the best worker we had. She'd been working at Silver Goose since she was sixteen, adored kids and was great with Daisy. A perfect fit.

She and I sat on the deck of the wine bar, discussing the upcoming schedule.

"Jessie and Rob are getting married in four weeks?"

"The 5th of July. A bang-up wedding, as Rob teasingly says."

Claire laughed. "Daisy showed me the dress she's going to wear."

I smiled. Daisy was ecstatic about being in the wedding. Halloween was nothing compared to being dressed up like a princess for a real occasion.

"If we get real busy, my sister Annie can help out," Claire said. "She's looking for work."

"Great. I guess with your mother working at Silver Goose as hostess, it's become a family affair to work for us."

"Mom loves the new job," Claire said with a note of pride. "Janelle is the one who recommended her. Good thing, too, since she's taken off for Washington State."

I sat up straighter. "Washington? What are you talking about?"

"Mom got a postcard from Janelle this morning. She's applying for a job at Chateau St. Michelle winery in Woodinville, outside Seattle. Why?"

I attempted to sound casual but my whole body was on alert. "We wondered why she didn't come to the party."

"According to my mom, she was already on her way to Seattle."

We continued to discuss schedules and inventory, but my mind lingered on the news of Janelle. If she'd left before the party, she couldn't be the one who'd attempted arson.

I talked to Jessie and Blake about it. We agreed Lisa was, no doubt, the one who'd set the fire. Blake talked to the Fire Chief. Their investigation led them to believe the rag had come from an overflowing Goodwill drop-off box near the motel. That gave us an additional reason to think the culprit was Lisa. It made sense. There'd been no other attacks since then. For me, it was another reason to be glad Daisy wouldn't ever have to live with her.

The night before Daisy was to depart for LA, I carefully packed her clothes, making sure her black patent-leather party shoes were buffed, the blue sundress folded neatly and her lacy nightgown in place. I shampooed and dried her hair, reveling in the beauty of her natural blond curls as I pulled a comb through them. My thoughts strayed to Blake. He had blond hair, though of a darker shade. Was this another reason to think he might be Daisy's father? My feelings torn, I trailed my finger down Daisy's nose. Its upturned style wasn't at all like Blake's.

Daisy and I talked quietly as she lay in bed, waiting to fall asleep. Gently, I probed her thoughts about going on another trip so soon after her bad experience in Santa Fe.

"Jessie and I are going to have fun," Daisy assured me. "I'm going to meet all of Rob's nieces. There's a girl my age named Megan. Jessie said so."

I smiled and listened as Daisy repeated one thing after another that Jessie had told her. Knowing she would be well cared for and happy, I thought ahead to a special weekend alone with Blake. It would be wonderful to have some free time with him.

Early the next morning, Jessie and Rob came to the house to pick up Daisy. Daisy knelt and put her arms around Coalie, and straightened for my hug. Her eyes sparkled with excitement as she pulled away from me and ran ahead to greet Jessie.

I handed Jessie a box of Bellano chocolates I'd had specially made for the occasion. Each chocolate morsel had a white swirl on top in the shape of a wedding bell.

"I'll be thinking of you. Have fun."

Jessie gave me a hug. "Thanks for taking care of the businesses."

"Better hurry back!"

She laughed, and I waved good-bye until the car drew too far away for Daisy to see me.

I went inside, grabbed a cup of hot coffee and went out to the back deck. As I sat down, I heard the sound of a car door slamming. I smiled. Blake.

I rose and went to greet him.

Seeing me, a wide grin creased his face. “Has the weekend begun?”

I laughed, as eager for time alone as he. “We’ve got exactly one hour before I have to open the gallery.”

“No problem,” he teased, giving me that sexy smile of his. “It’ll only take me a few minutes.”

“Like hell it will.” I grinned. “Follow me.”

Upstairs, he proceeded to demonstrate how wonderfully he’d understood what taking it slow could mean.

With the hour up, I breathlessly ran down the road to Treasures, barely arriving in time for my first customer.

I had no time to think of anything else as the day spun with customers coming and going at both locations. That afternoon, I hung around the gallery long enough to assure myself that Claire knew all the procedures for closing. Margaret was on standby at Sweet Talk, if Claire needed her, and Stu was on duty.

I picked up Coalie at the house and headed out to Silver Goose. In addition to my suitcase, the car was filled with a collection of items from Treasures to sell at the tasting barn.

As I drove between the stone pillars into the Silver Goose parking lot, I appreciated once more what a remarkable job Blake had done in just ten years, The amount of work involved in running a winery like his, with the retail and hospitality functions rolled into it, was unbelievable.

I parked the car, let Coalie out, and went to find Blake.

He was on the phone when I knocked and opened his office door. His face lit with pleasure when he saw me. He cupped his fingers over the phone. “I’ll be with you shortly. Have someone help you carry your things inside.”

I left him to go downstairs. The tasting barn attracted a more eclectic group of customers than the gallery, but the idea of selling featured items from Treasures was working.

One of the salesclerks followed me out to my SUV and lifted a box of merchandise out of the back. I followed, carefully holding an acrylic painting by a local artist known for his countryside scenes. Inside, I helped the clerk put the new items into the electronic inventory. I wanted everything to be done right. Sales from Silver Goose were making a big difference in our budget, allowing us to purchase more selective items to sell.

I was in the midst of hanging the painting upstairs, when I felt arms wrap around me. Turning, I smiled into Blake's blue eyes. He gave me a light kiss on the lips. "You'd better come with me into my office. I have something to tell you."

My hands grew cold. I almost dropped the painting. "You got the results of the DNA test?"

"I have an in with someone at the lab."

At the worried expression on his face, my heart thumped wildly. I put down the painting and followed him.

Blake closed the door behind us and faced me. "Exactly as I thought, it's not me, Allison. I'm not Daisy's father. When you came in, I was talking to Todd Schaeffer for legal advice regarding Daisy. Technically, she'll become a ward of the state until guardianship is established legally. He thinks it shouldn't be a problem for her to stay with you, but I would hate to see any interference on the part of the state."

Ice ran through my veins. I'd hoped a positive test result from Blake would give us an easy answer for Daisy's future. The idea that I was back to square one in finding Daisy's father hit me like a blow to the belly. Frightened for Daisy's future, I sank onto the couch in Blake's office.

"What am I going to do? How can I find her father? Why couldn't Kristin have been more open?"

Blake shook his head. "It doesn't make sense to me."

"Are...are you disappointed?" I asked.

Blake's eyebrows rose in surprise. "Not to be Daisy's father? Maybe, a little. It would have made things so easy for all of us." He leaned over and gave me a kiss on the cheek. "I know you're upset, but we can't do anything about it over the weekend. Why don't we enjoy the time we have, and on Monday, after Jessie and Daisy return from LA, we'll sit down with Todd and come up with a plan."

I let out a sigh. Blake was right. Friday evening was not a good time to solve this dilemma.

"I'll help you with the painting, and then let's relax at The Manor House. I've got a special evening planned."

"Okay." I shook off the cloud of gloom that hovered above me.

He offered me his hand. I rose, content to know Daisy was having a good time with Jessie. Somehow I'd find a way to keep her safe with me.

The staff closed up as we finished hanging the painting.

"No activity at The Manor House?"

Blake grinned. "Just you and me. You packed a suitcase?"

"Exactly as you suggested. So what's the surprise?"

He chucked my chin playfully. "If I tell you, it's not a surprise."

I laughed. "Okay. I'll wait. But not for too long."

Pepper wandered over to us. Coalie played at her side, looking happy to be reunited with her mother.

"Nice they can see each other occasionally." Pepper was a good mother I thought, watching her lick Coalie's face.

Blake carried my suitcase and we walked over to The Manor House.

"Why are we staying here?" I asked.

"You'll see."

"That's the surprise?"

Blake chuckled. "You must be an awful pest at Christmas."

I couldn't help laughing. I was known in the family for shaking presents well before Christmas morning.

We entered The Manor House to silence. As Blake had promised, no staff was present, though the aromas drifting from the kitchen indicated the chef had been there earlier.

Blake led me up the wide stairway. Near the top, he stopped. His eyes danced with mischief.

"We've just finished redoing the rooms upstairs. Brides wanted a special place where they and members of their wedding parties can rest and change before the event. We even refurbished one of the rooms into a wedding suite."

Delighted with the idea, I grinned. "Is that the surprise?"

His lips curved. "I wanted to try out the suite before anyone else."

"Perfect." I was touched by his sweet gesture. "Show me the rooms."

I inspected each of the four rooms set aside for brides, enchanted by the special touches each contained. Painted in varying soft, peaceful colors, the rooms held plush couches and chairs and contained oversized closets and marble bathrooms with plenty of lights and mirrors. Tissue dispensers, a selection of expensive perfumes, baskets of snacks, and other amenities were discreetly placed throughout.

"The rooms are beautiful,"

Blake gave me a look of satisfaction. "You haven't seen the last of it. On to the Honeymoon Suite."

He led me to double doors at the end of the hallway and swung them open to reveal a room breathtaking in its elegant simplicity. A mammoth king-sized bed with a tall, carved wooden headboard occupied the center of one wall and was flanked by marble-topped night stands that matched a long dresser and armoire. An Oriental rug in luscious shades of blue complemented a paler blue on the walls. But my eyes didn't remain on the furnishings for long. They were drawn to the French doors that led out to a balcony that I soon discovered overlooked green rolling hills covered with row upon row of grapevines. I drew in a breath of fresh air, redolent with the distinctive, earthy smell of the rich soil surrounding us.

"Beautiful, isn't it?"

I turned to Blake with a smile. "I feel like a member of a royal family, overlooking my kingdom."

He grinned, pleased. "That's what we were hoping for. This room is quiet and private, away from everything else. I wanted us to have the whole house to ourselves tonight so you could feel like the princess you are." Blake's lips came down on mine, and my kisses said more than words ever could.

When we pulled apart, Blake let out a shuddering breath. "We won't get to the rest of the evening, if I don't stop now."

"There's more? Is that why you wanted me to dress for dinner?"

"This *chateau* is ours for the night. Let's make good use of it."

"I agree." I was pleased I'd brought the black dress he'd once admired on me. If dinner was going to be elegant, I wanted to be ready for it.

After freshening up and changing into my dress, I stood in front of the mirror and pulled my hair into a loose knot behind my head so my pearl earrings would show.

Blake came up behind me. "Hmmm, you're looking a little bare."

I gave him a puzzled look, then, gasped with pleasure when he slid a string of pearls around my neck.

"What are these?"

Blake grinned. "Aunt Penny gave them to me to give to you.

They're Mikimoto pearls a gentleman admirer gave her many years ago. She wanted you to have them."

"That's so sweet." I was deeply touched by her generosity. "Why me?"

"She's convinced you're the one for me. When she thought you and I had broken up for good, she phoned and gave me hell."

"So that's the only reason you wanted to get back with me?" I teased. "To please your aunt?"

He grabbed me with mock roughness and pulled me to him. "You know better than that."

I chuckled. I certainly did.

Downstairs, we entered the library to find a bottle of red wine decanted. A tray of little appetizers on a silver tray sat alongside the cut-glass decanter.

Blake poured me a glass of wine and indicated a leather chair in front of the fireplace, which glowed with a small, flickering, gas fire. He filled his glass and sat opposite me.

"Here's to you." He raised his wine glass.

"And to you," I quickly answered, relishing this moment with him.

We took sips of the wine, and Blake cleared his throat. "I've been doing a lot of thinking this week while I awaited the results of the DNA testing for Daisy. It has made me think about the value of family. Like you said, it's so important." Blake gave me a crooked grin that made me want to melt.

We shared more wine and appetizers, and then Blake stood. "I believe dinner awaits us," he said with exaggerated formality. He took my arm, and, playing along, I walked back to the kitchen with him. In a corner, away from all the commercial equipment, sat a small table draped with crisp white linen.

As if he were the maitre d', Blake seated me. "I've been

given strict instructions how the *Boeuf Bourgignon* should be served. The chef threatened me with my life, if I marred his reputation by being so carried away with making love to you that I ruined the meal, like we almost did one night."

Recalling my first dinner at The Manor House, I laughed.

The crisp green salad that followed the main course was tart enough to cleanse my palate, as required, for the light lemon tart that Blake presented for dessert.

Having Blake clear and serve our dishes gave an added sense of intimacy to the meal I found charming. Or, maybe, it was because I loved him so much.

Darkness drew a comfortable cloak around us as we made our way to the Honeymoon Suite. I was mellow from the good food, wine, and the simple pleasure of being together.

"You don't have to do another thing to make me believe I'm a princess. It's been a wonderful evening."

Blake lifted my hand to his lips. "It's not over." His steady gaze sent a shiver of anticipation through me.

He ushered me into the suite and over to the balcony. We leaned against the wrought iron railing, surveying the undulating hills beneath us, silvery in the moonlight. Blake put his arm around me and pulled me close.

"This is mine—my kingdom—all I have to offer you." He smiled and indicated the vineyard with a sweep of his arm. "Will you share it with me?"

I gazed up at him, wide-eyed, my pulse pounding. "Do you mean ...?"

"I love you, Allison. I want you to be my wife."

His look of tenderness brought tears to my eyes. "Oh, yes..." I began and stopped. "It's not only me, you know. It's Daisy, too. Does that make a difference?"

Blake shook his head. "Not anymore. I know how you feel about her and I promise to love her and take care of her, too.

It doesn't matter that I'm not her father in fact; I'll be the real father she never had."

I flung my arms around his neck. "Oh, Blake. Yes, I want to be your wife. I'd be your wife even without this...this kingdom. It's you I want."

He smiled, started to say something and choked up.

"No matter what happens," I said, caressing his cheek, "I will always be here for you. I promise."

"I know," he whispered, and as his lips pressed down on mine, I realized I'd finally won his trust, just as he'd won mine.

We moved from the balcony inside to the large bed and there, Blake and I made a commitment to each other with our bodies.

Afterwards, lying in the darkened room, lit only by moonlight, I thought of the miracle of real love. In an innocent way, Daisy had opened my heart to it.

Blake awakened me with a good morning kiss. "Even princesses have to wake up some time, lazy bones."

I rolled over and smiled up at him. He stood by the bed holding a tray of food.

I sat up and stretched. "What do we have here?"

"A special breakfast. Move over."

He set the tray down on the nightstand and sat on the bed next to me.

"Coffee, Madame?"

"Oh, yes," I answered, continuing to play along with him.

He held up an empty cup and frowned. "Something's not right. Will you check it out?" He handed me the cup.

I gazed into it and let out a gasp of surprise. A huge diamond winked up at me.

"See if it fits." All pretense of the game disappeared. "You didn't give me a chance to give it to you last night, you wanton woman."

I slipped the ring on my finger, admiring the large stone in a simple, modern, platinum setting. "This is good enough for a queen, not a princess." My voice shook with emotion. "It's beautiful."

"*You're* beautiful." Blake pulled me down beside me, and all thoughts of breakfast evaporated in a rush of pleasing sensations.

CHAPTER TWENTY FIVE

Rob's truck pulled into my driveway. All smiles, I hurried outside to show Jessie my diamond. Daisy waved at me from the passenger's side window and jumped down from the truck in a burst of energy.

"Hi, Allie! I had fun!" she cried, running over to me.

"Good." I hugged her to me. "It's great to have you home."

"I know." Daisy dashed away from me, across the lawn toward the house. Coalie pranced at her heels.

Rob came from around the truck, a grim expression on his face.

"Where's Jessie?" I asked.

"Her place. We've had a fight, and I'll be damned if I know what it's all about. Something happened during our visit to LA. Jessie tells me she wants to cancel the wedding." He looked as if he was about to cry. "You gotta help me, Allison."

Speechless, I stared at him, unable to imagine what might have caused a rift between the two of them. They were my idea of a perfect couple.

"Will you go to her?" Rob asked. "If you go down to the apartment, I'll stay here with Daisy, Maybe you can get Jessie to talk to you about it. I can't."

"Sure." The situation had to be very serious. "I'll go there right now."

I left Daisy and Rob in the kitchen, feeding Coalie. As I walked down the road to Jessie's apartment above Treasures, I wondered what could have gone wrong. The Jessie I knew was true to her word. What in hell had happened to make her want to back out of marrying Rob? No doubt her mother would be pleased with her change of heart, but that couldn't be the reason for this sudden decision.

I went around the gallery and knocked on the door leading to the upstairs apartment. After waiting several minutes, I tried the door. Unlocked. I opened it and called up to Jessie. She came to the top of the stairway and, even from a distance, I could see how swollen her eyes were.

Alarm thrummed through me. "Jessie, what's wrong?"

She burst into loud, noisy sobs. "It's awful, Allie, simply awful. I don't know what I'm going to do. I can't marry Rob now."

I reached her and put my arm around her. "You'd better sit down and tell me everything."

She took a seat on the edge of the living room couch. I sat in a chair opposite her, shocked by her haggard appearance.

"Start at the beginning," I prompted.

"First of all, you know how much I love his family. There are so many of them it's hard to keep track of who goes with whom, but they're all friendly."

"How was the shower? Rob's aunt was excited about giving it for you."

Jessie sniffed and blew her nose. "Perfect, absolutely wonderful. We got all sort of gifts. Now, I'll have to return them."

"Stop, Jessie. Why would you want to return them?"

Tears streamed down her cheeks. "Because I can't marry Rob. That's why. Not after what I found out."

I gently clasped her hand. "You'd better tell me about it."

"After the shower was over, Rob's mother and I stayed at his Aunt Barbara's house. She brought out a family album to show me pictures of Rob's grandparents. It was supposed to be such a wonderful occasion."

"And? What happened?"

"In one of the photos, his grandmother was holding a baby. An older girl stood next to her. Rob's mother, Betsy, was the baby. The older girl was someone they called Babe." Jessie took a deep breath and closed her eyes. When she opened them, they were full of pain. "I swear to God it was Daisy in that picture. Babe and Daisy look so much alike it's uncanny. I was speechless. Barbara kept on chatting about the other pictures while I sat there, sick to my stomach."

"What happened then?"

Jessie drew a deep breath, fighting tears. "Finally Rob's mother noticed something was wrong and asked if I was all right. I told her I wasn't feeling well. We left and went back to their home."

"Did you say anything about what you saw?" My mind tried to grasp what this meant.

"I asked about the little girl Babe and learned she'd died of polio the year after the picture was taken. I didn't dare say anything about her similarity to Daisy to anyone. I couldn't, until I'd sorted things out in my mind."

I gripped Jessie's hand harder. "You're certain they look enough alike to think Rob must be Daisy's father?"

"Babe's hair was dark, but her facial features were Daisy's. I don't understand how the others didn't see it."

She rose and moved around the room restlessly, clasping and unclasping her hands. "What am I going to do, Allison? You know how many times we've talked about the need to find Daisy's father. Rob has never indicated in any way he might be the one. If Daisy is his child, she was conceived when Rob and I were supposedly committed to one another. He'd already said he loved me and that we'd be married someday. If he fooled around on me then, why wouldn't he do the same thing now? Maybe he's been screwing around behind my back the whole time we've been engaged."

"Whoa!" I turned her around to face me. "You're making all kinds of projections that might not be true at all. As Samantha would say, 'first things first'. Have you talked to Rob about this?"

Jessie shook her head.

"Okay, then, let's have him get his DNA tested to make sure he's the father."

"What if he is?"

I took her by the shoulders, and looked her in the eye. "Has he ever done anything to indicate he's been unfaithful?"

"No-o-o-o, but, Allie, I'm not ready to have a family. Not this way. Not raising someone else's love child with my husband."

I swallowed hard. I understood how that might make a woman feel. "You have to talk to Rob and get him to agree to the test. Wait for the results before making any decisions. Okay?"

Jessie blew her nose and let out a sigh. "I guess I have no choice."

"Good, that's settled. Rob is watching Daisy at my house. He asked me to come see you; he has no idea what's going on. Should I send him down here?"

"Might as well," said Jessie forlornly. "First, let's have a cup of coffee while I calm down. Otherwise, I might kill him."

I followed her into the kitchen and sat at the table while she got the coffee going.

Jessie turned and let out a yelp. "Allie! What's that on your finger? Don't tell me Blake popped the question! Let me see!"

I grinned and held up my left hand.

She grabbed it and traced the outline of the diamond. "It's beautiful" Her lip quivered. "I'm so sorry. It's your big moment and here I am, crying on your shoulder."

"Jessie? It'll work out. You'll see."

She slumped down in her chair. "I don't know. I just don't know."

I left her some time later and hurried up the hill, filled with whirling emotions. If Rob were Daisy's father, would I have to give her up? How could I? She'd become a child of my heart.

Rob greeted me at the door. "What did she say?"

"She'll talk to you now. She's waiting for you at the apartment."

"Is it going to be all right?"

"I don't know." I had no idea what this revelation meant for either him or me.

As I unpacked her suitcase, Daisy chatted about the shower presents she and Rob's niece Megan had helped Jessie open. Poor Jessie, I thought. It must have been horrible for her to hold everything inside while pretending she was fine.

Unaware of the turmoil taking place between Jessie and Rob behind the scenes, Daisy talked on and on about Rob's big family and how much she liked her new friend, Megan. Listening to her, she sounded so grown up. The past few months had made a big difference in her life. She was becoming more flexible, more open. But I wondered how she'd feel if Rob were her father.

The thought of losing Daisy sent a piercing pang of sorrow through me. I decided not to think about it until I had more facts. Perhaps nothing would change. Jessie wasn't sure she wanted her. I'd felt that way once myself.

After Daisy fell asleep, I wandered out to the front porch, deeply troubled.

If Rob was Daisy's father, it would only be right that she live with him. She'd indicated she wanted that and she trusted me to find him. But Jessie and Rob might not even marry, and that wouldn't be good for Daisy. If that were the case, she'd be better off living with me, and eventually, Blake and me.

I swallowed hard as another scenario came to mind. If Jessie and Rob decided to go ahead and get married and fight for custody of Daisy, would I be able to rise above it and maintain my business partnership with Jessie?

My thoughts circled endlessly.

I tossed and turned throughout the night. Unable to sleep, I rose early, and while Daisy was still sleeping, I called Jessie.

"How are things?" I asked tentatively.

"Awful. In a weak moment last night, after Rob left, I talked to my parents. If Daisy is part of the package, my mother is dead set against me marrying Rob. She's never liked him, anyway. You know how she is."

"Did you ask Rob if he could be Daisy's father?"

"Yes. At first, he was totally surprised by the idea. Then, he admitted there was one time, when I was away at college, that he and Kristin went to a party and got totally wasted. They ended up in bed. He told me it didn't mean anything to either of them, and it was never mentioned between them again. He didn't think anything more about it because Kristin was dating around."

"He agreed to take the test?"

"Oh, yes." Jessie's voice caught. "He told me he'd do anything I wanted, as long as I kept my promise to marry him."

"So, he's having it done today?"

"I suppose so. I told him I didn't care when he got it done, that I had to have time to sort through my feelings. He got mad and left."

"Oh, Jessie, I don't know what to think."

"Right now, everything is on hold, including the wedding. It was going to be a small wedding, anyhow. I figure I have a week before I have to cancel everything." Her voice broke. "I can't believe this has happened!"

"If you want to stay home this morning, I'll open up Treasures. Take some time for yourself. We'll manage."

"Thanks, I will." Jessie's voice quivered.

I hung up the phone determined to talk to Rob. Why hadn't Kristin mentioned anything to Rob about the possibility of his being the father? After pouring myself a cup of coffee, I sat at the kitchen table sorting through my thoughts. The truth was Daisy didn't look like Rob. Well, maybe her smile. Her blond hair and blue eyes were not at all like Rob's. He had dark-brown hair and green eyes. He hadn't known the aunt who'd died before he was born. A nagging thought entered my mind and staggered me. If I was right, there was a good reason Kristin didn't mention anything to Rob.

I checked the clock and though it was an early hour, I called him. He answered on the first ring.

"Jessie?"

"I'm sorry, Rob, it's me. Allison. I need to ask you something. You had already begun dating Jessie when you had the one night with Kristin, right?"

"Yeah. God, I wish it'd never happened. As a matter of fact, I was so out of it, I wasn't even sure if anything had actually happened that night. I woke up and there she was."

"She knew you wanted to marry Jessie, didn't she?"

"Oh, yeah. Kristin knew all about it. She hadn't met Jessie yet, but I'd told Kristin all about her."

"I'll be damned ..." I whispered. Tears came to my eyes. I knew exactly why Kristin had never mentioned a word to Rob. God! It was so like her! Knowing he was truly in love with someone else, she hadn't wanted to mess up his life. And she knew they could never have a normal marriage.

"Allison? You okay?"

I sniffed. "Yes, but I need to ask you something else. If

Daisy is your daughter, are ... are you going to want her to live with you?"

My stomach churned as I waited for his answer. I wanted to be fair to everyone involved, but I also wanted him to consider my fragile feelings.

He cleared his throat. "Listen, I know what this means for you, Allison, but I've been awake most of the night. If Daisy is mine, yeah, I want her to live with me. It's only right. Jessie has to understand that. Daisy and I have always had a special thing between us, you know? I didn't realize ..."His voice cracked, and I understood the tremendous emotional strain he was under.

"Okay, we'll talk later, after the test results have come through."

"Allison? Will you help me with Jessie?"

I heard the pleading in his voice, but didn't know what, if anything, I could say to her. Not until we'd both had more time to resolve our conflicting emotions. "I'll try, Rob."

I hung up the phone. The reality of the situation was chilling. My body shook so violently my teeth rattled. Feeling as if my heart was about to be ripped out of my chest, I sank onto a kitchen chair. Dear God, what was I going to do? The child I hadn't wanted might be taken away from me. How could I bear the loss? She'd become mine in spirit.

Daisy padded into the room, followed by Coalie. She gave me a worried look and ran over to me. Not wanting to frighten her, I reined in my churning emotions.

She crept into my lap and laid her head against my chest, sleepily. "I dreamed about my mommy," she said in a sad little voice.

I rocked her in my arms and listened while she told me in her dreams her mother had liked meeting Coalie. The dog seemed to know we were talking about her. She sat at my side and laid her head in my lap alongside Daisy.

"I love you, Allie." Daisy snuggled closer.

Her words tore at me. I wanted to throw myself down on the floor and kick in frustration, like Daisy used to do. But I had to be strong. If changes were going to occur, I'd need to help Daisy through them.

"I love you, too," I murmured, meaning it with all my heart.

After a few more snuggles, Daisy ran into the living room and turned on the television. Dully, I assembled her breakfast, wondering how we could survive another emotional upheaval.

Claire stayed with Daisy at the house while I worked behind the counter of Treasures. Jessie sat at the computer in the office, working on a new ad for the local newspaper. She'd told me she needed something to keep her preoccupied, and I was grateful for her work.

After the gallery closed, I walked into the office to check on her.

"How are you doing?" I asked, taking in her puffy eyes.

She buried her face in her hands and let out a heartrending sob.

I started to rise to go to her.

"No, no, I'm all right." Jessie lifted her head. "I'm so mixed up right now." She gave me a helpless look. "Do you think I could be a good mother to Daisy? You said you weren't ready to be a mother, but look at what you've done with her..."

My heart clenched with pain.

"Do you think I could do it, too?" Jessie's expression grew hopeful.

I knew what Jessie was asking of me, but I couldn't respond. Not yet. I jumped to my feet.

"Allison?"

I raced out of the building, not sure where I was going. I stopped and forced myself to slowly breathe in and out, reaching for calmness. I loved Daisy and wanted the best for her, I really did, but it would break my heart to watch Jessie become her mother, when I still wanted Daisy for my own.

Jessie came up behind me. “God, Allie, I’m so sorry. I didn’t mean to place you in such an awkward situation. No matter what decision I make, I’m going to hurt someone. I don’t know what to do.”

I turned to her and gave her the best advice I could. “Follow your heart, Jessie.”

Her eyes filled with tears. “Thanks.”

Over the next few days I continued to live in a state of uncertainty. Jessie and I were like robots, performing our duties, talking very little. Blake had little he could offer as consolation. Until we had concrete news, we were stuck in a cycle of waiting.

One afternoon Blake and I arrived at Treasures for a meeting. When we walked inside, the gallery was empty. I called out for Jessie. She emerged from the bathroom, her eyes red-rimmed.

“What’s wrong?”

She sniffed, trying not to cry. “Rob called. It’s positive. He’s Daisy’s father.”

I stood a moment, not knowing how to react. “What can I say?”

Tears rolled down Jessie’s cheeks. “Congratulate me. I’m going to be a mother.”

The finality of her decision caught me off guard. The room spun in sickening circles. My knees weakened.

Blake’s strong arms came around me. He led me to a chair.

"Better sit." He knelt in front of me. I leaned my head against his shoulder and let the gut-wrenching sobs come.

"I'm sorry. So sorry," Jessie murmured like a chant.

I fought for control, my emotions so confused I could barely speak. "You're marrying Rob? I'm ... I'm so happy for you."

Jessie clasped my hand. "I love him more than anything. I have for a number of years. Don't worry. I'll be a good mother to Daisy. I love her, too. Rob made it clear the two of them are a package deal. I can't have one without the other."

I held back another sob, though I could feel my heart breaking. "Funny, I told Blake the same thing." After a moment, I said, "Promise me you'll give me time to help Daisy prepare for the change. Okay?"

"Rob will talk to you about it." Her eyes filled once more. "He's so excited about the whole thing. We've always talked about having a large family. I just didn't know it would start this way."

Hearing the quaver in her voice, I rose from my chair and wrapped my arms around her. She would, I knew, be a good mother to Daisy. As Rob had told me earlier, he and Daisy had always shared a special bond. It would be a good situation for Daisy.

When I stepped away from Jessie, Blake drew me to him. "You okay?"

I nodded numbly. Like he kept telling me, it would all work out. But I didn't know if I could stand the pain of it.

Outside, Blake held my hand. "I know how hard Jessie's news is for you, Allison. You love Daisy like your own."

Unable to speak with the huge lump in my throat, I merely nodded. She was *my* little girl. *Mine.*

He gently wiped a tear from my cheek with his thumb. "It'll be all right. You'll see."

I hoped Daisy would believe that, too. In order for her to leave me, I needed her to feel that way. At the moment, though, I didn't know how I could let her go.

Rob called me as I was doing the dinner dishes. "You got a minute?"

I glanced at Daisy, sitting on the living room couch, watching television. "Sure."

"Are you all right with the news that I'm Daisy's father? And that Jessie and I want her to live with us? It can't be easy for you."

"It's not," I admitted, "but I understand it's the right thing to do. Kristin loved having you in her life. I believe she thought you were Daisy's father all along, but didn't want to come between you and Jessie."

"Really? Jeez, I didn't think of that. Now that I know she's mine, I want to move as quickly as possible to move Daisy into my family. Jessie and I have decided we're going to elope. It sure as hell makes it easier on everybody. But we don't want to disappoint Daisy, so we'd like to take her with us to get married. Then, we're going to take her to Disney World in Florida. Under the circumstances, it's the best kind of honeymoon we can think of to start the family off right. But I want to make sure you're okay with everything."

I put my own painful feelings aside and forced enthusiasm into my voice. "She'll love it. Why don't we tell Daisy together? We'll give her a few days to get used to the idea that you're her father. She'll want to know where she's going to live and all."

"Not a problem. She deserves to know about it."

Rob was a good man. I'd always known it, but I admired him more than ever before because he had Daisy's interests at heart and was putting her first.

"Do you want to come over to see Daisy? If the timing is right, we'll tell her tonight."

"Thanks, Allie. I knew you'd be kind and understanding. I'll be there soon."

I hung up the phone and gripped the counter until my knuckles turned white. I'd always heard that real love meant giving a child both roots and wings, but I'd never understood how deep the love must be to let someone go. I prayed I'd be able to do it with enough grace and assurance that Daisy wouldn't be afraid. It would, I knew, take all my strength.

Rob arrived a little while later.

Daisy was in her pajamas, ready for bed, watching her favorite movie. When she saw him, she jumped up from the couch and ran to him.

"Rob! Rob! Come see what I made with Claire today." She took his hand and led him toward the kitchen.

Rob and I exchanged glances, and I observed raw emotion in his eyes. This whole scenario was as hard on him as anyone else.

Daisy showed him the elbow macaroni she'd strung on a shoe lace. "It's my necklace. Isn't it beautiful? Tomorrow we're going to paint it."

"Very nice." Rob patted her on the back.

"Time for bed. Rob is going to help me tell a story." I'd decided that might be the best way to introduce the subject.

Rob glanced at me and nodded, turning the situation over to me.

"Lift me up, Rob." Daisy held her arms up to him. "I want to ride on your shoulders."

Coalie and I followed behind as he climbed the stairs with Daisy perched atop him. In her bedroom, Daisy snuggled under the covers. I sat on one side of the double bed while Rob sat on the rocking chair beside it.

Sensing the tension in the room, Daisy asked me, "Is this a special story?"

I took her hand and held it. "It's a very, very special story. Do you remember I told you I would look for your daddy?"

Daisy nodded solemnly.

"Well, I've found him, exactly like you wanted. It's someone you already know. Someone you already love."

Daisy's eyes widened. She turned to Rob. "Are you my daddy?"

He started to answer, then simply nodded, too choked with emotion to speak.

"You're so very lucky, Daisy." I forced myself to continue. "You're lucky because Rob and Jessie want you to live with them like a real family—with a mommy, a daddy and a very special girl named Daisy."

"And Coalie?"

I looked at Rob.

He smiled at Daisy. "Of course. Every little girl needs a special dog."

"And Allie?" She eyed me uncertainly.

I shook my head. "No, I won't be the mommy. I'll be your special godmother, like always."

"But I want to stay here," said Daisy. "I like this house."

"We'll see. Maybe that can happen." Rob turned to me, and explained, "This house is going to be put up for sale. That's one of the things I wanted to talk to you about. With you marrying Blake, Catherine wants to sell."

"So can we stay here?" Daisy asked.

Rob shrugged. "I don't know yet. We might have to stay in Jessie's apartment for a while."

Daisy lay back against the pillow, looking from one of us to the other.

"Where's Jessie?"

I brushed a blond curl from her forehead, hoping this child would understand and accept all we were asking of her. "She's at home, waiting to hear if you're happy about the news."

"I had a mommy," she said pensively.

"Yes, Kristin will always be your real mommy. Jessie is going to be the mommy your daddy chose for you. A special, new mommy."

She turned to Rob, and I held my breath, waiting for her to speak.

Daisy nodded seriously. "I like Jessie, too."

"I'm glad." Rob's relief was obvious. "We'll make a good family. I promise."

Daisy bit her lip. "Allie? Where will you go?"

"I'll live with Blake at his house at the winery." Saying the words sent chills up and down my back. Until now, the reality of our marriage had seemed so distant.

Daisy's expression continued to be uneasy. "Can Coalie and I come visit you?"

"Any time."

"Sure," said Rob. "Allie is very special to you. I know that."

Daisy smiled at him. "You're really my daddy?"

"Yep." He reached over and hugged her. "And you're really my little girl."

I left them calling Jessie on Rob's cell phone. It was a private, family time.

My heart felt as if it were shattering, one sharp-edged piece after another.

CHAPTER TWENTY SIX

Arrangements fell into place. Daisy, unaware of the turmoil behind the scene, was thrilled with the idea of being part of a secret wedding and traveling to Florida to see Mickey Mouse and all his friends.

On her last night with me, I helped her pack her suitcase, telling myself this was a good way to say good-bye, to deal with the reality of it all. The lump in my throat almost choked me. Tears threatened to blind me.

Sensitive to my feelings, Daisy kept asking, "Are you all right, Allie?"

I nodded, unable to speak. How could I tell her that her happiness was breaking my heart? That I'd never be the same?

The next morning, Rob and Jessie picked up Daisy to go to a judge's office to be married. Blake stood at my side. I could feel the tension in him as he put a protective arm around me.

Daisy climbed into the truck and waved cheerily as they pulled away.

My legs grew wobbly. I leaned back against Blake's strong chest.

"You didn't want to join them for the wedding ceremony?" he murmured. "Jessie invited you to participate."

I shook my head. It was too much to ask. I couldn't do it without breaking down completely. It would upset Daisy.

As I turned to go inside, Blake lifted my hand and brought it to his lips. "You're going to make a wonderful mother someday," he said, pulling me into his embrace.

"I'm a mother already," I whispered, and fought to hold

back fresh tears. Though my heart didn't seem to know it, I'd cried enough in the last six months to last a lifetime.

We went inside, and I lay down on the couch, too tired, too much in a funk to do much else. Blake sat in a chair nearby, keeping an eye on me.

When the phone rang some time later, Blake answered it.

He handed me the phone. "It's for you."

I listened and hung up, emotionally ripped in two.

"Rob and Jessie are dropping by with Daisy to say good-bye before taking off for Florida." I hugged myself, trying to keep from breaking apart. "I can't say good-bye. I can't do it. I just can't."

Blake put his arms around me. "Yes, you can. You'll do it for Daisy. I know you."

How had my life become so mixed up? I hadn't wanted the responsibility of Daisy when Fate plopped her into my unsuspecting lap. Who knew what a change she'd make in my life? I once thought being successful was about running a business. I'd been eager to prove to myself that I could do it. Now, I understood real success was about giving and receiving love.

I let out a shaky sigh, thinking of what I was being forced to do. Heading to the wedding, Daisy had looked like an angel with her blond curly hair, tilted nose and big blue eyes. In truth, she was anything but—she was difficult, easily frustrated, temperamental and spoiled, along with her natural slowness. But she'd wiggled her way into my life in unexpected ways. No matter what happened from here on, Daisy would always be my first child.

At the sound of Rob's truck pulling into my driveway, I clasped Blake's hand, needing his strength. He squeezed it and gave me an encouraging smile.

"You can do it," he murmured.

He opened the front door and, inhaling deeply, I stepped out onto the porch.

Daisy stood outside the truck, staring at me, looking as uncertain as I felt. I moved forward in slow motion, as if I could delay this moment from happening.

Jessie and Rob stood to one side while I knelt in front of Daisy to say good-bye. I struggled to maintain my composure as she wrapped her small arms around me and hugged me tight.

"I love you, Daisy," I whispered, meaning it with all my heart.

She looked up at me, her blue eyes filled with concern. "Will you always be my fairy godmother?"

"Always," I managed to say, though tears rolled down my cheeks.

Solemnly, she wiped the wetness away with her little fingers, and I felt like the child not the adult.

"Can I come visit you when we come back?" She stood still, awaiting my answer.

I knew she was asking much more of me than that. I nodded emphatically. "I'll always be here for you. You can count on it."

She smiled, and it seemed as if the grayness of the foggy morning disappeared. The day I'd arrived in Sarita she'd looked like a little cherub to me. She was much bigger now, more grownup. *Oh, Kristin, you'd be so proud of her.*

I rose to my feet and watched as Jessie helped Daisy into Rob's truck. Blake put his arms around me.

"They'll be fine," he said, as they pulled away. "You've done a good job with her."

I swiveled in his arms, and let my tears flow. My life had taken another turn. Time to move on. But Daisy would always be part of me.

"Allison," Blake said softly, his voice comforting, "we'll have children of our own someday." It was the sweetest talk I'd ever heard from the man I loved with all my heart.

I searched his eyes, noticing the moisture gathered there. "Do you mean it, Blake? Are you sure?" Until I asked the question, I didn't realize how incredibly important his answer was to me.

His expression filled with love. "There's nothing I'd like better than to see you carrying my child inside you."

I lifted my face to him, and his lips came down on mine—firm and sweet. I reveled in the wonderful future we would have together—we would have children and I would love them dearly. But whatever the future held, it wouldn't diminish my feelings for the sometimes difficult little girl who'd taught me what it was to love a child.

"Come." Blake held his hand out to me.

I took it, filled with the promise of what was to come.

I hope you enjoyed *Sweet Talk*. If you have, please let other readers know by writing a review on Amazon, Goodreads or your favorite site. It's such a nice thing to do for authors. Thanks!

An excerpt from *Straight Talk* (Samantha's story), Book 3 of the Hartwell Women Series follows:

CHAPTER ONE

A bruising hand gripped my upper arm and jerked me around. Startled, I dropped my purse. A tough guy glared at me with glassy eyes. His thin lips curled into a sly sneer that turned my mouth dry.

A young drug addict. My stomach fisted. Damn! I should have been paying more attention to my surroundings. The chill from the rainy Tuesday evening in Boston crept into my body stiffened with fear.

"You're Samantha Hartwell, ain'tcha?" the druggie demanded. His eyebrows angled into a fierce scowl that sent fear skittering down my spine.

I nodded, surprised he knew my name. Not a good sign.

He moved his face close to mine. His warm breath reeked of garlic and alcohol. I swallowed hard and yanked against his painful grasp.

"You stay the hell away from Caitlin, you hear?" he snarled. He jerked me closer, making me stumble. "Stop fillin' her head with all that art stuff. She's not doing that no more."

My mind took a moment to grasp what he'd said. This was about Caitlin? The guy was shouting and practically wrenching my arm off because of Caitlin Rafferty?

"I don't know who in hell you are, but Caitlin has real talent." My voice shook, but I forced myself to stand my ground. Nobody was going to tell me what I could or could not do.

He jabbed a finger at me. "Stay away from Caitlin, Bitch. She ain't no artist. She's my woman and she does what I tell 'er. If I hafta come back and find you, you're gonna be sorry."

He shoved me against my car and marched away as if he owned the sidewalk beneath his feet.

Adrenaline left me in a torrent of tumbling waves, turning my bones to jelly. I collapsed against the car and glanced all around, but the leather-jacketed goon who'd threatened me was nowhere in sight.

Gathering strength, I picked up my purse and made my way up the stairs to my fourth floor office on Marlborough Street in the Back Bay. I'd need to calm down before I could drive home. Caitlin had told me about her boyfriend, Anthony Carbone, but I had no idea he was such a controlling jerk.

Inside my office I paced restlessly, trying to shake off the fear that clung to me like a tiger's claws. I'd founded Straight Talk, my non-profit consulting business, to help other young women grab a foothold in business and get a grip on their unsteady lives. For some, the task was easy, but for others, like Caitlin Rafferty, the challenge was overwhelming.

Taking a deep breath, I told myself to be strong. But Anthony's sharp-edged words, the way he'd so easily bruised my arm, and the sickening odor of his breath made my stomach churn. I eased myself into a chair. It would take more time to gather my wits before I attempted to return to my car.

I wouldn't call the police. That would cause problems for Caitlin and might hinder what I was doing for the other women who'd asked for my help. I'd come too far to let anyone ruin my plans. Running Straight Talk was what kept me focused... and sober. Without it, I didn't know what I'd do. It wasn't until I'd stated my name before a circle of people that I began to understand what I'd been given— another chance at life, an opportunity to help others, a reason for living.

Friday afternoon, I replaced the phone receiver and sighed. I'd told no one Caitlin's boyfriend had threatened me. Too many people would tell me to forget her; it was too dangerous. But I couldn't do that. As I saw it, her entire future rested in my hands.

Advising troubled women in start-up businesses was no easy task. I rose to stare out the window of my office and watched college crews in their shells row steadily along the Charles River, dipping their oars in the water in a regular rhythm that soothed me.

Zach Adams stuck his head into the office. "Tough day?"

I turned and smiled at my best friend. "Tough week. Glad it's Friday."

"Me too. Let's get out of here and party."

I laughed. Zach was a recovering alcoholic like me and our idea of partying was to have an extra Diet Coke.

"Derek Roberts' photographs are showing at the Winthrop Gallery on Boylston Street. I said I'd drop by. Want to come?"

"Sure. He's famous and I'd like to see his work. Anything to shake off this bad feeling I've got about Caitlin."

He raised his eyebrows.

I was still at a loss as how best to handle the situation. She hadn't shown up for our meeting yesterday. Her absence could be due to any number of reasons. I hoped Anthony Carbone wasn't one of them. "Between her family problems, her boyfriend and her drinking, she's like a freight train running out of control. There's no stopping her."

"Some people just don't know when they're on the right track." Zach grinned at me.

I groaned at his usual wacky sense of humor and picked up my purse. "You're incorrigible. Let's go have some fun and meet this Derek guy. 'Could be interesting."

"You sure you won't marry me?" Zach's voice was teasing, but his expression told me he might be serious.

"You know how I feel about you." I gave him a little punch on the arm. He was my best friend and I adored him.

"Yeah, you think of me as some damn brother."

We looked at each other and smiled. I never would have made it through recovery without him, nor he without me. I could give him friendship, loyalty and a kindness he didn't receive at home, but I couldn't give him the type of love he desired. There was no mystery, no magic, no moving of mountains between us. I couldn't imagine sex with him.

"You deserve the works, Zach Adams, not my kind of love. You'll see. Some woman is going to knock you off your feet and I won't even be able to get you to say hello to me."

The corner of his lip lifted in a lop-sided mock grimace. He didn't believe me.

"Zach, I've seen the way girls look at you. You just don't notice."

"Not with you around, I don't. Not with those smoky gray eyes of yours."

I shook my head, wishing I could give him what he desired. "You're hopeless. C'mon, let's go."

As we walked along Boylston Street to Winthrop Galleries, I noticed our images reflected in the glass windows of the store fronts. Zach's outline was tall and muscular, his strong facial features definitely a plus. Any girl would be lucky to have him. Next to him, I seemed short and slim, though no one would call me fragile. My dark straight hair, I noticed, swung back and forth in rhythm to our brisk stride.

"So tell me about Derek Roberts. How do you know him?"

"We went to prep school together. He wasn't one of the jocks, but used to spend his time taking photographs of various sports. In college, he won a Pulitzer for a shot he took of the Bruins' goalie catching the puck in overtime play, taking the win away from Montreal."

"It's supposed to be a great show." I'd read about it in the *Globe.* "I'm pleased for the gallery. I know the owner. He's been struggling to attract a younger crowd, and this may be one way to do it."

"Is he still helping you with your art project? We're putting together an art show of paintings done by women in recovery. It should help fund the new proposed shelter in Southie."

Zach pulled me to a stop. "See why everybody loves you, Sam?"

My thoughts flew to George Hartwell, my elderly father. "Not everyone."

"Well, most people do." Zach took hold of my shoulders and gave me a long look. "I know all about your father, but, Sam, you can't let one person destroy how everyone else feels about you."

He was right. My relationship with my father was an old story. Most likely it was why I worked hard to excel at everything I did and might even have been the reason I'd turned to alcohol at an early age. No matter what I accomplished, I'd never be what my father really wanted. Thank God my mother, Adrienne, was as sweet and as strong as they come. She'd counter-balanced my father's unreasonable attitude as best she could, but she couldn't prevent the damage done to me.

Determined to have some fun, I looped my arm through his

and skipped along the sidewalk with exaggerated steps.

Zach grinned and hurried to keep up with me.

The Winthrop Gallery was deceptively large, extending deep into the storefront from the street. Inside, I took a moment to get my bearings. The high-ceilinged rooms were discreetly lit and the walls, of varying shades of neutral colors, were the perfect backdrops for the colorful photographs mounted on them.

The gallery owner waved his hand in recognition and broke away from a group of people to greet us.

"Samantha! Glad you could make it."

I smiled and accepted his hand. "Me, too."

As I was introducing Zach, someone called out, "Hey, Zach!"

Zach grinned. "Hi, Derek.

I turned to find a tall, dark-haired man striding toward us. He smiled at Zach then turned his gaze on me. Our eyes met and shivers traveled down my spine. Derek Roberts was one of the most attractive men I'd ever seen. The contrast of dark hair with light brown, almost gold eyes was intriguing. They lit with pleasure as his crooked smile settled on me before turning back to Zach.

About the Author

Judith Keim enjoyed her childhood and young-adult years in Elmira, New York, and now makes her home in Boise, Idaho, with her husband and their two dachshunds, Winston and Wally, and other members of her family.

While growing up, she was drawn to the idea of writing stories from a young age. Books were always present, being read, ready to go back to the library, or about to be discovered. All in her family shared information from the books in general conversation, giving them a wealth of knowledge and vivid imaginations.

A hybrid author who both has a publisher and self-publishes, Ms. Keim writes heart-warming novels about women who face unexpected challenges, meet them with strength, and find love and happiness along the way. Her best-selling books are based, in part, on many of the places she's lived or visited and on the interesting people she's met, creating believable characters and realistic settings her many loyal readers love. Ms. Keim loves to hear from her readers and appreciates their enthusiasm for her stories.

"I hope you've enjoyed this book. If you have, please help other readers discover it by leaving a review on Amazon, Goodreads, or the site of your choice. And please check out my other books:

The Hartwell Women Series
The Beach House Hotel Series
The Fat Fridays Group
The Salty Key Inn Series
Seashell Cottage Books
Chandler Hill Inn Series
Desert Sage Inn Series

ALL THE BOOKS ARE NOW AVAILABLE IN AUDIO on Audible and iTunes! So fun to have these characters come alive!"

Ms. Keim can be reached at **www.judithkeim.com**

And to like her author page on Facebook and keep up with the news, go to: **https://bit.ly/3acs5Qc**

To receive notices about new books, follow her on Book Bub - **http://bit.ly/2pZBDXq**

And here's a link to where you can sign up for her periodic newsletter! **http://bit.ly/2OQsb7s**

She is also on Twitter @judithkeim, LinkedIn, and Goodreads. Come say hello!

Acknowledgements

Through the years of writing there have been people from all parts of my life who've encouraged me when I've wanted to stop, to give up , to step away from the disappointments. And now when I've dared to present one of my stories to the public, I wish to thank them with all my heart. You know who you are, you who are so dear to me. Thanks.

Made in United States
North Haven, CT
05 October 2024

58384410R00189